RUSSIAN BRIDE

RUSSIAN BRIDE

DOC RICHTER

atmosphere press

CHAPTER 1

Moscow, Post-Soviet Perestroika, 1993

The ancient trolley rumbled down the center of Cherkisov Street toward the general area of Natalia Melnikova's building. Absorbed in thought, she was in high spirits despite the other commuters' impassive faces. People had long-learned to hide their thoughts and emotions, but they couldn't mask their eyes. The eyes around her showed despair and anger, but the feelings of others wouldn't depress her mood, not that night.

She enjoyed January's freezing cold as much as the springtime. At this point in the school term, her better piano students pulled away from the ordinary learners. The best pupils' initial clumsiness had passed, and natural talents exerted themselves, which always pleased her. Fresh talent meant hope, rare these early days of post-Soviet Russia.

Natalia loved music in a nation that adored song, and she possessed a fulfilling job. Of course, teaching didn't pay much, which made her life a struggle. Even doctors only made the equivalent of fifty dollars per month. If she didn't live in her retired mother's small apartment, it would be impossible to survive the crushing inflation and lack of rubles. Inflation ran at a hundred percent per month.

When the streetcar groaned to an abrupt, shuddering halt at her stop, she stepped onto the boulevard and searched for oncoming traffic. Automobiles had the right-of-way, and they took it. Crossing the three lanes to the sidewalk was hazardous, worse at night. Most drivers negotiated the dark streets with their headlights off to conserve gasoline. Pedestrians were often hit. Fleets of ambulances cruised the thoroughfares and sought to find a "prize" before a competing unit arrived.

Natalia checked up and down the street and made her dash.

The trek to her building hidden in a forest of other twelve-story structures called a korpus would take a half-hour. Naked trees lined the narrow lane into the complex with decrepit cars and tiny, ice-coated portable garages.

Many people walked their dogs. Muscovites preferred large ones for personal security. Other people carried sacks for their night's meal and vodka. Almost everyone drank a bottle a night, but Natalia didn't imbibe because of the cost.

Natalia kept her brisk pace through the crisp snow and thought about Mr. Jacob Wilder from the United States, and excitement warmed her. He had landed in Moscow and would meet her soon.

Natalia thought about her first letter to Mr. Jacob, as she referred to him in her mind. She made fifteen attempts to write the message. Even then, she didn't believe the words were sufficient to express herself well, but she hoped Mr. Jacob would forgive her limited English. After that came the post-age, oh, so much postage, followed by the excruciating wait for his reply if he wrote her back. But he did reply, and her dreams of a good man soared.

But one thing disturbed her: she hadn't been honest with him. The Moscow correspondence agency she used, International Friends, which was one of dozens such agencies, demanded she lie and not tell Mr. Jacob about her four-year-old son, Alexandr. They said keeping Alexandr confidential was necessary to increase her chances for an American gentleman. Natalia would tell Mr. Jacob later if he chose her. She'd agreed though believed it was wrong and felt guilt for her deception. She wanted him to be truthful with her, yet she didn't reciprocate. *What will he think of me when I tell him?*

She worried that he would meet others and didn't want to compete with them, but she appreciated his honesty. He had every right to meet anyone he wanted. He'd come all the way from America, and she'd be a fool to think a man would make such a trip to meet only one woman. But Mr. Jacob told her he liked her letters the best and would spend the most time with her, which made her happy and ever-so-nervous.

Natalia passed through the dark paths to her "Khrushchev" apartment building, one of thousands of nondescript cement towers erected during the time of a Soviet premier Natalia had only heard about in school. But at least she, Alexandr, and her mother had a place to live. So many people from the country came to Moscow to hunt for jobs that housing was in critical supply. There weren't enough places to house Moscow's nine million residents. A place to live, however small, was needed to survive.

She walked into the dim hallway, trudged up six flights of stairs, unlocked the door, and was surprised her mother stood in the entryway. "Is everything okay, mama? Alexandr?"

Her mother gave a slight smile and said, "The angel sleeps." Her worried brow returned, and she handed Natalia a note. "This came for you."

The note was from the agency, and they ordered her to come to their office immediately. *But why? I have no time for this. Mr. Jacob is in Moscow, and I have much to prepare.* She didn't know why they wanted her to come but had no choice.

Natalia looked in on the sleeping Alexandr, his toy car clutched in his hand, and gave him a kiss. She grabbed a piece of buttered bread from the kitchen for dinner and started the long walk back through the snow. The further she traveled, the more anxious she became.

What does the service want now?

Has Mr. Jacob changed his mind about seeing me?

* * *

Natalia entered the old brick building on Rus Street across the Moscow River from Red Square, stomped the slush off her boots, and climbed the steep concrete steps to the offices. Before, she had waited for her interview in the cramped, cold lobby, but this evening the receptionist ushered her ahead of the others who sat on hard chairs.

The door of the small, poorly-lit room closed, and she hesitated. Blue tobacco smoke filled the air from quality foreign cigarettes. A man sat behind a table, his face only partially visible in the shadows. His black leather coat and silk shirt were expensive. Her eyes went to the flash of gold from his wristwatch.

He was a New Russian, one of the recent breed everyone despised but wished to become. They were the people who drove Mercedes or Saabs or Jeeps and talked with loud voices in restaurants and flaunted their cellular phones and beepers. They paid policemen outrageous sums to park their fancy autos on the sidewalks to be guarded by those same officers. They displayed their wealth while most people starved.

What does such a person want with me?

The man took a long drag, and his face was illuminated by the cigarette's glow. He had dark hair and looked in his forties, which was all she saw before the light faded.

"Sit," he commanded.

The KGB was not too far removed from her memory, and he spoke with sharp authority. She sat.

The man obscured in the smoky shadows said, "Natalia Melnikova, you have corresponded with a Mr. Jacob Wilder. He is in Moscow to see you and three other women."

Natalia heard the surprise in her voice. "How do you know about the others?"

The man spread his hands, and she noticed his smile. "We

know many things, more than you want, but that is not relevant. What is important is Mr. Wilder chooses you. We don't represent the other ladies because they use other services. You must be the one for him."

"But what if he doesn't select me?"

The man's voice turned hard. "You don't want to think of the consequences. Jacob Wilder selects you, or you will forever weep." He gave her a dismissive wave. "That is all. For now. Keep your son a secret and do what we tell you. Understand?" She didn't but said, "*Da*," the only answer she could give.

CHAPTER 2

T he tram seemed colder, dirtier than earlier, and Natalia felt sick to her stomach. All she dreamed of was a reliable mate, somebody different from Vitaly, but she hadn't gone to a service for the expected reason of an easier life. She went because she'd heard men from America were compassionate and caring. They were gentlemen and made fine husbands. Moscow was her home, though she struggled. What she valued most was a good man to share her life with, one who'd treat her like a lady and appreciate her. And be a real father to Alexandr. If she could find such a man in Russia, she would never consider leaving.

And Mr. Jacob had landed in Moscow, and she would at long last see him. She thought his arrival would be wonderful and exciting. Until tonight.

Natalia understood the agency man was a "mob boy" who didn't tell her everything. There had to be more because the Mafia always wanted money. Her insides gave a sickening twist. She was poor. Only Mr. Jacob would have cash for the mafia.

The crowded car lurched and halted though they were not at a regular stop. Word spread through the trolly of a pedestrian lying on the tracks, but she couldn't see through the steamy, mud-covered windows. An ambulance would come to claim the victim, and the passengers would be stuck while the police sorted out the incident.

She wished she could talk to someone, anyone, but such conversations were not possible. With whom could she discuss her predicament?

Natalia lowered her chin, bit her lip, and tried not to weep. She hated to cry. She willed herself not to.

* * *

Dmitri Chekhov lit another Marlboro and called for his car. Time to leave the agency and go to his casino on Tverskaya Street.

His personal meetings with Natalia Melnikova and two other special women were brief and pleasurable, like the seventy-eight other such encounters he conducted over the past months. He so much relished their desperate fear in the darkened room and savored the US dollars they would make him.

* * *

Ivan Rublev smiled as he drove his immaculate white Corolla south on Interstate 5 out of Sacramento, California, and into the Central Valley's fog-shrouded farmland. His car wasn't new but was in exceptional condition. Automobiles in the US were easier to keep in top working order versus the crap Moskvichs and Ladas back home. Americans and Russians both loved their wheels, but here the cars were so much better. The little Toyota was nondescript and quick, ordinary yet reliable, and his long, meaty legs fit well enough.

The US offered more than fine autos. Here, he lived in a nice apartment, made far more money than possible in Moscow, and was an important man compared to when he had been back home. Everything was superior here. Unfortunately, that included the police. He needed to be careful in The States, not like Moscow, where bribes solved any problem.

Russia was the Wild West now that the Soviet Union had collapsed from its inefficient, ponderous weight.

These days, gambling, drugs, and extortion flourished.

Fine young prostitutes cost one thousand dollars a night, which mystified Ivan. One night pumping some teenager for what the average Russian earned in fifteen years? Craziness, but excellent crazy, the kind of insanity that made his boss, Dmitri Chekhov, rich and brought Ivan to America.

Rublev glanced at his image in the rearview mirror. His butch emphasized his large, round head. He would *never* wear his hair this short back home. Too fucking cold. The corners of his blue eyes crinkled in a smile, and he winked at himself as the dormant vineyards slid past.

Ivan eased the Toyota onto I-205 at Stockton and turned toward the San Francisco Bay Area. The fields along the highway were frost-covered alfalfa and harvested corn. He faced a full day's drive to check out his target including time at the destination, Milpitas. But the trip was most likely worth spending a day in his vehicle.

If everything checked out, Mr. Jake Wilder would soon be another easy kill, and more cash would be deposited into Ivan's German account.

CHAPTER 3

Thirty-three-year-old Jake Wilder retrieved his luggage from Sheremetyevo Airport Number Two's single carousel and waited as the lone customs inspector X-rayed his suitcases. He exited through the only unpadlocked door into the airport's enormous arrival lobby. Exhaustion from the overnight flight from San Francisco to Frankfurt followed by a late-afternoon flight to Moscow, weighed on him like an extra pair of bags. But this was too great an adventure to let tiredness overcome him. *Moscow in January? I must be nuts!*

The arrivals area was poorly lit, and Jake searched the cavernous room for the interpreter he hired through his travel agent. The translator, car, chauffeur, and apartment came as a package costing less than cheap lodging back in Silicon Valley.

Jake spotted a plump, cigarette-smoking young woman with thick glasses and knit cap who held a cardboard sign that displayed his scrawled name. Next to the woman stood a middle-aged, broad-shouldered man under a corduroy jacket and ragged wool hat. The woman noticed him, and Jake lugged his suitcases to the pair. "Hello, I'm Jake Wilder."

The woman crushed her cig out on the muddy floor, shook his extended hand, and said, "I am Tatyana Filiminova. I recognize your red hair from agency's description. This is Victor. He owns the vehicle you will use."

Victor's last name wasn't offered, nor was his hand. The man nodded and turned to the only unlocked exit out of dozens. Jake lifted his suitcases, and he and Tatyana followed. *I guess the driver doesn't handle the luggage.*

Jake asked, "Why are all the doors chained except one? It

would be a challenge to get everyone out of here in an emergency."

Tatyana shrugged and answered, "Security."

Outside, they walked into the night heavy with snowflakes. The brittle cold stung Jake's ears, face, and nostrils. Tatyana watched him over her glasses, smirked, and led him through the frozen mud to the parking lot. They slid and crunched their way to a weathered, yellow Lada, which was a Russian-built Fiat. Victor forced one suitcase into the trunk and wedged the other into the back seat leaving scant room for Jake. While Jake and Tatyana sat in the well-used auto, Victor took the doors' rearview mirrors and windshield wipers from inside and reinstalled them. Tatyana lit a new cigarette and volunteered, "Thieves take them."

Victor climbed in and coaxed the small engine to start. The Lada bounced and careened onto the ten-lane boulevard that led to the city. The road was rough, but Victor seemed adept at avoiding potholes, at least the largest ones. Jake wondered if a wild maneuver would give his suitcase enough momentum to squash him. That is, if the door didn't pop open and spill him onto the ice-covered street. The latch did have a suspicious rattle, but so did the left back wheel bearing and the transmission.

Massive apartment complexes loomed in every direction on the hour drive, many festooned with enormous Marlboro signs. Though the falling snow was white, the city's grayness struck Jake. Light from an occasional streetlamp filtered to the ground, and automobile headlights weren't bright enough to illuminate the dark road.

While Tatyana and Victor chatted in Russian, Jake shivered in the cramped back seat, both from the cold and from anticipation. He'd flown to the other side of the world to be introduced to four young women on the chance he might find one to marry. *Now that sounds insane! Might be the dumbest thing I've ever done.*

He shook with cold again as Victor swerved to miss yet another gaping pothole, and the suitcase pinned him against the loose door.

Tatyana turned and asked Jake, "Is this your first time in Moscow?"

"Russia, actually."

"I have coordinated with the women you will meet. You will have a very good time, I promise you."

"Do many Americans come to Moscow to find a wife?" Jake asked.

"Oh, yes. Many women want to leave because the economy and inflation are so bad here."

"Just wondering if agency advertising is true. You been interpreting long?"

"Studied English at university and have offered my services for four years. The foreign money is good compared to what most women have to survive on. Times are not good here, so women want to leave for a better life."

Jake had corresponded with nineteen Russian women over the last eleven months, and the people he would meet were of particular interest. Each attracted him in different ways, and they would take trains to Moscow if needed.

Larisa was a thirty-one-year-old bank economist from Gorky with a daughter who was six. Jake believed having a child would be wonderful.

Next came the young and smart Irina, full of youthful enthusiasm, from St. Petersburg.

The intelligent, capable, and attractive Olga, whom he planned to see third, was a Moscow psychiatrist. She would make a "showcase" wife.

But he thought of Natalia in Moscow last and longest. He had exchanged more letters with her than anyone else. Natalia was sensitive and hopeful.

Still, he couldn't believe he was doing this. *You're nuts, Jake.*

Tatyana lit another cigarette, and the bitter smoke brought Jake back to the moment in the uncomfortable Lada. Victor braked and turned off the street. They entered a warren of snowy paths and meandered through an endless forest of twelve-story apartment buildings. People walked everywhere, many with dogs. Some people tugged little carts for shopping or children on sleds. Some carried satchels and bags. Men held vodka by the bottlenecks. All dove out of the way when Victor hit the horn.

After another thirty minutes, the car squeaked to a stop, and Tatyana took the last drag from her current smoke. While Victor sat in the Lada, Jake picked up his two cases and trailed Tatyana up several flights of dark, freezing stairs to a door with more locks than San Quentin. He stamped his feet and pulled his coat tight as Tatyana went through the sequence of keys to open the door.

After they stepped into the small hallway and wiped their mud-covered shoes on the inside mat, Tatyana turned on the lights.

If this place has a refrigerator, it's redundant! Jake thought.

The apartment was poor and shabby compared to Moscow hotels, which were among the most expensive in the world because the mobs controlled them. Jake didn't care about the money. As the long-time computer applications vice president for SmartSystems Corporation, he lived a comfortable life, but if he stayed nearer Red Square, he would have difficulty meeting the ladies. The Mafia ran the hotel prostitutes and didn't allow female visitors who might take their guests' minds off the in-house offerings. Jake had heard stories of prospective wives being roughly treated and even dragged away at gunpoint.

Tatyana gave Jake a quick tour of the small rooms. The

tiny kitchen contained a table for two, gas stove, and refrigerator.

I bet the fridge is warmer than the rest of the room.

The compact bathroom came next. The living room appeared like a sitcom set from the fifties. The five-socket ceiling light had one low-wattage bulb that cast shadows across the thin, worn, flowered linoleum. Jake paused at the bedroom and scratched his head. He rented a two-bedroom apartment, though he remembered the travel agent said "Russian standard." Apparently, "Russian standard" included the couch.

The tour complete, Tatyana said, "Bye-bye," took her invisible cloud of cigarette odor, and slammed the solid door behind her. Jake gazed around the dim, frigid space, and his tired body again trembled from the deep cold.

Yeah, I'm crazy.

CHAPTER 4

On Natalia's two-hour walk and trolly ride in the dark to work, her mind was consumed by her predicament. *Why did I choose a Bratva company? I didn't know, but a terrible decision!*

Last night, Mama agreed she should not go the police. What would the *politsiya* do against the Russian Mafia other than troll for bribes? And she couldn't identify the man in the shadows. Yes, if she involved the authorities she would put herself in more danger.

Dust drifted across the classroom as Natalia's beginner pupils attacked their exercises on the ten old pianos, but she couldn't focus. Their discordant notes fit her feelings. Of course, she wanted Mr. Jacob to select her. In his letters, he seemed a strong, capable, honest, and caring man who would be a trustworthy husband and father. Before, she had felt uncomfortable deceiving him about Alexandr, and now she feared what might happen because she had been untruthful. She ran her fingers through her blonde curls in frustration.

"Please start again," she directed her students.

Natalia gazed past the rows of Russian-made, Cohet-brand pianos and through the classroom's dirty windows. Somewhere in the city Mr. Jacob would be with another woman. She wouldn't meet him for several more days and fretted.

God, help me escape the mob boy.

* * *

Jake awoke cold, tired, and hungry after fitful sleep. He slid out of the narrow bed, put on his long underwear and heaviest clothes, and padded to the living room. He checked the radiator under the window. Tepid.

He grabbed a handful of trail mix from the bag he left on the kitchen table. *Maybe a shower will melt off this damned cold. If it's hot.*

Hot steam filled the small bathroom. Jake managed to adjust the temperature to a tolerable level, and the marvelous spray cascaded over him. *Why is the bathroom's water so hot and the radiator isn't?*

He closed his eyes, and his thoughts settled on what had driven him to travel to Moscow.

Loneliness. While building his Silicon Valley career, he never thought much about marriage. But now, he understood he seldom dated because of his shyness with the opposite sex. He was an ordinary—some would say, boring—executive who believed he would never be in the kind of relationship he longed for.

How would he find someone? His softball buddies continued to try to match him up with women they knew. His friends' intentions were good, but he had no interest in anyone he met, especially the gold-diggers.

He tried to keep his personal life from affecting his work, but Sergey Nazarov pointed out in his irreverent way, "You need good woman."

Jake frowned. "Why?"

The Russian software engineer twisted his long, brown beard. "So obvious. Happy men are better managers."

Jake had no retort and, after months, succumbed to his friend's campaign. Through correspondence with Russian women, he realized his employee might be right. Jake chided Sergey that he only wanted free present-delivery to his friends. One of the suitcases he had brought to Moscow was half-full of packages from Sergey and his wife, Veronika.

Jake finished showering and felt the steam evaporate off

him. He dressed and ate several pieces of jerky with his instant coffee.

Larisa Galkina, the bank economist from Gorky, would arrive that morning to spend two days with him.

He gazed at himself in the mirror and smiled.

* * *

Dmitri Chekhov sat in his office above his casino as loud music thumped through the floor. He fumed over the four-month wait for a network connection. Such commercial necessities should be easy to obtain.

Before Perestroika, the government controlled the Web. No matter. He did not need the Internet when he focused on smuggling and extortion.

He viewed himself as a businessman, not a criminal. He liked fine suits, craved American cigarettes, and envisioned retirement in luxury in Finland. Illegitimate businesses had been his only options under the Soviet system, and he pursued them without pity.

And, miracle of miracles, the vaunted USSR fell to earth and shattered into fifteen writhing pieces, the Commonwealth of Independent States. Only Russia mattered to Dmitri, and the past two years exceeded his wildest fantasy. After the collapse, his homeland became the Wild West—the term everyone used—with vodka instead of whiskey.

Men's true characters of greed and lust now ruled. Civil law enforcement was corrupt. Even the vaulted KGB had been cleaved into the ineffectual Domestic Counterintelligence Service, the FSB, and the Foreign Intelligence Service, known as the SVR.

At first, his protection business increased exponentially, though his black-market income evaporated. Private enterprises opened everywhere. Why smuggle if people could purchase what they wanted from trucks on the streets?

He chose to stay away from narcotics. Too few people had money for the wicked shit, and drug rivalries were fierce and bloody. No, let the uncouth thugs deal drugs. He would stick with protection as new establishments sprang to life like fields of dandelions.

Other gangs accumulated their own extortion customers, but Dmitri was not part of the wider Bratva. The rapid privatization created a bounty of targets for all the mobs. So far, his competitors left him alone, a measure of his vicious reputation.

He anticipated the illicit rings would turn against each other to continue their expansions. Human nature. When the mob organizations started to collide, the wars would be deadly. Because he was a newcomer, the others would come after him early. That didn't mean he would stop expanding. No, he would grow the protection business to the maximum while he completed his move into another racket.

Prostitution was not the answer. He developed a stable of young girls to cater to international businessmen, provide the casino's upstairs entertainment, and act as favors to officials he wanted to influence. But competition in the flesh trade was fragmented among the army of pimps.

Dmitri searched for a niche no one else had discovered, something to dominate without drawing attention. A business that required minimal manpower.

Entrepreneurs found opportunities where none appear to exist. He perceived one that so far escaped everyone.

He took a long drag on a Marlboro and perused his webmail.

The Internet promised reliable worldwide communications, and his FSB friends provided discreet access to mail passing through Moscow's Main Post Office. The internal spies couldn't handle electronics worth a damn, but they still read the mail. Too bad the same capability was not available in the rest of the country. For now, Dmitri contented himself with only a portion of the intelligence he sought.

He clicked through his email and contemplated Jacob Wilder. Two of the American's four dates resided in Moscow, and one, the Melnikova girl, belonged to his enterprise. His FSB contacts opened Wilder's letters and identified the other Muscovite, Olga Abramova. He did not know the other women's identities, but he dispatched three employees to persuade the psychiatrist to skip her meeting with Wilder. Natalia Melnikova was another potential gold mine, and he would not allow anything to interfere with her landing the rich American.

He rubbed his chubby, stubbled chin as rock music and the occasional shout from a satisfied or disappointed gambling patron came through the floor. Sporadic grunts and giggles emanated from the bedrooms down the hall.

Dmitri scrolled through his messages and smiled at the report from Ivan Rublev. Yes, Melnikova needed to make Wilder choose her. The stupid American would help make him wealthy.

CHAPTER 5

J ake tossed, turned, and shivered through another night. At least the constant snow made the air warmer than the brittle dryness.

After almost a week in Moscow, Jake awoke weary. Through the prior evening, televisions blared, loud music played, and families' voices came through the thin apartment walls. The sour smell of reheated borsch seeped from the stairwell. Somewhere, a youngster raced from room to room, hour after aggravating hour. *Bump, bump, bump, bump, bump. Bump, bump, bump, bump, bump.* He was astounded children possessed so much energy. The noise hadn't been as bothersome when Larisa Galkina visited three days ago, but last night his foul mood made the racket annoying.

He rolled over in frustration and buried his head under the stiff pillow. He enjoyed his time with the Gorky bank economist, but they experienced no "spark" between them. She was respectful, but they both knew they were not right for each other. He slept on the couch.

Irina Donskaya from St. Petersburg was sweet and attractive, but within an hour of her arrival, he realized they were wrong for each other. She proved to be emotionally and physically young, much younger than her correspondence indicated. He wondered if she had help with her letters.

He felt awkward with her, like a chaperone at a dance. They spent two days touring museums, and Irina constantly held his arm and pressed herself close. The first night, she asked him to sleep with her. Sergey had told Jake most Russian women viewed sex casually, but Jake couldn't do it. He would feel like an adulterer, so he slept in the living room. On the second night, she undressed in front of him and tried to take off his clothes.

He gently pushed her away and kissed her forehead. "I'm sorry, Irina, but I cannot."

She looked crestfallen. "Please, oh please make love to me. I want you!"

"It wouldn't be right, Irina. I can't."

The experiences with Larisa and Irina had been discouraging.

And last night Tatyana called. "I apologize to telephone so late, but Olga Abramova changed mind. She does not want to meet you."

"What?!"

"She refuses to see you and gave no explanation or apology. She spoke to me with rudeness."

Strange.

He exhaled. "Thanks for calling me."

Today, he pulled the bedcovers around him and listened as someone shoveled snow. The tool made long, irritating scrapes across the sidewalk. The day without meeting someone left little to look forward to, but perhaps he would deliver the gifts from Sergey and Veronika.

* * *

Red Square sat on a slope that rose from the Moscow River, and Jake followed Tatyana toward the city's most famous landmarks. The bitter, Arctic wind stung his face and nostrils. *Sure is different from sunny California.* The cobblestones were ice-covered and treacherous.

He stared at St. Basil's Church, which loomed ahead with its multi-colored onion domes. To the left stood the Kremlin.

The plaza opened before them, and Tatyana pointed to a

stone riser. "The raised platform is for public executions in the past."

Lenin's Tomb squatted halfway down the plaza, over-shadowed by the rust-red Kremlin Wall and Clock Tower. The white, multi-storied GUM Department Store stretched the length of the square on the right. A red brick administration building and an immense gate closed the far end.

He estimated a few thousand people milled across the square. Children bounced everywhere, many with parents and others in organized groups. The young people generated an energetic Christmas atmosphere. Happy laughter filled the air. Hawkers sold Polaroid pictures of people who posed in front of the attractions, and vendors peddled postcards from tables spread through the throng. He noted people avoided Lenin's tomb as if the granite edifice was radioactive.

Teenage prostitutes also worked the crowd. They approached him three times in the first forty yards. His quality clothes and unusual, bright-red hair marked him as an affluent for-eigner. Tatyana shooed them away with harsh words. The girls saddened him. *What an ugly way to spend their youth.*

Jake negotiated the slippery cobblestones toward the cathedral, where his interpreter and her plume of smoke led him up the steep, icy steps.

At the top, high above Red Square, she said, "St. Basil's is eight churches joined in common structure. One is in center, and seven smaller ones surround it. Worshipers stand. Takes less space."

Tatyana walked to a middle-aged woman who stood next to the ticket booth. The graying lady shuffled her five-foot frame to stay warm. She wore a scarf tucked into a long brown coat with years of wear. Jake took in her pleasant, round face.

The two women introduced themselves. The woman turned to him and extended her hand. Her gray eyes showed happiness and gratitude. Her English was slow and broken.

"Please to meet, Mr. Wilder. I Sveta Borisova. Veronika call me from America. She inform me you coming."

The woman appeared somewhat older than he had expected, or perhaps she seemed so because of the difficult life there. He shook her hand. "Delighted to meet you too."

The woman smiled. "*Spasibo* to bring gift to me and husband."

He gave her the shopping bag. "You are quite welcome. No problem at all."

Her eyes moistened as she handed him a small sack. "For you."

Inside he found a hand-painted matryoshka doll and a box of Red October chocolates. Modest, but he sensed their purchase had not been easy. "You are *so* kind. *Spasibo*."

The woman's smile beamed across her face. "You welcome."

The exchange accomplished, they said their good-byes, and the woman scurried away with her presents held close. As Sveta left, Jake scrutinized Tatyana, who stared at the departing woman.

He guessed the twenty-fiveish interpreter did not want the same difficult life.

CHAPTER 6

The Education Ministry was housed in a massive, uncompleted, seven-story structure in Lenin Prospect, near Moscow's highest point. The site lay across the Moscow River's horseshoe bend surrounding the Olympic Village built for the less-than-successful 1980 games. The white ministry building had been occupied for many years. On the south end, the habitable space disintegrated into bare concrete and exposed rebar. Like many government buildings, construction had been under-funded. Money ran out. Work stopped.

Natalia paused at the front entrance. The late-afternoon winter gloom gathered, which fit her feelings.

She did not know if a former student's father might assist her, but the assistant deputy director of Primary Education was the only official she knew. She had taught piano to Deputy Director Borovick's son, Ruslan, until he turned ten and became, like most boys, more interested in sports than music. She feared the man could not help, but she needed to try.

She wandered through the over-heated, dim corridors searching for Borovick's office until she found it. She straightened her fur hat, took a deep breath, and knocked.

"Enter!"

"Excuse me, Andrei Borovick, may I take a minute of your time?"

"Natalia Melnikova! What a surprise! Come in, come in!"

The short, heavyset man had thick brown hair, over-sized ears, and a meaty face. His smile was broad and sincere. His eyes sparkled. He extricated himself from behind his cluttered desk, ushered her to a chair, and telephoned for tea.

23

She settled in the seat as a babushka delivered the tea. The old woman poured the hot liquid into China cups and served them. They sipped in silence as the woman tidied up the tray and left.

"And how is your son?" she asked.

"Well, Ruslan likes wrestling, like his father. He is very skilled."

"Excellent. I am sure you are proud of him. Ruslan was exceptional at music. He will do well with whatever he pursues. Please give him my regards."

"I will." His eyes shifted from delight to curiosity. "So, what brings you out on this miserable afternoon?"

At the risk of her life and everything she held dear, she told him.

He listened, hands folded across his stomach, until she finished.

"I believe you are right not to go to the police because they cannot protect you. But why come to me?"

"Because I know of no other to go to."

He moved from behind his desk and paced across the small office. "I can do nothing against a mob boy. No one has such power."

The certainty of his words crushed her.

"This might be dangerous, Natalia." He hesitated. "But I have a dacha outside the city, a place for your mother and boy to hide. You may need to disappear, too."

She stared up at him. "You would do this for me?"

"You were an outstanding teacher to my son."

"But I have no money."

He gave a dismissive wave. "We will consider payment if my country place is needed."

She glanced down, afraid tears would surge to the surface. "Thank you for your generous offer, Andrei Borovick. If I need your dacha, I will somehow pay you for your risk. *Spasibo.*"

The deputy director smiled, but his forehead bunched with worry. "I am happy to help a friend."

She took a deep breath. She had reason to hope.

* * *

Dmitri Chekhov started his workdays in the afternoon, though the casino downstairs remained silent. The quiet did not bother him. In a few hours, boisterous gambling patrons would crowd the casino floor. His line of ten exceptional teenage prostitutes, who would sit seductively at the bar, would supplement his nightly income in the rooms down the hall from his office.

He shook his head and marveled at the swarm of young girls who flooded into Moscow and craved money in exchange for sex. He always selected the best of them for his stable.

Dmitri drummed his fingers on his wooden desk. He glanced out the window at the gritty view of the cityscape and blew smoke toward his office ceiling.

His first update of the day was from Vladimir Motorin, one of his collection agents, who sat in front of him. Dmitri thumped his desk harder as he grew furious. He was not upset with Motorin, only with the report. In fact, he expected Vladimir to become a reliable lieutenant or captain someday.

Motorin did not act or look like most of his Bratva employees. In his thirties, he was calm, smart, and executed tasks without bravado. His blond hair was well-cut, and he dressed in expensive suits. With his kind, blue eyes, Vladimir Motorin treated shopkeepers with respect as he made his collections. Merchants appreciated not having a goon enter their shops, which disquieted customers.

Except two clients.

Motorin said, "Fydor Kalita is again pleading for a reduction. He lies about his slow business and inability to feed his family. I checked. His profits are higher because people want quality Japanese electronics. What he lacks is money to fuck the whores as often as he wants.

"Yuri Belousov is a different problem. He didn't give me this week's collection. Claims there are too many auto parts stores to compete against. Another outlet opened two blocks away that cut into his sales, but I don't like his attitude. He should have told us so we could protect his establishment from the competition. Instead, he breaks our agreement."

Dmitri had his own ideas about punishing the recalcitrant clients, but, as a test, he decided to ask Motorin, "What would you do?"

Without hesitation, the bag man replied, "Tell Kalita if he doesn't want his rate increased, stop complaining and pay us. And when he hires a girl for sex, she must be one of ours and not freelancers.

"For Belousov, I would burn his establishment. If he says anything, kill him.

"I will go to the new store and sell them our services. We can point to Belousov's example of what happens when people cross you. Besides, we would have already eliminated their nearest competitor and boosted their revenue. They'd owe us."

Yes, Dmitri Chekhov believed Motorin had potential. He might be slight in stature and soft-spoken but ruthless. "Solve both problems as you suggest. Take whatever help you want."

Dmitri thought for a moment. Should he give Motorin a task beyond his current responsibilities as another test? He rubbed his chin. "In the morning at ten o'clock, a car will pick up a woman at this address. Blonde in her twenties." He leaned forward and wrote on a piece of paper. "I want the location where she spends the night. If she does not stay at least three days, I must know immediately. Use whomever you need on this, too."

Motorin read the note and slipped it into his pocket. "Anything else?"

Dmitri shook his head, and the collection agent left. He was not ready to trust fate or Natalia Melnikova's young body that Jacob Wilder would choose her. Added steps were necessary to make sure the American did. Motorin would be the tool to find the idiot's location.

Four of his associates had visited the Abramova woman and convinced her to withdraw meeting with Wilder, but the two women from elsewhere worried him. Once Dmitri knew where the American stayed, he would be watched in case one of the out-of-town bitches returned to solidify her relationship with him. If that happened, she would also experience an unwelcome encounter.

He had telephoned Melnikova at her work, and she told him where and when she would be picked up. If Wilder was interested, she would stay at his apartment.

Dmitri snuffed out his cigarette with a satisfied smile. He called for one of his fresh, younger girls to be sent to his office.

CHAPTER 7

T he Lada bounced through dim, slushy streets to a tavern, and when Victor, Jake's driver, activated the windshield washer, Tatyana inhaled and laughed. Victor had poured vodka in the reservoir to avoid frozen water, and the alcohol's scent filled the cramped car.

Jake stared at the occasional Christmas decorations that sparkled in the otherwise dark city. Tonight, he waxed philosophically about the lack of spark between him and Larisa, the mismatch with young Irina, and Olga's cancellation. *If nothing comes of this trip, at least I tried.*

With no plans for the night, Jake had asked Tatyana to call Sergey and Veronika's friends and invite them to dinner.

His interpreter said, "The Borisovs are happy to accept. I made certain they understand they are your guests."

Now, Jake rode on his way to the restaurant for the evening with the people to whom he had delivered the presents. After an hour of dodging potholes and rattling over cobblestone-lined trolly tracks, the Lada loudly screeched to a halt at a row of shops on the dark road.

People streamed from a storefront with loaves of unwrapped bread. Another shop sold frozen blocks of fish. A babushka hawked eggs from crates stacked on the sidewalk.

How does she keep them from freezing? Jake wondered.

Lampposts with Lowenbrau beer insignias stood by the tavern's door. Jake's spirits lifted because the brand had once been his favorite.

Tatyana set the time for Victor's return, and he drove away. "He will go to friend," she said.

They scaled the ridge of plowed snow separating the road

from the walkway, and Jake again noticed there were almost no smells in the city. Too damn cold.

Jake stated, "Victor doesn't like me much, does he?"

"It is not you. He was Army major, but there was no money. Soldiers often are not paid. His wife and daughter were hungry. He commanded a transportation division with many trucks, but now he drives foreigners so his family can eat. He is proud. This is hard for him."

Jake nodded as they entered the eatery. Short candles illuminated the five tables. A bar took up an entire wall because this was Russia. There were no other diners because this was Russia.

A bored-looking hostess in a revealing red dress showed them to a four-top table near the back. The bar's lights and table candles were the room's only illumination. Thick, heavy red and black curtains covered the windows to keep in the heat. The odor of burned tobacco permeated the air, and Tatyana's cigarettes added to the stink with gusto, which annoyed Jake.

While she buried one cigarette in the cheap tin ashtray and lit another, he eyed the Lowenbrau mugs, taps, and lamps. A slim waitress arrived to take their order. No Lowenbrau, which started a three-way Russian/English conversation between Jake, Tatyana, and the waitress. The place had not carried the brand in years or removed the accouterments.

Tatyana turned to Jake and shrugged. "This is Russia."

Jake settled for an Elephant Beer, the only brew they carried.

Tatyana exhaled a smoky cloud. "Disappointed about the women you come to see?"

"Things were not right with Larisa and Irina, which is fine, but I don't understand why Olga changed her mind."

Tatyana pushed her glasses up her nose and tapped her ash into the tin. "Olga Abramova was indignant and refused to talk. She would not explain why she would not visit after

29

you came so far to join her."

Jake's shoulders sagged in resignation.

The front door swung open, and two people stepped in. He recognized Mrs. Borisova by the patterned scarf over her head. Her tall, broad-shouldered husband wore an old, long, brown leather coat. His fur hat accentuated his height, and his bushy mustache made him look intimidating in contrast to his kindly spouse. Jake guessed the man was in his early forties.

Sveta Borisova's face brightened, and she waved. Her smile cheered Jake despite his romantic disappointments.

The couple came to the table. The man extended his hand and said in accented English, "I Sidor Borisov. Pleased to meet."

Jake took the firm but friendly grip. "Jake Wilder. I'm happy you two are here."

The man smiled with uneven teeth and turned to allow Sveta to shake Jake's hand.

Once seated and their orders taken, the two women conversed in Russian, so Jake asked Sidor, "Where did you learn English?"

The man's eyes took on a far-off stare. "Army. I was two years in Cuba." He tilted his head and nodded. "I, uh, studied your country."

"Studied?"

"Listened to military communications."

Jake's mouth dropped open a moment before he collected himself. *Of course they spy on us. We do the same to them.* "So, what was Cuba like?"

Sidor grimaced. "Stinking hellhole. We spent most time in barracks and went out only for work and baseball."

"You play ball?"

Borisov's mustache went up as his wrinkled face broke into a smile. His deep-brown eyes had an intelligent glint. "First base. Russians hate American game, but commander forced us play friendship games with damned Cubans. Baseball only thing they are better. But I loved when we sometimes won."

Jake pictured the scene on a hot, dusty Caribbean diamond. He envisioned how Borisov's long arms and body worked well at first base. "I play ball, too."

"You do?"

"Have for years. Fast-pitch softball on my company's team. Used to be shortstop, but now third base. My legs are slower, but my arm can still fire a bullet to first."

The Russian gave Jake an approving nod. "I not miss that hot sewer Cuba, but I came to love baseball."

The arrival of their food interrupted the conversation. Jake's sturgeon baked with crab, egg, cheese, and the ubiquitous potatoes smelled wonderful. He scanned the table. All the enormous, steaming meals looked rich and delicious.

Sidor finished his beer with two swallows. Jake motioned to the bartender, and replacement cans soon appeared. While the ladies chatted, the two men discussed famous Cuban batters, and, after desserts, they moved on to talk about their jobs over vodka. Jake was surprised Sidor was a police lieutenant and now realized why he seemed threatening. An occupational requirement.

And Jake understood he must be careful about how much more he drank. Sure, he was on vacation, enjoyed the banter with his new-found friend, and didn't have to drive.

But tomorrow he would see Natalia.

* * *

Natalia packed for her time with Mr. Jacob. She folded the best dresses she and Mama had sewn. New boots she could not afford sat by the table, which held the cake she made. She put a small box of Red October chocolates and a bottle of champagne for one of the evenings into a shopping sack.

Her clothes went into the old suitcase her mother had before Natalia was born.

Alexandr played on the rug with his toy car, and Natalia smiled as she watched her happy son. His gentle disposition, bright smile, and curly yellow hair brought her much joy.

But Natalia's excitement about Mr. Jacob had been stolen and replaced with dread. She would spend four days plus nights with the man who, through his letters, seemed the one she had dreamed of. They could now be in danger. Her only hope was that Andrei Borovick might help her with his dacha if needed. She knew of no other protection from possible Bratva wrath. She would have to leave Moscow.

CHAPTER 8

J ake paced the small flat and paused to stare out the window at the snowy, frozen landscape. The roads and paths below were crowded with people going about their daily lives. Workers. Shoppers. School children.

Still can't believe I'm in Moscow, 'specially in winter!

He turned and paced some more. Up before dawn because he couldn't sleep, and time had crawled all morning. *Natalia should be on her way by now.* His heart quickened a notch. The frigid apartment didn't feel so cold.

He grinned as he re-lived his joy when he went to his mailbox back home each day after sending those initial letters to Russia. One day, an envelope with red and blue stripes on the edges of the cheap paper arrived.

The woman described herself. Twenty-five. Piano teacher. Divorced. Natalia Melnikova wanted to learn more about him and apologized for her poor English.

He recalled his gasp when he held the photograph she had sent. Her thumbnail photo in the Russian Introductions catalog had caught his attention, but this full-body picture was stunning. Petite, with smokey-blue eyes and clear, fair skin. Her delicate mouth carried a slight, almost shy, smile.

Insecurity had washed over him. *Why would she want anything to do with me? Cripes, I'm six years her senior!* He'd relaxed a little after he remembered the words in the catalogs had said Russian women preferred older men because they provided stable, more secure homes.

His mind back in the cold apartment, Jake stomped another lap around the room and hoped Natalia would be interested in him once they met.

He thought of her passion for music. Unlike the other women, she thought highly of her country despite the "temporary difficulties." An optimist. And she had written of her search for a reliable, devoted partner, the same as he did.

Before he left The States, he decided to meet her after the others and spend the most time with her. He prayed the time with Natalia would be different than with Larisa and Irina.

The familiar screech of brakes roused him. He stared out the window for the hundredth or so time in the last half hour. *She's here!* His pulse quickened.

From above, he watched Victor park the car, and Tatyana and Natalia got out. Natalia carried a small suitcase and a bulky shopping sack.

He bolted to the door, jammed himself into his greatcoat and boots, and raced down the stairs. He went out the building's thick wooden door as the women reached the steps. He did not register the cold's bite on his face and ears.

They all hesitated a moment. "Hello. May I take your things?" he said.

She's more beautiful in person than in her photos. Sensuous lips and blonde curls framed her fresh face. *She might be mistaken for a movie star.*

A hint of fright flashed through her eyes, which he understood because she was here to stay with a foreign stranger. But her smile widened, and her eyes showed pleasure.

"Hallo, Mr. Jacob." She spoke in halting English.

She blushed and talked to Tatyana in Russian, who translated, "She is sorry. You are Mr. Wilder. She thinks of you as Mr. Jacob. Please forgive her mistake."

He almost laughed, but Natalia's embarrassment appeared profound. He shook his head. "No apology needed. You can use whatever name you wish. To most people, I'm 'Jake.'"

Tatyana translated for Natalia, who nodded. "If you agree, I will call you 'Jacob.' I Natalie."

"Why Natalie?"

"Natalie is your equal to Natalia. Easier for you," Tatyana explained.

He realized the grin hadn't left his face. He tilted his head and softly said, "I can only think of you as 'Natalia.'"

The bitter wind across his uncovered ears finally registered in his mind. "Let's go in." He took Natalia's bags and led the two women inside.

He put the luggage in the bedroom and allowed Natalia privacy to unpack. This had to be more awkward for her than for him. While he and Tatyana waited, the interpreter gave him an approving nod.

Yes, Natalia is exceptional, Jake agreed.

* * *

Natalia unpacked her bag and hung her dresses in the small, worn wardrobe. She didn't want to keep Jacob waiting but fidgeted with her appearance in the mirror.

Jacob was handsome with his red hair, green eyes, and smooth face. *He does not have the rough Russian look. He is polite and his expression honest. No guile in his eyes.*

Her fear of the Bratva intruded, made worse by her dishonesty about Alexandr, but she vowed to hide those worries while she and Jacob were together.

And, somehow, she would find a way out of the trap.

She went into the living room and announced, "I ready."

* * *

Jake sat in amused silence as the Lada lurched through the gray streets. The women chatted about where to eat. Curls of Natalia's hair escaped from under her fur hat and bounced as she laughed.

Tatyana turned to him. "We planned day. First, we will go to sport facility near the Kremlin."

"Sport facility?"

"Yes, the building has all sports inside, but restaurant is excellent. It is best for lunch. Next, you will visit the Tretyakov Gallery. Dinner will be Pizza Hut."

"Pizza Hut?"

Worry crossed Natalia's forehead, and she answered, "*Da.* I have not before."

Those blue eyes. He was helpless. "Perfect!"

Natalia's smile returned. "I happy."

"Me, too."

The vast dining room in the basement of the multi-storied, city-block-sized complex was permeated with the aroma of wonderful food. The entertainment alternated between a television blaring Mexican soap operas dubbed in Russian and a duo belting out tunes on a piano and violin. What the pair lacked in musical sophistication, they countered with volume. Talk was impossible.

Jake contented himself with the sight of Natalia across the table.

The women were correct about the food. Jake's garlic chicken was the best ever. And something else he appreciated—Tatyana smoked less and only outdoors. He welcomed the change from her chimney over the past several days.

The slow-arriving bill came to the equivalent of eight dollars for the three of them. Jake peeled bills off his wad of rubles and left a generous tip.

Outside, he was comfortable in the cold. He wasn't sure if that was because of the meal or Natalia. Perhaps both.

They climbed into the waiting Lada and rode over the Moscow River and through narrow, ancient alleyways. When they arrived two blocks from the Tretyakov, Victor parked, and Tatyana informed Jake, "Victor and I will come for you in four hours."

"Four hours?"

"*Da.*"

Jake assisted Natalia out of the grimy car, and they strolled down the broad snow-covered sidewalk to the plaza in front of the Tretyakov. Though many people plodded down the walkway with purpose, quiet enveloped Jake and Natalia other than the crunch of snow under their boots. She took his arm, and he smiled to himself despite the self-doubt that swirled inside him. *Why would such a beautiful woman want anything to do with me?*

He glanced at her, and she beamed at him. Snowflakes clung to her hat, curls, and fur collar of her heavy coat. He fought the urge to stop and hug her. He inhaled her sweet perfume.

Her face turned anxious. "Admission expensive. Ten thousand rubles."

With an average fifty dollars a month salary, ordinary Russians could not afford the two-dollar admission. He enunciated slowly, "Do not worry. Have you seen the Tretyakov before?"

"*Nyet.*"

"Me neither," he said. She gently squeezed his arm, and his unease evaporated.

Her body brushed against his as they walked up the stone steps and entered the gigantic brick building. After they entered, Jake floated with the stream of well-dressed people down the marble stairs to a lower level. They checked their coats, he bought tickets, and they tied strange-looking felt slippers over their shoes. The coverings laced at the toe and heel and looked elfin. "Protect floor," she explained.

They shuffled their way to the first gallery. The massive paintings and sculptures impressed Jake. Most depicted life and nobles, but many works evoked profound human emotion. Suffering. Triumph. Betrayal. The simplicity of peasant life. They traded clipped comments of, "I like," or, "Famous." But he felt at ease with her as they wandered arm-in-arm. Her eyes sparkled, and she moved with grace.

She's delightful.

By the fifth gallery, the art pieces blended in Jake's mind. After eighty galleries in the massive, multi-storied building, the three-thousand-piece collection was a blur to Jake, and his feet ached from the tight shoe covers.

CHAPTER 9

Natalia and Jake walked to where the car would pick them up. She embraced his arm and thought about the long tour, though she was not tired. They spoke little, and he was attentive. He opened doors for her. He held her chair. He helped her with her coat. He seemed nervous but was as kind as she imagined. *Why can't I find such a man in Russia?*

Jacob was a soft-spoken person. She liked his eyes and unusual red hair full of deep fire in contrast to his gentleness. And he was wealthy, like all Americans. *This man can take any girl he wants. Why would he choose me?*

A shadow passed over her heart. She feared the consequences if he did not select her.

Jacob's driver had parked on the street, and she smiled to herself as Jacob hurried to open the door for her.

* * *

Jake looked forward to riding in the cramped Lada with Natalia. In addition to sitting close to her, his feet throbbed because of the gallery's bizarre slippers that required him to shuffle and slide across the floors. He wondered if the shoe covers weren't actually intended to polish instead of protect the hardwood.

Victor drove to a boulevard lined with up-scale clothing and accessory stores and turned into a small square crammed with cars and people. The early night had descended, and Christmas lights brightened the sidewalk. Victor had nowhere to park, so he stopped in the street.

Tatyana stated, "We get out here."

Jacob, Natalia, and Tatyana climbed out and joined the long, outdoor Pizza Hut queue. The car disappeared into the traffic. Jake stamped his feet to stay warm in the chilly breeze, but he didn't feel as cold as he had. Natalia's closeness warmed him from within.

An armed guard stood at the restaurant's door to prevent diners from entering until a table became available. The well-lit restaurant was packed.

As they inched forward, Jake took in the shops. Their lights glowed brightly through the falling snow. His heart smiled because Natalia appeared happy to be with him.

"You like Moscow?" she asked.

No, I don't. What to say? "I like being here, especially with you."

Natalia's cheeks turned a soft red.

They talked and shuffled for an hour to reach the door. Once inside, the loud chatter struck Jake. People laughed and enjoyed themselves.

Other than the menu being in both Cyrillic and English, the pizzeria was indistinguishable from its stateside cousins. A waitress took their order of individual pan pizzas with different toppings.

After excusing himself to go to the men's room, he came back to find Natalia and Tatyana speaking rapid-fire Russian. Natalia said, "Excuse please," as she got up and went to the restroom.

Tatyana toyed with her cigarette lighter. Jake knew she would kill to light up but was thankful she didn't.

She gazed at him over her glasses. "She likes you."

"She does?"

"And you like her. I know such things."

He didn't dispute Tatyana's opinion about his feelings. Natalia captivated him. His real wonder was her attraction to him. "But we just met."

She shook her head. "Does not matter. This is common. When people hunt hard for something, they know when they find it."

The thought he might be what she sought pleased him. So did Natalia's smile when she returned to the table.

* * *

Natalia closed the door and hugged herself in the small bedroom, happy and afraid. She thought about the man in the next room, with his gentle eyes and white teeth. He was a real gentleman who treated her like a lady. *What an extraordinary day.* Meeting Jacob had been so much better than she expected.

She would remember the fabulous Tretyakov the rest of her life, and the incredible treat of Pizza Hut sated her constant hunger. But the best for her came at the end in the apartment. He prepared his bed on the couch. This simple action confirmed what she believed in her heart about the tall American. *He is a good man.*

He desired her. She saw it in his eyes and heard it in his voice, but he was different from men here who had tried to force themselves on her. His eyes flattered. The other glares did not. He cared about her, and the others pursued her only for sex.

Natalia undressed in the cold and slipped on a flannel nightgown. She wouldn't need her negligée because she would sleep alone. She wanted to make love with Jacob and would if he asked. But he would be in the next room, which made her want him more.

Her son and the mob boy jumped into her thoughts, and the fairy-tale shattered into shards. *Why did I lie to Jacob? If I only told the truth...*

* * *

41

The kiosk vendors who lined Moscow's sidewalks huddled around buckets of burning coal. Policemen directed traffic, pounded their hands together, and stomped their feet to keep warm. Frost clung to mustaches and beards.

Bundled in his greatcoat, Jake smiled, and Natalia's eyes sparkled.

Victor drove them and Tatyana to the Old Moscow Circus, which Natalia had seen as a child. As they arrived at the tall building, Tatyana spoke sharply to Victor, who accelerated and pulled the Lada to a stop on the sidewalk.

"Easy to buy tickets, but militia here," Tatyana said. "I don't want you involved if problem happens. Wait here."

She climbed out and scurried away. Several minutes later, she returned. "Give me one hundred thousand rubles," which he did. The equivalent of twenty dollars for admission seemed reasonable. Back in the car, she handed him two slips of thin paper.

Jake helped Natalia out, and they strolled arm-in-arm up the avenue. As they approached the building, young militiamen with submachine guns surveyed the people who milled near the entrance.

The couple walked into the noisy lobby and checked their coats and hats, as was the custom. She squeezed his arm as they descended the steep stairs to their seats. The usher took them to the front row, inches from the round, ice-covered stage.

How can a circus performance be on ice? Jake wondered.

Natalia clapped her hands and beamed with girlish excitement.

The lights faded, music began, and clowns sped around the rink. All the performers wore skates. Acrobats, dancers, and men riding unicycles. The best acts were the clowns, the funniest Jake had ever seen.

Too soon, the houselights went up. He was sorry the fun

ended but happy when Natalia kissed his cheek.

"*Spasibo*. That mean 'Thank you much,'" she said.

"You are welcome. I loved the show." *And the kiss.*

Though early, they exited the building into the dark, bone-aching cold. Tatyana's smoke caught Jake's attention before he spotted her under a streetlight. She tossed her cigarette. "Circus good?"

"Delightful, and our seats were in the front row. *Spasibo*," he said.

She waved him away. "Your money, but I didn't want problems for you. They try to stop illegal sales. Impossible. Would you like to go to restaurant?"

"Whatever Natalia wishes."

The two women began a long exchange. Tatyana smirked and informed him, "She would like to prepare dinner tonight if you agree."

Natalia gazed up at him with hopeful, smoky-blue eyes.

"Of course! *Da!*"

CHAPTER 10

They stopped at a so-called supermarket, which proved to be a challenge because most of the small store's shelves were empty. After waiting in line to enter the market, they quickly acquired what they needed and went back to the car for the ride to his apartment. Jake placed the groceries on the tiny table. "Can I help?"

Natalia cocked her head in a quizzical expression. After a moment, she shooed him out.

While she hummed and prepared dinner, he tidied the apartment and swept up the dirt and mud that had come off their shoes.

"Ready!" she announced.

Braised chicken, cabbage, and mashed potatoes filled the table along with a plate of pickles, glasses of fruit juice, and dark bread.

He spoke no Russian, and she struggled with English, so they talked little during the meal other than his repeated, "Superb," and her asking, "More?"

Jake finally couldn't eat another bite. The flavors were different from what he was accustomed to, but the savory feast satisfied him. Miming with his hands to communicate his meaning, Jake said, "You are an *excellent* cook. I will wash the dishes."

"*Spasibo.*" She went to the bedroom and came back in her robe as he dried the last plate. He would have thought her changing into a house robe was provocative except Larisa Galkina, his first date, explained that robes were the usual household attire. Regular clothes were too expensive to wear at home.

He lit the stove under the water kettle. "Tea?"

"*Da*. Cake, too?"

"*Da*."

She took her cake out of the refrigerator and cut generous slices while he dropped teabags into cups. They moved gingerly around each other in the tight space. His upper arm brushed her breast, and her hips touched his abdomen when she turned. Natalia blushed, and Jake felt heat in his face. He wanted to hold her but didn't. He feared he would spoil everything.

They relaxed side-by-side on the couch with their dessert and tea. Jake opened his Russian-English dictionary, and they began a tortured, slow conversation. He appreciated the effort she had spent writing to him.

"Please tell your life," Natalia said.

He had shared much in his correspondence but was happy to talk to her slowly in simple, precise English. He grew up without a father, or, as his mother always called him, "the bum." His mom died during his second year at college, run down by a drunk teenager whose parents provided both the souped-up Mustang and the alcohol.

"The main things in my life are work, my dog, Silky, and baseball."

"Like job?"

He nodded. "I am lucky. I joined SmartSystems after college when the company started."

Her eyes showed fascination. "What else?"

"There is not much more."

Her forehead creased in a slight frown. "No married?"

"*Nyet*." He sensed from her expression she wanted more. Though the translation took effort, he enjoyed talking with her. "I focused on my job, and I am shy around women."

She regarded him in disbelief when he pointed to the dictionary word for "shy."

"True! I guess that is common for people in software engineering. Sometimes we do better with computers than people."

She set down her teacup. "Why interest to marry now?"

"I have always been interested but never found the right person. Now I am lonelier than before."

She reached over and ran a finger down his jawline. "Sorry."

He shook his head. "My fault, but if I had someone, I would not be here." *And I wouldn't have discovered you.*

Careful, Jake.

He swallowed hard and tried to change the subject. "What about you? You live with your mother?"

"*Da.* Papa die when I young, as I told in letters. My mother was music teacher. She retire."

"Could we take your mother to lunch? I would like to meet her."

"Not possible," she said with a forceful timbre in her voice.

He turned his head in surprise and disappointment. Perhaps she did not like him enough to meet her mother.

She said, "Mama at friend in another city." She tried not to look sad at her flagrant lie.

Satisfied, he asked, "You like your work?"

Her face became a portrait of delight. "I love music and teaching piano. Good for soul."

"I have no musical talent."

"Important to start young."

They paused for more cake. "Can you tell me about your marriage?"

Her face turned earnest. "I tell. You need know all." She took another swallow of tea. "Vitaly army officer. I thought he be happy with me but no. He drink too much vodka and stay out nights with other women.

"After Soviet Union, we had freedom but little to eat. Many starve. Vitaly gave money for me to take train to aunt in Ukraine. She had food.

"I return in three months. Apartment a mess." An undertone of anger crept into her voice. "Stinking clothes in piles. Vodka bottles. All garbage." Her chin quivered. "The bed stained with wine and fluids of other women."

She bowed her head, moisture in her eyes. She bit the inside of her lip.

His heart ached for her. To divert the topic, Jake picked up her empty cup. "Would you like more?"

She forced a smile and answered, "*Nyet.*" Her face brightened. "Would you like Russian tradition?"

He did not understand what she meant, but no matter. "*Da.*"

Her bad memories apparently pushed aside, she seemed to float to the kitchen. He heard cellophane rustle and a cork *pop.* She motioned him to join her.

A small candle illuminated the room. On the table sat a box of chocolates, two flutes, and champagne. She indicated he should pour, which he did. His toast, "To dreams."

"*Da.*" They clinked glasses. She smiled, ate a piece of candy, and sipped. "Russian tradition."

Jake followed her lead. The chocolate tasted different, halfway between milk and dark, but he liked it with the champagne, though it was a cheap Russian vintage. "This is wonderful!"

Natalia's curls, eyes, and smile glowed in the candlelight. He wondered if his special someone sat before him. *Does she feel the same?*

By their third glass, they laughed and giggled about the absurdities in each other's country. The half-constructed Moscow buildings. The cost of driving in Russia and the terrible roads. The lack of public transportation in the US, which mandated cars. Russian soap operas. American soap operas. Inconsequential stuff. Silly things.

Soon, no chocolates remained, the bottle sat empty, and the hour had grown late.

When they stood, he gently pulled her to him and hugged her. "*Spasibo.*"

After the hug, she busied herself to put things away. He smiled and made his bed on the couch.

She entered the living room. "Goodnight."

He put out his arms, and she came to him. He kissed the top of her head. "Sweet dreams." He let her go, and she went to her room. He looked at the closed door a moment before he undressed, climbed under the old quilt, and turned out the lamp.

Sleep did not come. Jake adjusted the bedding to get comfortable. Hopeless. He stared at the furniture, the ceiling, the wall.

Her door squeaked. "Jacob?"

"Yes?"

"I 'fraid." She stood in the dark doorway.

Jake vaulted out of bed and jammed on his pants.

He held her. "Why are you afraid?"

She didn't answer, only clung to him and trembled.

He couldn't help himself. In the faint light, he saw fear but also longing. He kissed her, and she kissed him back.

Their embrace intensified.

He slipped his hands under her robe and caressed her warm, soft skin.

She undid his clothes, which slid to the floor. She let her robe slip off her shoulders.

* * *

Dawn came late as always that far north, but Jake wished this night would last forever. He held Natalia close under the narrow bed's disheveled covers.

His prior sexual encounters differed from last night. *Why?* After a few sleepy minutes, he understood. Passion was different from plain intercourse. Sex with Natalia was breathtaking passion, which he wanted for his life.

He stroked her hair as she lay still beside him, her eyes closed. He draped his arm around her.

* * *

Natalia felt the steady rise of Jacob's chest as he slept. She pressed closer against him and breathed his scent.

Perhaps an illusion, but she felt safe in his arms. The mob boy didn't seem so terrifying at that moment. She thought about Jacob and knew she could be happy and grow to love him.

How can this man from the other side of the world be everything I want? Am I what he wants? What if I am not?

She pulled his arm tighter against her body.

CHAPTER 11

The Moscow air terminal spotlights glowed in the pre-dawn snow. Ice crusted the Lufthansa jet's wings that would carry Jake to Frankfurt. He fidgeted in his seat because the wait for the de-icing truck seemed interminable.

Most passengers appeared as exhausted as Jake felt. Many drowsed, but he stared into the snowy gloom. Somewhere in the dark, Natalia rode home, and a hollow ache clenched his stomach. Victor and Tatyana had picked them up at three AM for the long ride to Sheremetyevo Airport for his flight.

Jake had left generous dollar tips for Tatyana, Victor, and the person who owned the apartment where he had stayed. He knew the additional cash would be significant for them.

Recalling the past five days, he and Natalia had enjoyed their time together. He extended his stay an extra day to spend more time with her and wondered if he dreamed and would wake to reality. In his weary stupor, he hoped not. He had no doubt he wanted Natalia as his wife. He thought about when he proposed to her in a candle-lit restaurant. He took both her hands and asked, "Will you marry me?"

Delight swept across her face. "Da, Jacob. I will marry. Thank you for wanting me."

"Thank you for wanting me, too. I know you are worried about leaving Russia."

"Da, but I want to be with you."

Jake felt happy and in passionate love. Something he had never experienced.

Their time together raced by, especially the hours they walked, talked, and planned her trip to America. Their communication and understanding improved as the days passed.

Their six-year age difference didn't matter to him, and when he raised the issue, she assured him she was happy with him regardless of how old he was.

He had found someone exceptional he'd hungered for. *I'm a lucky man.*

Telling Natalia goodbye at the airport was torture. They would not reunite for months because of how the US fiancée visa process operated.

She implored him, "Forget me no."

He gave her a long hug and kiss and held her creamy-white cheeks. "How can I forget you? I won't be happy until we are together again."

He didn't know what words she understood but knew she comprehended his feelings.

And this plane would start him on his long journey to the other side of the world. Boring Jake Wilder had come to Russia and found a beautiful woman he planned to marry. An incredible adventure. He could now do anything.

* * *

Natalia said goodbye to Tatyana and Victor, and both congratulated her as she got out of the Lada in front of her apartment high-rise.

She climbed the silent stairs to her apartment and thought about Jacob. She bit her lip. She had almost told him about Alexandr a dozen times or more, but fear still strangled her tongue. A guilty ache writhed beneath her happiness.

Everything they said about American men proved true, at least for Jacob. He came here and chose her and insisted she take five hundred dollars to cover the costs of coming to the United States. Yes, there would be expenses, but five hundred! She couldn't believe he trusted her with such a fortune.

She left her suitcase in the darkened entryway and tip-toed to Alexandr's small bed. His covers had slipped off him, so she pulled them up and tucked him in. She stroked his back. She missed him so much these past days.

The bed in her mother's room creaked, and Mama came to the bedroom door. They embraced.

"Oh, Mama, he is perfect."

"Is he a good man?"

"He is an excellent one."

Her mother gave her a relieved smile. "Come, let's have tea. You must tell me all about him."

* * *

Vladimir Motorin craved strong coffee and sweet pastries this Monday morning. He took a table in a café near the Metro Station on Sukharevskaya Street, one of his preferred places. Though not a Chekhov account, he came to this eatery often. The two waitresses and cook greeted him as a friend. He was no one's comrade, but they liked him, doubtless because of his expensive clothes and generous tips.

He came here because of the clientele. Many worked at the European embassies, and he admired their clothing and mannerisms. These people were cultured and sophisticated compared to the oafs he usually dealt with. He observed the patrons to understand their ways and habits because he didn't plan to remain a bag man forever.

A new country bloomed in front of his eyes, yet few fathomed the seismic change. His boss, Chekhov, did and had positioned himself to exit at the right time. Why else would he keep his money in German banks?

Vladimir envisioned a different future. Leave Russia? No. He would build his own constituency and become a leader in the Bratva to come. He would exert god-like control over any

Russian bank that held his deposits. He would rule.

Until then, he would make his daily collections, relax in this café to study the Europeans, and capitalize on additional opportunities certain to come. A few lay ahead this week. No surprise. Vladimir had every confidence his quiet professionalism was watched and valued. His upward climb was underway.

He paid his bill and visited the electronic outlet store owner about the man's request for a rate reduction. He explained with sympathy, "My employer is furious, Fydor Kalita, and wants your head with a bullet inside. I, myself, persuaded him otherwise and to keep your fee unchanged, though you must use only our prostitutes to feed your urges. You would now be dead if I did not argue on your behalf. You owe me your life. Don't ask favors again."

Another personal constituent.

* * *

Vladimir ordered two enforcers to shoot the auto parts proprietor, Yuri Belousov, in the head when he opened for business. He had them drag Belousov's body to the sidewalk before they burned the store. No witnesses, of course. But the new, nearby automobile supply proprietor was most willing to do business with soft-spoken Vladimir when he introduced himself the next day.

The two assignments were the first where the boss had asked his opinion and allowed him to act on his own. A significant step. And the thugs in the organization sensed his new power.

His thoughts turned to Chekhov's interest in the Melnikova woman. Why did the boss care about how many nights she stayed with the foreigner with odd red hair? Vladimir decided to find out. Whatever this entailed, he assumed the scheme was both lucrative and wicked.

CHAPTER 12

Tired to his soul, Jake drove Highway 237 along the southern stretch of San Francisco Bay on his way home from San Francisco International. The rhythm of the windshield wipers made him drowsy. The reflections of oncoming headlights off the wet pavement hurt his eyes. He had slept little on the journey from Moscow. He was happy but weary. *Going to be a challenge getting to work tomorrow.*

He picked up his dog, Silky, from one of his softball teammates in Palo Alto. She had bounced and run in circles when she saw him. Her short tail wagged, and her brown and mottled body shook with excitement. She had lost a pound or two, but she should be fine now he was home. She perched on the pickup's passenger seat and alternatively glanced at the surroundings and back at him. She seemed to search for familiar landmarks while she made sure he was still there.

In Milpitas, he cruised straight through the town's commercial center. Many high-tech companies, including SmartSystems, headquartered in the city just north of San Jose.

Jake was luckier than most because he owned a house in the hills off Piedmont Road with a panorama of the bay. He had purchased the home when he landed the job at SmartSystems, back before housing prices went stratospheric. New homes up the street now sold for millions.

He believed Natalia would like his home and the spectacular vista. A perpetual spring flowed below his property, and the resulting unstable hillside precluded other homes that might obstruct his view. A fifty foot retaining wall kept the house and lot stable, and at the bottom, masses of blackberry vines grew around and over the water. The thought of picking blackberries with Natalia and making jam brought a grin to his face.

Silky whined as they approached his house. "Yeah, girl, we're almost home." He smiled and scratched her behind the ears, and she licked his cheek. "There's going to be some changes, girl. I hope you like Natalia. *I* sure do!"

He pulled into the garage, unloaded his suitcases, and they entered the house. He poured kibble into Silky's bowl, listened to the dozens of messages on his answering machine, and browsed through his personal email. Jake realized he must write "Sorry, but I selected someone else" letters to Larissa and Irina. He regretted that, but nothing could lessen his joy about Natalia.

Later, he lounged in his favorite chair and gazed at the rainy landscape. Car lights sparkled on the shiny streets far below. His German shorthair pointer sat with her head on his lap while Jake swirled a brandy and petted her. He thought of Natalia and their coming new life.

"This will be wonderful, Silk."

* * *

Jake awoke groggy and disoriented at three in the morning. He heard the rain drum against his bedroom bay window and saw the shadow of Silky's head rise from her bed on the floor next to his. The eleven-hour time difference from Moscow proved too great for normal sleep. "Sorry Silk, I know it's early but I'm awake and can do nothing about it."

A smile washed across his face as he thought about Natalia. Though it was almost the middle of the night in Milpitas, he knew she had already started her day. Thoughts of her contented him.

"Rainy here, but a *lot* warmer than Moscow," he muttered

to himself. He involuntarily shivered from the frigid Moscow remembrance.

Jake stumbled out of bed, shaved, and took a steaming shower in hope the scalding water would get his blood flowing. He dressed and gave Silky an extra ration of kibble. She wolfed it down, and he expected her to regain the weight she'd lost while he traveled to Russia.

Jake drove down the steep hill to the Milpitas business district to drop Silky off at the doggy daycare. Like many Silicon Valley businesses, the dog spa was open twenty-four hours to support the swarm of hi-tech workers. He knew he had a long day ahead of him, too long to leave her home. Besides, she could play and socialize with other canines.

Traffic was heavy, as always, on the drive to SmartSystems.

After Jake parked in his assigned space, he went into the main building and greeted a dozen or so engineers who worked through the night. He was at his desk by four AM. Good thing, because over six hundred emails clogged his inbox. He sighed, filled his oversized coffee mug in the break room, and went to work. Fortunately, most messages were informational only. No need for him to act. He whittled that group down to eighty-seven to-do messages by eight o'clock.

Sergey Nazarov tapped on Jake's office door and didn't wait for an invitation to enter, which Jake liked about him. The man was irreverent about trivial protocol. He was also the best software engineer in the company.

The tall, slender, bearded Russian with unruly brown hair and sharp brown eyes had left the Soviet Union as its government convulsed toward its inevitable—in Sergey's outspoken opinion—collapse. He had abandoned his homeland for economic and religious freedom. The man reveled in both.

Sergey plopped himself into a chair across from Jake's desk and asked in his thick accent, "How was trip?"

"Excellent." Jake couldn't suppress his smile. "I found someone."

Sergey leaned forward, slapped the desk, and pointed a nimble finger at Jake. "I told you. Didn't I tell you? Russian women are best! Which one did you choose?"

"Yes, Sergey, you told me repeatedly. Natalia Melnikova will come here."

"The blonde with blue eyes?"

"*Da.*"

The two men broke into laughter, and Sergey said, "You will learn much more Russian soon, my friend. Congratulations." Sergey twisted his long beard and added, "Thank you, too, for delivering gifts to my wife's friends and taking them to dinner."

"My pleasure. I hope the Borisovs enjoyed the meal. They seem like nice people."

"Yes. Sveta Borisova called. They did enjoy. A treat. The husband can seem hard, but he is policeman." Sergey's voice turned to stone on the word "policeman." He then said in a normal voice, "We will tell her about you finding someone when we call again."

"Please give them my best when you do."

Sergey nodded and ran fingers through his scattered hair.

They both needed to get back to work, but Jake sensed Sergey had more on his mind.

The software engineer said, "A Russian wife will make you happy man."

Jake smiled. "Natalia already has."

CHAPTER 13

Natalia was glad to be back at school and her daily habits, though life now would be anything but routine. Soon she would leave Russia for a new life with Jacob.

Her list of tasks was daunting, and the process for a United States visa seemed complicated and difficult.

A substitute teacher had handled her classes over the past week in the cold piano studio, but Natalia flung herself back into teaching *her* students. She planned to teach in America. Music was a universal language, but Russian was not. She would use some of the dollars Jacob gave her to attend English instruction. She hoped he would understand and had included her plan in a long letter to him. If he objected, he would tell her.

The headmistress came to the classroom door and gruffly announced, "Natalia Melnikova, telephone call!" The heavy, middle-aged woman with a dark mustache wore a sour expression.

"*Spasibo*." Natalia told her class, "Continue." She followed down the dim hallway to the woman's office, which had the school's only working phone. Natalia's insides wrenched into a knot as she walked. *What could this call be?*

She picked up the receiver.

"Natalia Melnikova, I believe congratulations are due! Yes?" The mob boy. His voice sounded pleasant, but she was not fooled. She felt sick and wanted to scream.

"*Da*."

"Outstanding! Do what you are told and all will be well. First, you must complete America's Immigration documentation. The agency will assist you."

"And the cost?"

"Nothing, of course! Part of the package for you. And understand, we cannot control the time US takes to authorize entrance to their country, but we can provide some influence."

She sighed. With help, she would be with Jacob sooner. But she expected bad news and was compelled to ask, "What must I do?"

The voice turned unpleasant. "Don't ask unnecessary questions, Natalia Melnikova. You will be told when we are ready. All will be well if you follow instructions and keep your son a secret from the man. Your boy will remain here to ensure you cooperate."

She felt as if she had been punched in the stomach. She grabbed the desk to keep from collapsing as she shuddered in terror. Her mouth moved, but she could not speak.

"Come to the office tonight for help with the forms," the mob boy told her. The line went dead.

* * *

The Melnikova woman's success with Jacob Wilder started Dmitri Chekhov's workday on a cheerful note. She'd apparently done her job well. Americans were such fools for beautiful girls who spread their legs.

Dmitri indulged in a satisfied smile. With the hard times, Russian women by the thousands emigrated to become wives of foreign men. They traded their beauty and bodies for a better life. He held no grudge and didn't care what they did with their miserable lives. But whenever someone wanted something, there was money to be made.

Best of all, his scheme did not rely on Russia's economy. Ironically, the worse things became here, the more he stood to profit.

He had established International Friends and, like the

dozens of other such agencies across Russia, affiliated with the American firm Russian Introductions. He helped these women find husbands, and they paid for the service. On a select few, he received huge returns.

Dmitri powered on his computer, selected the mail icon, and typed a message to his associate in Sacramento.

Dimitri contemplated Ivan Rublev. All of Dmitri's US associates were prior KGB, people trained to blend in and hide in plain sight. Rublev was a former KGB officer but had been assigned tasks requiring more muscle than brains. The brute was effective.

Embedded in Sacramento's extensive Russian community as a part-time mechanic, the man's cover was plausible. He didn't have to mix with non-Russians, and Dmitri could not complain about Rublev's results. The man was faster and more efficient than his compatriots, though not as intelligent nor sophisticated.

And now, Ivan Rublev needed to discover exactly what Jacob Wilder was worth.

* * *

Natalia arrived at work from the blustering dark and dusted the pianos. The students wouldn't take their places for a half hour, so she had time to sip tea and think. Tomorrow would be twenty-nine long weeks since she said goodbye to Jacob. Such a wait to be with the man she knew she could grow to love! Her days seemed endless as she waited for his next letter or call, though both were frequent and always reassuring. She had arranged with a girlfriend who owned a telephone and went to her apartment each Sunday to not-so-patiently await Jacob's calls. Her poor English and his limited Russian made the weekly conversations brief, but she heard his sincerity, though she couldn't understand all he said when he talked too fast. She prayed he sensed her genuine feelings and appreciated her improved English. So many words and pronunciations she had not mastered but was determined to.

Time crawled by for her immigration paperwork to be processed. The correspondence agency helped prepare the documents, but the US Embassy took months to review them. The agency also expedited her Russian foreign-travel passport, which involved a bribe, for which she used some of Jacob's money.

Next came the US Embassy interview, which had taken a month to arrange. She stood in the long line outside the building, whipped by freezing wind, before she entered a stuffy, dirty waiting area. She presented her Russian passport and waited three hours to be interviewed by a rude woman with black hair and constant frown. Natalia politely answered every question through the nasty encounter. The woman regarded her as a whore who would do anything to go to the United States, which shocked and disappointed Natalia. She anticipated such treatment from Russians, not from Americans.

Her US K-1 Visa arrived after five months.

A final meeting with Andrei Borovick was required. The Assistant Deputy Director of Primary Education agreed to let Alexandr and her mother use his dacha after she went to America. Natalia and her mother both believed hiding was necessary since she did not know what the Bratva planned.

Borovick insisted on much money because of the risk, and she could not argue. The only alternative was her aunt, but the mob boys would search for Mama and Alexandr in Ukraine.

Borovick took the rest of what Jacob had given her. There was nothing left for her trip's incidental costs. She had to ask Jacob for more money, which pained her. He immediately wired more than she needed.

CHAPTER 14

The airplane was enormous, much larger than Natalia ever imagined. *How can something that holds so many people be so clean?* A mystery.

"Something to drink?" The attendant's question brought her back to the moment.

"Tea, please."

Natalia sat in the middle section of seats an incredible five places wide. So much room and comfort. And polite service! Perhaps her experience at the American Embassy was unusual.

She missed Alexandr. Their parting had been painful.

"Why can I not come with you, Mama?" He did not comprehend why she would leave him.

"I have to go alone, but you will be with me soon. I promise."

"But I want to come now!" He cried and hugged her, which broke her heart.

She wouldn't be free to tell Jacob about her son until she somehow broke the Bratva's hold over her. But with Barovick's help, she at least had done everything possible in Russia. Next, she would work on the problem from America. If only she understood what awaited her there.

* * *

Jake thought about his hard day but knew Natalia's was tougher. From the time she left Moscow to her arrival in San Francisco, she would travel twenty-four hours. She would be disoriented and weary. And, he hoped, happy. He checked the flight status board. Her plane had arrived early, though it would take time to clear Immigration and Customs. *We're almost together!*

He paced across the lobby and stared at her airplane through the windows. The passengers had disembarked.

He hoped Immigration would be kinder than she experienced during her embassy interrogation. Though they handled her case faster than normal, his temper flared and cheeks warmed when he remembered what she told him about the interview. The US government tolerated tens of thousands of illegals who flooded into the country, yet treated educated, legitimate immigrants like dirt. He emailed messages to his congresswoman on *that* issue.

Jake willed himself to think of other things, sat, and smelled the dozen red roses he had bought for Natalia. They were fresh and fragrant with beads of moisture on the petals.

He glanced at the monitor again and tried not to fidget.

They had three months to decide their futures. If they married within the time limit, Natalia stayed. If not, the visa mandated she leave the US. He expected her to stay and trusted their marriage would succeed. According to Russian Introductions, their clients suffered only seven divorces out of two thousand weddings over the past five years. *I can live with those odds.*

Jake shifted in the worn chair and observed people meander around the arrival area. International flights cleared Immigration and Customs in clusters, and travelers staggered into the reception hall, fatigued from their long journeys. He searched the throng for blonde curls and blue eyes.

A new stream of travelers came in.

"There she is!" he whispered.

Natalia came through the doors dragging an old suitcase and carrying two shopping bags. She wore a gray skirt and white sweater and looked bewildered and exhausted. His throat constricted. She had come so far to be with him. He wanted to pick her up and carry her off in his arms.

He bolted toward her.

Natalia saw him and flashed a bright smile.

Jake's voice choked. "I am so glad you are here."

She put down her things, took the flowers, and kissed him on the cheek. They embraced. His heart accelerated as she looked up at him and said, "I happy to be here. Flowers beautiful."

"So are you," he said, which caused her to blush.

People flooded past them. "Let's go home." He took her luggage, and Natalia carried the bouquet as they worked their way through the dense crowd.

A huge guy with close-cropped hair and nasty expression wouldn't move out of their way. The man forced them to go around him.

"Asshole," Jake muttered.

He loaded her belongings into his pickup and exited SFO. Once on US 101 down the peninsula, Natalia perked up.

"So many new cars! And the road is wide and smooth," she said. "Everything is clean. This is beautiful place. This is different for me. The air is clear, and people smile here. The glass buildings sparkle. The houses and apartments look nice." On and on she spoke.

Jake smiled and made a couple comments but let her experience her wonder.

They turned east onto Highway 237 for the short stretch along the southern tip of the bay toward Milpitas and up the hill. Jake was thankful Natalia arrived while the hills were green and covered with wildflowers. In a week or so, the grasses would dry and turn brown for the summer.

Jake pulled into his driveway and Natalia grew silent, her hand over her mouth.

"Welcome home, Natalia."

"This is your house?" A tear streaked down her cheek and

dropped off her chin. "It so beautiful. And view is wonderful."

"This is *our* home, now. With you here, it's no longer just mine."

The moment he stopped the car in the garage, Natalia leaped across the seat and kissed him with warmth and tenderness. Oh, how he had missed her. He kissed her back and held her.

They entered the house, Silky barked, and Natalia went wild. Her slow, careful English vanished into an English-Russian jumble. "*Oi*, what beautiful *sobaka*!" which Jake assumed meant dog. She went down on her knees, stroked Silky behind her ears, and hugged her. Silky responded with face licks, and Jake grinned to himself.

After Silky calmed down, he gave Natalia an affectionate hug and kiss, which she returned. She seemed so fragile. "I missed you," he told her.

"I miss you, too. I miss you much."

"How was the trip?"

Her eyes pleaded with him. "I sorry. I too tired for English."

"I understand. You need to rest."

He showed her upstairs to the master suite and the spaces in the closet and drawers he'd made for her clothes. He left to put the bouquet in a vase.

Jake shook his head and smiled. *I can't believe she's here!*

When he went back to the bedroom, he found Natalia curled up, asleep. Silky dozed on the floor next to her. Jake covered his fiancée with the comforter and tip-toed out of the room.

Later, he sat on the bed and watched her. *She's so beautiful. I hope I can make her happy.*

Natalia awoke and reached for him. She gave him a peaceful smile.

He leaned over and nuzzled her ear. "Thank you for being with me."

They undressed each other with care. Their bodies pressed together, and they embraced. As her warmth enveloped him, he became lost in her sweet fragrance and touch.

Their passion rose like a tidal wave. After the months of waiting, he could not get enough of her.

They made love the rest of the night and did not sleep until the sky lightened.

CHAPTER 15

Ivan Rublev had enjoyed his little bump into Jacob Wilder, the American prick. Make the fucker go around him at the airport. He didn't believe getting so close was unwise. He made the point for fun with every target.

Chekhov had sent an email with Melnikova's itinerary plus her digital photograph. Pretty, more attractive than most. And petite. Small girls were always his favorites, though he relished them all.

Ivan had driven down from Sacramento to see the man because the men always met the women at the airport.

He would call Melnikova Monday after the groom-to-be left for work to tell her he would watch her every move. Keep her in line so she would not cause trouble.

If this woman was like the others, she would do what she was told, whatever he demanded. He would fuck her a time or two for sure.

* * *

Natalia looked at the view out the living room bay window. She had received many shocks. The traffic, the freeways, the panorama, and especially the house. Compared to her Khrushchev apartment, this was a palace in a movie. So much room. She marveled that this was Jacob's home and now perhaps hers.

They had spent Sunday shopping for clothing and food, which overwhelmed her. She now possessed more new clothes than ever before, and the selection and variety of foods in the gigantic market left her in awe. But today, Monday, Jacob went to work. This was her first opportunity to explore the house.

The telephone rang near noontime. Jacob had already called twice to talk to her. She went to the strange, complicated contraption. Numbers glowed on a small display. The calling number showed, "pay phone."

She picked up the handset as a loud beep from the attached device startled her. "Hallo?" She must work on her pronunciation. She needed to say the "e" sound, not "a."

Silence, followed by a rough Russian voice. "Welcome to the United States, Natalia Melnikova."

She almost dropped the phone. The room shrank around her, and fear made her speechless.

"Come, come. Don't be surprised to hear from your friends. We will protect you."

Still, she said nothing.

The man's voice hardened. "Nothing has changed. Marry as soon as possible and all will be well."

Natalia's anger surged over her terror, and she screamed, "What do you want of me?"

"To follow instructions," the man yelled. "Do what we say, or your worthless son dies."

* * *

Jake understood life would not be the same with Natalia here, and so far the differences were wonderful. As he walked in the door after work, the aroma of garlic chicken and rice soup welcomed him. His stomach proclaimed hunger, and he knew he would not miss his former staples of carryout food and microwave dinners. The house was also spotless, with everything neat and in its place.

Silky's bark greeted him, and he scratched her mottled-brown side. "Smells like you got a bath, girl."

Natalia tended the stove and wore a new skirt and blouse protected by one of his old barbecue aprons, the one with,

"Kiss the cook," on the front. He intended to. He smiled. "Hello."

She turned and gave him a smile traced with sadness.

"Are you okay?"

"I fine."

"You sure?"

She nodded and went back to dinner preparation.

He frowned. Something bothered her. "Any calls?"

She hesitated. "Only yours."

He would have to show her how to operate the answering machine because the *beeps* told him their conversations were recorded. He punched the erase button since the messages were all his. He realized he should teach her how to set the house alarm, use the microwave oven, and run the dishwasher. So many things Americans took for granted.

Jake put his arms around her waist and kissed the top of her head. "I love you."

Her shoulders slumped, and his joy vanished as she choked back tears.

He turned her around, held her, and let Natalia bury her face in his chest. "What's the matter?" he asked.

"Nothing. I am silly woman."

"Talk to me, please."

She shook her head and turned back to the stove without speaking.

Did I do something I shouldn't have?

* * *

Ivan Rublev strolled down the wooden sidewalks of Sacramento's Old Town, the original section of the city along the river. The restored district resembled the Gold Rush days. The McDonalds and Burger King had storefronts to fit the western motif. Rublev liked Old Town because it projected the essence of the Old West without the motion picture fakery. A statue of a Pony Express rider marked the end of the long overland mail route. A riverboat converted to a hotel and restaurant floated at the waterfront. The massive California Railroad Museum with its steam locomotives added to the aura of authenticity.

Old Town was a pleasant place to walk, and Ivan blended in among the many foreign tourists. He loved coming here, too, because a store that sold Russian dolls and lacquered trays had opened on 2nd Street. The woman who owned the place came from Vladivostok, which was closer to Sacramento than Moscow. How could Russia be so enormous and impoverished? And why was America so rich yet so fucking stupid?

This country paid him for being a poor immigrant. He collected government assistance worth more than a doctor's wages back home. Of course, his real income came from the money Chekhov deposited in a German bank after each assignment to ensure his comfortable retirement. Plus, his father and mother got a generous monthly stipend courtesy of their overseas son.

He smiled and planned to take the Vladivostok woman a coffee. She was married but drawn to strong men. He figured he would one day soon give her something to remember. *That will put a smile on her face.*

Old Town also attracted him because of the sidewalk public telephones, including the one outside the Russian shop. The few working street phones in the south of the city where he lived were never available because of the filthy drug users and dealers.

He chuckled to himself. He had enjoyed his first call to the terrified Melnikova bitch. As long as she remained scared, she would cooperate.

But he didn't dwell on her. He had another obligation up the valley in a town called Red Bluff. Business was brisk.

He would deal with the Melnikova woman later.

CHAPTER 16

"What did you think of the game?" Jake asked Natalia. She had arrived a month ago, and they were inseparable.

Natalia stared straight ahead and both hands gripped the steering wheel as she drove toward the Milpitas turnoff and home. Silky held her nose to the wind, and her ears flapped as she rode in the back with his baseball gear. "Is interesting. I do not understand all, but you did well."

Jake nodded. He had hit a double, a single, and threw five runners out at first. The first game of the summer league, SmartSystems won against a friendly rival technology company. "I'm glad you came. I hope the game wasn't too boring."

"No. Fun to watch action and people but hard to talk with your friends. I sorry."

He leaned over and kissed her on the cheek. "Don't be. You're doing terrific!"

"I try," she smiled.

"You succeed, and you drive well, too."

Natalia would soon take her behind-the-wheel test, and he would buy her a car, whatever car she chose. With her driver's license, she would be mobile and not stuck at home.

He took in her beautiful face and grinned. Everything was going right for them. He still struggled with small things, like her requirement he remove his shoes in the house. He understood she wanted the floors to stay clean, but occasionally he forgot, which earned him a shake of her head.

They shared much happiness, though something bothered Natalia. She was sometimes forlorn and had not opened up to him about the cause despite his entreaties.

Jake chewed the inside of his lip. Again yesterday, he came from work and found her almost in tears. Was it because of her captivity at the house and loss of her friends and mother? *What can I do?*

He forced away those thoughts. "You look forward to meeting the Nazarovs?"

She checked over her left shoulder, signaled, and changed lanes to pass a semi. "Yes, but I nervous."

"Why?"

"What if they not like me?"

He laughed. "Of course they will like you. You are a charming person! Besides, you need to spend time with people who speak your language. I wish we could have visited them earlier, but I sent Sergey to Seattle for training." Jake knew the custom for Russians was to first meet socially as a couple. "He's worked for me for almost four years, and he's the best. With more training, he'll be exceptional."

He hesitated before bringing up an old topic but charged ahead. "Can your mom go to your girlfriend's like you did so you can call her?"

"Would be difficult."

"Why don't you?"

The corners of her mouth turned down, and she nodded. "I try."

"I'm sorry it's hard for you here."

"Not your fault. I am silly woman." She glanced at him. "You good to me."

"And you're wonderful to me. I love you."

"I love you, too, Jacob."

"You still want me?"

She fingered her engagement ring and spoke with a playful note in her voice. "I have four weeks to wedding to decide. Maybe surprise!"

"Okay, keep me in suspense... as long as you keep me."

* * *

Natalia wanted to scream. How could she find so fine a man yet be in such a trap? And no letter from Mama. *Are my letters getting through? How can I set up a call without mail?*

The only communication she received from Russia was a note from Andrei Borovick asking for more money. Three hundred dollars to compensate for his personal risk. She couldn't complain about the demand, but Mama and Alexandr hid at his dacha with no phone.

She looked again at the diamond on her left hand, which sparkled in the sunlight. Yes, Russia had diamonds, but only New Russians could afford them. Yet here she wore a jewel costing more than a Russian house. Jacob's generosity astounded her. She did not need an expensive ring. She would be happy with a simple band.

Deep guilt gnawed at her because she deceived Jacob and the need to ask him for money. *How can I explain? And what will happen if I don't send what Borovick demands?*

And there was the Bratva. The thug had called her again and told her to marry as soon as possible.

* * *

Sergey and Veronika Nazarov lived up Highway 880 from Milpitas in the town of Fremont. Electronic assembly companies crowded the city's southern half, and the joint-venture auto plant owned by General Motors and Toyota dominated the town's economy. Less high-tech meant lower home prices. Though Jake paid Sergey well, his friend spent on his church and private schools for his children, not a house. The modest, well-cared-for home was not what one would expect for a high-level Silicon Valley software engineer.

Natalia pulled into their driveway off Mission Boulevard,

and Silky barked from the back. Sergey's old Dodge was parked in front of the garage, which had long-since been converted to a play room.

Sergey, Veronika, and their three adolescents flooded out of the house the instant the pickup stopped. The kids ran to Silky, who jumped out of the truck to greet her friends. The two boys and their sister grew at an astonishing rate. Jake once believed he'd never be a father. *Now, perhaps?*

He did the introductions, which concluded the English-language dialog. The children rushed to the backyard with Silky as Sergey and Veronika addressed Natalia in their native tongue, which was the purpose of the visit from Jake's standpoint. As he hoped, Natalia's mood brightened. Her slow English morphed into rapid-fire Russian. She gave him a quick smile.

Jake followed the plain and kind Veronika inside for the obligatory house tour. As always, the small but comfortable home was spotless. Because he had visited Russia, he now realized this house was enormous compared to what their Moscow apartment would have been.

In minutes, the two women were well-launched on their own, and Sergey slapped Jake on the back. "Like beer? 'Course you do." He went to the kitchen before Jake answered. He never felt like "the boss" around Sergey, a brilliant employee and fascinating person.

"Thanks for having us over," Jake said as Sergey opened the refrigerator and handed him a cold Budweiser.

"'Course." Sergey lowered his voice. "Apologize we will speak so much Russian."

"That's why we're here! I don't mind being on the outside for once. I can only imagine what Natalia experiences every day." Jake sighed. "I sure wish she was happier."

"What do you mean?"

"Often, she's upset when I come home. She won't talk to

me and shuts me out. I'm concerned about her."

Sergey gave a knowing smile, twisted his beard, and held up two fingers. "My wife cried for two years when we come to US."

"Really?" Veronika didn't strike Jake as the long-suffering type.

Sergey took a swallow of beer. "Yes. Terrible time, but she got over it. She is away from mother and friends, true, but this is America! She knows here better for sons and daughter. Do not worry, my friend. They are all sad at first. Their nature! They adjust."

"I hope so. I don't want her to be so unhappy."

Sergey chuckled. "All Russian women are unhappy in same way. Like they carry the sorrow of their mothers and their mother's mother. Do not judge her by American standard. She understands she is lucky to be here, and she loves you. Obvious. Believe me, she happier here than in Moscow."

"Yeah, you're right. Still bothers me, though."

Veronika ejected the men from the kitchen to complete the dinner preparations.

* * *

The two couples and the children ate a chicken feast in the dining room, with Natalia and Veronika chatting in Russian. Sergey sporadically joined their conversation but let the women talk.

Jake did not understand the Russian, so he engaged with the kids. He asked the boys, twelve and ten, about summer vacation and school next year and repeated the question for the nine-year-old daughter. Three children, each with different plans and perspectives, talked to him with enthusiasm. They were well-behaved and good-natured.

The children cleared the dishes while Sergey and Jake

adjourned to the living room. Natalia and Veronika continued to talk at the dining table.

"From her tone," Jake said, "Natalia is opening up some to Veronika."

"Yes, they discuss many things about Russia and here. I think they will talk much longer tonight."

"Fine with me. Natalia needs this, and thank you for inviting us."

Sergey stroked his beard. "But of course! Natalia is new friend for Veronika, too. This helps both."

Because his wife-to-be now had someone to talk to, a weight lifted off Jake's heart.

CHAPTER 17

Today was THE DAY, and Jake fidgeted and paced around his living room after he ran out of things to keep himself occupied. Outside, he took another tour of the backyard preparations, avoided the busy set-up crew, and decided to retreat to the house.

He put on his tux with care. He didn't have much else to do but wait.

As he viewed the outside chaos through the floor-to-ceiling window, the wedding planner walked up and patted his arm. She was fortyish, smartly dressed, smiling, and would blend in among the guests, her low heels the only giveaway.

"Your bride is beautiful and so happy," she told Jake. "I checked on Mrs. Nazarov and Natalia. She has a trace of nerves, but that's natural on a woman's wedding day."

Jake let out a breath. He was elated and relieved about the planner recommended by a woman at work who recently wed. The professional had shepherded Natalia through the wedding dress selection, deftly guided her and Veronika on the décor and menu, and now supervised the caterers, musicians, and everything else. Natalia had told him she appreciated the help.

The planner nudged him. "I made sure everything is the way Natalia wants. Now relax and leave the worries to me."

Jake laughed. "Thank you so much!"

The woman went off to her duties, and Jake turned back to the window.

The two months since Natalia's arrival had passed so fast. Life with her was better than he imagined possible. She adapted well to American life, especially after meeting Veronika. Some days she was upset and closed him out, which he disliked, but she often called Veronika for advice about one thing or another. And her driver's license helped. Now she wasn't confined to home. He guessed he would have gone nuts if their circumstances had been reversed.

Jake remembered when they shopped for her vehicle and smiled. Natalia appeared lost in the vast dealer lots, but at the end of the day, she fell in love with a red Mustang convertible. Her decision surprised him, but why not? He admitted the car suited her. Blonde curls in the wind. Girlish smile on her face. Disbelief and excitement in her eyes. He took dozens of pictures of her in, besides, and in front of the shiny Mustang. The car reminded him of the thrill he felt from his own first new car.

She had been so distraught when she asked for money for her mother. He agreed without hesitation. She scoured the newspapers and looked for piano teaching positions to repay him, which was unnecessary. Jake's only concern about sending his almost mother-in-law three hundred dollars was that it might not be enough. He encouraged Natalia to tell him whenever her mother needed funds. In his soul, he didn't feel he was being taken advantage of. The money was a pittance.

He peeked into the crowded kitchen and expected his bride would re-clean everything no matter how spotless the caterers left it.

He chuckled to himself. Despite everything Natalia had learned, the answering machine still confounded her. He gave up explaining it to her and left it on.

Silky sulked out of the kitchen, ejected by the cooks, and stared back with a confused expression before coming to him for pets and reassurance. He rubbed behind her brown ears.

"Don't worry, Silk, they'll be gone soon, and we'll be a real family." He checked his watch. "Guests should start arriving. You behave and some of the leftovers will be yours."

* * *

Natalia fussed at the dresser mirror. Almost done with her hair, but not quite. She wanted everything to be perfect for Jacob. He cared for her, and her heart warmed at the thought of him.

The mob boy trap and her dishonesty about Alexandr jumped into her mind yet again. The lack of letters from her mother deepened her dread. *Mama promised to write. Should I ask Veronika what to do? If only I could.* She willed herself not to cry. Tears would spoil everything.

She tucked two locks of hair into place, satisfied. Today she would marry her Jacob and gave herself a smile touched with sadness about her son. *And I wish mama could be here.*

"You are beautiful," Veronika told her as she straightened Natalia's dress.

The doorbell rang, and Silky barked. The first guests had arrived. Natalia was ready, and he would be hers. The US government wouldn't force her back to Russia, though that was not her fear.

Her terror was much deeper, as was her guilt.

* * *

A light mist hung over San Francisco Bay, but the fog burned off to provide a breathtaking sight from Jake's back yard. At the shore, mountains of salt from the evaporation ponds reflected intense white. Across the water reared the giant hangers of Moffett Field. Silicon Valley spread beyond the vista.

A cool breeze fluttered the flowers woven into the white trellis. Chairs lined the lawn.

Jake waited at the altar with Sergey and the minister. The seats filled and some people stood. Cameras clicked. Through the living room window, Silky watched the three dozen guests.

She knew everyone from softball games and company picnics, but now they had invaded her domain and left her to stare through the glass.

"You nervous?" Sergey asked Jake.

"A little. Still hard to believe this is happening."

"You made excellent choice. Natalia is good woman."

"I know. Thanks to you, I found her."

An audible gasp interrupted their conversation. Jake felt his smile stretch across his face as Natalia walked up the aisle more beautiful than ever. Golden hair framed her face, and the white gown showed off her slender figure. Lace at the neck and sleeves complimented the tight-fitting satin, and a string of pearls added an elegant touch. Stunning.

Veronika followed as matron-of-honor. Russian custom dictated Natalia not smile, but she gave him a shy grin.

"I love you," he whispered.

He marveled that she would blush when he voiced his affection. He could not believe he was such a lucky man.

* * *

After the ceremony, people mingled and chatted with plates of food and flutes of champagne. Jake found a moment to be alone with his wife. "This is wonderful. We're married!"

She batted her eyes. "Of course!"

Jake laughed and kissed her.

Veronika came up to them as they gazed out at the bay. "You ready for the trip, Jacob?" She gave him a surreptitious wink.

Jake trusted leaving the Nazarovs with a key to his house much more than his baseball friends. He could never tell what kind of mischief they might pull while he and Natalie honeymooned in Maui.

He grinned. "I feel like I've been ready for Natalia my whole life." He gently squeezed Natalia's hand.

CHAPTER 18

The house echoed with music as Natalia played with passion. She and Jacob had returned from the sun, flowers, and rainbows of Hawaii, and here in the living room in front of the glass wall sat a Steinway grand piano. A stunning surprise! She was speechless.

"Veronika took care of this while we were gone. Do you like it?"

Natalia took a moment to compose herself. "Magnificent. But why?"

"It's my wedding gift to you."

Her cheeks warmed as she blushed. "I did not know about presents between us."

Jake smiled. "*You* are my gift."

She sat at the piano, composed herself and hummed as her fingers danced across the finest instrument she had ever touched. If she was her present to Jacob, she would give herself freely and often. She felt more special, feminine, and wanted than ever before in her life.

And now she might also give music lessons to earn money to repay Jacob. She understood Andrei Borovick might require more to hide Alexandr and Mama. The piano would help her with that.

She truly loved Jacob, despite little frustrations like when he failed to remove his shoes in the house. He was generous beyond imagination, yet not demanding. He did not insist on sex during her woman's holiday, which here was called her period, as her first husband had. And Jacob did not demand his clothes be ironed or the house scrubbed each day or expect dinner to be ready when he arrived from work. He seemed happy to be with her, which made her want to give herself even more.

* * *

Ivan Rublev sat at his computer in Sacramento with a cup of coffee and performed his morning target checks. US federal, state, and local governments uploaded public information to the Internet. An efficient system.

His first query brought a surprised smile. The Melnikova bitch and Wilder had recorded their marriage. *Excellent!* His irritation was that the nuptials occurred two weeks ago. *Dammit.* A little lost time, but not that important. With one finger, he typed an email to Dmitri Chekhov, who would take the next steps to ensure Melnikova's cooperation.

Rublev knew Chekhov would be pleased, and the little Muscovite would set him up for another bonus. The only question was how much he would be paid. He imagined his best payout yet because the value of Wilder's house gave the man a net worth of over three million dollars. *Rich bastard.* If the new bride did her job, his payday would be fat. He rubbed his thin, bristly hair.

Such a land of opportunity, America.

Ivan had driven to Milpitas twice to follow and photograph the Melnikova whore while she drove her red sports car, shopped for groceries, and wandered in the mall. With the photos she would know there was no escape.

Protocol was for him to wait until the husband was dead before visiting the wife and giving her the photographs, but he could not help himself. As he cruised down I-80 toward Richmond, he wanted to fuck her *now*. Chekhov would never approve, but his boss was far from California. The further Rublev drove, the more aroused he became.

* * *

Silky's bark and snarl interrupted Natalia's morning piano. A heavy knock sounded on the front door.

She opened the door, and a large man with wide-set eyes and broad face, a Russian, stood in the doorway. The muscles in her throat constricted as he thrust a foot against the door. She tried to force it closed. Impossible.

"You alone?" he demanded.

The smell of the man's sweat nauseated her, and she couldn't speak.

He shoved her hard, and she toppled backward to the tile floor. Agony shot up her spine and ricocheted across her shoulders.

The man stepped inside and grinned with brown stained teeth.

No escape.

"Now, you and I are going to have some fun," he said.

As he reached down to pin her arms, a deep rumble filled Natalia's ears. A brown and white blur leaped over her. Silky chomped into the man's thigh. Deep.

"*Oi! Fuck-your-mother! Oi!*" Rublev squealed. He twisted and turned, but Silky held fast. He slammed Silky into the wall to dislodge her, and they both yelped.

Natalia had understood the man's sexual avarice, but Silky's defense changed everything. When he freed his leg, he turned to flee. Silky lunged again and bit his butt. The man scraped her off against the door and ran.

Silky went after him.

God, I hurt. Natalia got to her knees, stood, and staggered outside. She feared for their dog, who growled from the backyard. Natalia stumbled around the side of the house in agony and found Silky stalk along the back fence from one end to the other.

Where'd the Russian beast go?

* * *

Rublev wanted the woman, wanted her so badly. But that fuck-your-mother *sobaka* spoiled everything! He was aware of the dog from his surveillance, but it looked like a gentle, playful creature, not a vicious cur. The animal still pursued him.

Instead of delivering Melnikova the hardest fuck of her life, he bolted. The yard to the street was open, and the *sobaka* would chase him. He sprinted to the back and saw the four-foot, ivy-covered fence at the end of the lot. Rublev vaulted over a second before the fuck-your-mother beast caught him.

Nothing but air! A steep retaining wall rushed past Rublev. He accelerated toward a mass of berry brambles and ripped through the thorny bushes.

Splat!

He landed in a stream of water. Acrid filth filled his mouth. He spit again and again to expel the nasty slime. Blackberry barbs had shredded his clothes and skin, and the slimy muck stung his wounds.

Rublev's body screamed as though sliced by a thousand knives, and his ankles, shoulder and head pulsated with pain. Mud covered him. His blood mingled with the foul water.

The fucking beast barked and snarled above. Rublev surveyed the damage to his body and ego. Impatience and stupid lust had caused him to break the rules and act. And he didn't deliver the photos he'd taken of the woman. They were now ruined in his soaked pocket.

He rolled to his back and received more punctures and scratches from the thorns. He had to get away from this place and call the Wilder woman before she did something stupid.

Ivan turned back to his stomach and began the painful crawl out of the reeking, thorny thicket.

* * *

Natalia struggled to bring Silky into the house and calm her. The dog limped and had a bloody ear. *What will Jacob say? How do I tell him?* "A man came and Silky chased him away." The truth, but only part of the truth.

Twenty minutes later, her back ached more than when first assaulted.

She jumped when the telephone rang. *Jacob? Will he hear my fear?*

The screen on the kitchen telephone again displayed "pay phone." Not her husband. Worse. She was afraid to answer. She dreaded not to. Natalia picked up the receiver as the recorder beeped. "Hallo."

The man sputtered with fury. "I will kill your *sobaka!*"

Natalia startled herself with courage fueled by rage. "Stay away from us!"

"Control your tongue! We will release you when we are ready. Obey instructions or you will never see your son again. He is with us, and he will be dead. Understand?!" he yelled.

She fought back tears and wouldn't cry. She wouldn't give the mob boy the satisfaction. "*Da,*" she whispered.

She heard triumph in his enraged voice. "Say nothing about your son, and all will be well. Your husband must change his life insurance policies to make you beneficiary and his will to leave everything to you. Soon. Call this number any Thursday at four PM when it is accomplished."

Anger and panic jolted Natalia. She realized the Bratva wanted Jacob dead.

CHAPTER 19

M oscow. Though he never showed it, Vladimir Motorin disliked meaningless errands. He enjoyed the extortion racket because of the direct link between his friendly shop owner meetings and the weight of the leather satchel delivered to Chekhov. Clear and simple. Cause and effect.

Of course, whatever was asked of him, Vladimir did with enthusiasm. No option, there. He craved to move up in the organization. Today's task was more interesting than most because it related to a familiar name: Natalia Melnikova.

Vladimir was pleased with himself. After months of cautious observation and careful inquiries, an understanding of Chekhov's strong interest in the women leaving Russia formed in his mind. Chekhov owned the correspondence service, International Friends, which was legitimate. He did not believe his boss would involve himself in anything other than a crooked scheme. Against Chekhov's nature. What was the source of the money?

The Education Ministry was across town, but he decided to handle this personally. Vladimir found Andrei Barovick's office after wasting time wandering through dim hallways and entered without invitation.

The man behind the cluttered desk sat up straight in his chair, startled, and, though older, seemed fit enough to inflict heavy damage if motivated. Vladimir wasn't worried. His expensive suit and confident demeanor were all the authority he needed.

Vladimir perceived uncertainty on the Deputy Director of Primary Education's face. The bureaucrat asked, "Why do you enter my office so rudely? Who are you?"

Vladimir didn't respond. He sat in the padded chair and straightened his fashionable Italian slacks and coat. He raised his head and glared, pleased with Barovick's growing discomfort.

"Who I am is not important," he said in his quiet, cultured voice. "What is relevant is your dacha and your relationship with Natalia Melnikova."

Barovick's eyes widened, which confirmed to Motorin that the woman had confided in him. The man attempted an innocent smile. "She taught my son piano. She asked to rent my dacha." Sweat gathered on Barovick's forehead, and he shrugged. "I agreed."

"No other reason?"

He shook his head. "No! I'm an honest man who minds his own affairs."

"I am happy to hear that. And the dacha is no longer needed by Melnikova." Vladimir reached inside his coat and took delight in watching the man's body tense. He retrieved his wallet, not his gun, removed three American bills, and laid the money on the desk. "This is for minding your own business."

Barovick's relief appeared profound. "Of course!"

Vladimir rose. "Forget about this." He left the stuffy office certain the Deputy Director of Primary Education would follow his wise advice.

* * *

Jake drove into his garage, parked next to the Mustang, and smiled. Natalia kept the red car polished. She had rags and cleaner in the trunk to remove every bug and spot whenever she stopped.

Though still preoccupied with money, she seemed happier. She'd had no apparent depression since the wedding, and in the days after their return from Hawaii, the house echoed with passionate music.

He walked into the kitchen and remembered to take off his shoes. He stopped. The house was dead quiet.

"Natalia?"

No answer except Silky's bark from upstairs. Jake dropped his briefcase and sprinted to the second floor two steps at a time. Silky met him at the master suite's door, and he noticed her cut ear and stiff movements. "What happened to you, girl? Natalia? Natalia!"

He rushed into the room. Natalia was on her side, face crushed against a pillow, eyes puffy and red.

He knelt beside her. "What's wrong, sweetheart?"

She turned away from him.

"Natalia, don't do this! Talk to me, please."

She shook her head, so he touched her arm and tried to roll her back to face him, but she pushed his hand away.

He almost cursed but bit his lip and said, "What is it, Natalia? Please tell me. Don't shut me out."

No response.

Dammit!

He hated when she did this and loathed the feelings it gave him. "I don't deserve to be treated this way." He left the room before he said something he would regret.

A pensive Silky waited in the hallway and winced when he patted her. "What's the matter, Silk, you get in a fight today?"

He almost turned back and asked why Silky was hurt but changed his mind. He stomped down the stairs, and his dog gingerly followed.

Jake had known a Russian wife would be a challenge. Differences in cultures and tastes were sometimes difficult to bridge, and conversations were often fraught with misunderstandings. But he reminded himself how loving and compassionate Natalia could be. He couldn't remain angry with her.

Of course this was hard for her. *But why does she do this? God, I hate it.*

He pulled a beer out of the refrigerator, took two long swallows, and poured the rest down the sink. The brew tasted bitter and didn't satisfy.

Jake eyed the kitchen answering machine. Two messages. One was his call that morning. His company name displayed. He punched "erase" and saw the second number. *Pay phone?* The recording started with Natalia's frightened greeting trailed by a choleric voice spewing Russian, then plaintive pleading from her.

Jake felt his mouth drop open.

What the hell is this?

When the message ended, he ran up to the bedroom. "Please tell me what's going on, Natalia. Please."

Each shake of her head was like a slap to his face.

"Natalia, I love you. I'm sorry you don't trust me enough to talk to me. I'm not a bad man. I'll leave you alone if you want, but closing me out is not right."

She buried her face deeper into the pillow.

Jake went downstairs and grabbed the cassette out of the machine after he took care of Silk's wounds, which were not serious. Torn ear. Tender hindquarters. "Come on, Silk, let's take a ride."

* * *

Cars and trucks inched up I-880 during rush hour, though "hour" was a gross misnomer in Silicon Valley. Traffic congestion lasted well into the evening. Jake pounded the steering wheel in frustration. Silky rested on the seat, uninterested in the scenery. At last, he exited at Mission Boulevard and drove up the hill in a crawling line of cars. When he pulled into Sergey's driveway, he left Silky in the truck before he went to the front door and knocked.

Sergey answered, napkin in hand.

"Sorry for interrupting dinner. Do you have a minute?"

He wiped his mouth. "Of course! Come in."

Jake hesitated. "No, but I need you to translate something."

Sergey said something over his shoulder to Veronika, placed the napkin on the table by the door, and came outside. They climbed into the pickup, and Jake inserted the tape into the cassette deck. "Listen to this."

Sergey stopped his perpetual beard twisting and listened. The color drained from his face.

"What? What is it?"

Sergey waved him off until the end. He was a religious man who never swore, but his friend scowled into space and whispered, "Fuck-your-mother."

* * *

The evening had blurred into darkness when Jake and Silky returned. The house was silent. Silky headed to her water bowl as Jake went up to Natalia.

His shock and fury made him miss a step and stumble. Someone wanted him dead, which was not a comforting thought, and Natalia was somehow trapped in the situation.

She hadn't moved, still curled up on the bed. He sat next to her and stroked her hair. She kissed his hand. "I sorry, Jacob."

Jake took a deep breath and said in a soft voice, "Tell me about your son."

CHAPTER 20

N atalia bolted upright. "How you know?"

The pained, helpless expression on her face. The fear and desperation in those blue eyes he loved. His anger evaporated. "I'll explain later. But first, tell me about my stepson. What's his name?"

Her face became a forlorn smile. "Alexandr. He is four, almost five. That is why I went to visit aunt in Ukraine for food before... before I divorce Vitaly. I was waiting mother and needed good diet to keep health."

His throat constricted and eyes moistened. "Do you have pictures?"

She went to her jewelry box and pulled an envelope from the bottom drawer. She fought tears, thumbed through the contents, and handed him several photos.

He took them, and his hands shook with each heartbeat. Small boy with a toy car. Smiling boy on a sled in the snow. Natalia holding her son, his arms around her neck, both grinning. The handsome lad had his mother's eyes and blond curls.

And his name was Alexandr.

Jake tried a feeble joke. "Strange way to discover I have a son."

Natalia lost control and sobbed. He pulled her to him, hugged, and comforted her. "It's okay. I think I understand."

When she calmed enough, he said, "Tell me the whole story."

Natalia turned to sit on the edge of the bed, her head bowed. "When I go to agency, they say me not tell about Alexandr. Child would scare away men." He almost protested but let her speak. "It was not right. I wanted to tell you him, but they demand no.

"When you come to Moscow, they say me again to keep Alexandr secret, but this time was evil threat."

Jake stood and paced back and forth across the bedroom floor.

"So, I try to make my mother and Alexandr safe. I know man with dacha. I pay him all the first money you give me to hide them." She swallowed hard. "He wanted more dollars. That is why I asked again.

"But now the mob boy say me get you to change your will and insurance or they kill Alexandr."

Jake grimaced as his fingernails cut his palms from his clenched fists.

Natalia stopped talking and stared at him in fright.

He unclenched his hands and took a deep breath. "Please continue."

"A man came today. Silky bite him." Her smoky-blue eyes were desperate. "He call and say me they got Alexandr and to do what they say."

Jake froze, every muscle rigid.

Natalia fell to her knees and clutched his legs. "I understand you hate me. I go back to Russia. Let you go on with life."

Her words surprised him. "Why would I hate you? I love you!" She looked at him with surprise. He reached down and lifted her to her feet.

"I lie to you. I believed them about keeping Alexandr from you. I had no choice. I spent so much of your money. I did not understand what they wanted until today, but I lie to you. I sorry. I have son."

Agony etched her face.

"No, Natalia, *we* have a son."

* * *

The kettle whistled on the stove in the otherwise quiet house. Natalia went to the teapot while Jacob sat at the breakfast table and sipped his black coffee, deep in thought. Silky curled up under his chair. The sky remained dark, but dawn would soon lighten the horizon. Silicon Valley buildings and headlights flashed below in the gloom.

Natalia prepared tea for herself and pondered the fact this country had no strong tea. She thought it strange to think of such a thing at a time like this. She felt like she had crawled out of hell, and the gentle man she married helped her. She believed she was not so isolated and helpless as she sat with him.

She cleared her throat and said, "I want to tell you many times about Alexandr."

He took her hand and said, "Tell me more about him."

"He is fine boy. He loves toy cars and learning piano. Always happy. Laughs much. But, Jacob, I was trapped in cage my dishonesty built. I relieved now you know, and I expect you to divorce me and send me back to Russia.

"That won't happen, sweetheart. I love you!"

Natalia sat back and marveled. He would not throw her away. And though the mob boy wanted Jacob dead, her husband was not afraid. His eyes showed anger and determination. "We'll find a way to save Alexandr. I promise, Natalia."

After that long night, she could barely think. She dropped her head because of exhaustion and the sick feeling in her stomach.

Jacob slurped his hot coffee. "The first thing is to establish whether they have Alexandr. Sergey and Veronika's friends, the Borisovs, will help. Sidor Borisov is a cop."

"No! Police work for Mafia."

"I know the man, Natalia. He didn't seem like someone who might be bought."

"But you not understand, Jacob." She twisted her hands. "All police are corrupt. The *politsiya* are not trustworthy, ever."

Jake persisted, "Sidor Borisov is a fine man, I know it, and we need help. I assume none of your letters made it through, and you've received no mail from your mother, correct?"

"*Da.*"

"She must be frantic. You need to tell her not to worry, but more important, we need to learn what she can tell us about Alexandr's and her situation. We can't do this alone, Natalia."

"I don't trust man I have never met."

Jake held her hand warmed by her tea. "But I have spent time with him."

Jacob's conviction reassured her. She spoke with more strength in her voice than she felt. "Do what you must. I have faith in you. You best husband, Jacob."

* * *

"You look like shit," Sergey Nazarov proclaimed.

"You're not much better," Jake replied. The exhausted engineer seemed ten years older than yesterday, and Jake was utterly drained.

Sergey slumped into a chair, hoisted his feet onto Jake's desk, and twisted his beard. "So, what are you going to do?"

He didn't answer. Instead, he asked, "Do you trust Sveta and Sidor Borisov?" Jake watched and wondered how Sergey's beard would survive that day's punishment.

Sergey reflected a moment. "She is Veronika's friend since school and is good woman. Husband is policeman." The last sentence did not sound complimentary.

"I hope he can help us. We must try."

Sergey gave Jake a tired smile. "Veronika and I came to same conclusion."

"That's reassuring." Jake rubbed his eyes. "We have to find

out everything we can. Will you help?"

Sergey raised his head, offended. "Of course! Will you contact police here?"

Jake shook his head. "Not today. What do we tell them? An unknown man assaulted Natalia? They would take a report, but that won't get Alexandr out of Russia. There's the answering machine tape, but I think we must first determine if the boy is safe."

"Alexandr? Good name."

Yes, my stepson's name, and some lowlife may have him.

"Natalia okay?"

"No, and under the circumstances, she won't be opening the door to strangers anytime soon."

Sergey slowed his beard-twisting. "I will tell Veronika to ring Sveta now."

Jake bowed his weary head. "Thank you."

CHAPTER 21

The telephone startled Natalia awake, and she rolled across the bed to pick up the receiver. The bedroom phone didn't show the calling number like the one in the kitchen, so she couldn't tell if the caller was Jacob or not. "Hallo?"

The call was from Russia—only her homeland had such poor phone connections—and she heard the taunting voice she recognized from International Friends.

"Congratulations, Mrs. Wilder. Now the US government cannot force you to leave. They require their interviews, but you can stay. You should be happy."

"Where is my son?" she demanded.

The man chuckled. "He is right here. Speak to your mother!"

"Mama?"

Natalia's heart clenched and tears cascaded down her face as she strangled the phone. "Oh, Alexandr, are you well?"

His distant voice pleaded, "Where are you, Mama?"

"I am..."

"Enough for now," the man interrupted. "Your instructions are clear. Carry them out quickly, or you will never hear him again." The line clicked to a dead hiss.

"Alexandr! Alexandr!" she wailed.

She couldn't stop the tears.

* * *

Dmitri Chekhov dropped the handset into the cradle, took a long drag from his cigarette, and smiled. The boy stared up at him in fright and sadness, but the whelp didn't cry. Most cried.

He left the little bastard standing in the room and departed the former orphanage he now owned. All its residents had Russian mothers living in the US with their new husbands, the unsuspecting men who would make him rich.

On the ride to his casino, Dmitri thought about the man the Melnikova woman had snared. From Ivan Rublev's research, Jacob Wilder would be a huge payday. And did the stupid woman really think she could hide her son? *Dumb girl.* The intercepted letters from both Natalia Melnikova and her mother were in his office cabinet.

But no matter. Soon the ignorant foreigner would be dead. The woman would be allowed to keep a limited portion of what she inherited, and Dmitri's German bank balances would grow larger.

* * *

Ivan Rublev sprawled drunk and naked on his bed. He winced when he reached for the vodka bottle on the nightstand. Two empties lay on the floor along with a pile of his bloody, mud-caked clothes. He took another drink and dreaded going to pee. He considered using one of the empty bottles but doubted he could hold his penis steady enough to hit the hole. On his next agonized journey to the toilet, he would detour to the kitchen for something to urinate in.

Fuck, I hurt.

The deepest dog-bites on his thigh and butt continued to soak the bandages and rags he'd applied. The almost inaccessible injuries on his ass throbbed. In the mirror, purple bruises surrounded each bite mark. Those wounds didn't bleed now, but they had bled through his pants to the car seat. His prized white Toyota now had an interior stained with mud and blood. *Filthy fucking mess.* He couldn't yet gather the strength to clean his vehicle. His ankles were sore and swollen, his left shoulder wouldn't move without a gouge of pain, and his head and neck ached like a losing prizefighter's. And all the cuts and punctures from those terrible bushes! Ivan had so many holes he marveled that vodka didn't spring out of him like the stupid things the idiot Americans used to water their lawns.

He would not be able to work for a week or more other than monitor the pay phone. He took another gulp of vodka and prayed Dmitri wouldn't notice the reduction in messages from him.

"Fucking dog."

Easy to blame the *sobaka,* but the fault was his. Dmitri would have him killed if his boss found out he went to Wilder's house before the husband was dead. Fatal mistake on his part, but he wanted to get his big cock between the young Melnikova woman's legs.

He hoped the little bitch would not tell Wilder about his visit. That could foul up everything, and he would be shot in the head by Dmitri's men. *Fuck-your-mother!*

But his immediate concern was getting to the bathroom before his bladder burst or his ankles collapsed.

* * *

Jake felt over-the-edge and fought the urge to drive home from work, though his computer clock displayed only ten AM. *I should be home with Natalia.* But he needed to talk to Sergey and attend a crucial meeting. Jake also realized he might soon have to use all his available vacation time. So, there he sat at his desk unable to concentrate and accomplish anything. He craved sleep to think.

Russian mobsters wanted him dead to extort the inheritance from Natalia in exchange for Alexandr's life. He did the mental arithmetic. His net worth was millions.

A dark, sick feeling twisted his gut. He wanted to go home to Natalia.

Other emotions swirled inside him, including worry for Natalia and a new appreciation of what she'd lived through. He asked himself the inevitable questions about her feelings toward him, about her deceit. *Did she play me for the fool? Was I just a means to get money?*

He rubbed his eyes and knew he still loved her.

The gangsters were clever. They had made their demands in escalating steps for Natalia to follow. No, he couldn't condemn her.

Jake stared at the ever-growing list of emails on his computer and ignored them. Project deadlines, budgets, and corporate communications seemed irrelevant. Today, somewhere in Moscow, a small boy was in danger and needed help. His stepson.

He had longed for a family and often hoped he would be a father. He had determined to be a better dad than his own had been, but who could have expected something like this? Fury pushed through his tiredness. He wanted his son and would go through anyone to get Alexandr back. That decision was granite-hard.

Sergey entered Jake's office. "I talk to Veronika. She call Sveta."

"Thanks. Will she go to the grandmother's? I hope Natalia's mom, Regina, is at her apartment and not at the dacha."

The software engineer nodded and added, "Veronika will be with your wife. Natalia needs Russian woman close. It is necessary."

"I should be with her, too."

"No! They might be watching. You must act normal."

That was a new thought for Jake's weary mind. And what if he delayed changing his beneficiaries and will? Would he be safer if he did not do it? Would Alexandr live if he didn't? *How would I know? Fuck, this is hard.*

Jake flinched when the phone rang. "Hello?"

Natalia cried, "I talk to Alexandr. They have him!" She broke into sobs.

"Take some deep breaths if you can, sweetheart. Sorry I'm not there with you, but their call is not a surprise. Confirms what we thought. The Borisovs will find your mother and learn what they can."

No response.

"Veronika is on her way to our house, and I will be home as fast as I can, okay?"

After a pause, she said, "Alright."

"I love you, Natalia. We'll get through this, I promise." *I hope I can keep my word on that.* He hung up and solemnly told Sergey, "If this is what it seems, I swear I'll kill them."

CHAPTER 22

Vladimir Motorin sipped strong coffee and relished the taste of his cheese-filled sticky bun. He sat at his preferred Moscow café in the embassy district. The brew, pastry, and warm summer sun reinvigorated him.

He smiled at the two waitresses and watched the consular workers stroll by. He still came here to observe the fashions and manners of the European government employees, from which he patterned his own wardrobe and mannerisms. The Swiss were his favorite because they all dressed well.

The past two months had been busy and pleasurable for the former bag man. His boss had promoted him because of his consistent high performance. Motorin now had five underlings to do the detail tasks. A self-satisfied smile painted his face. His patience had paid off, and he now had opportunities to more quickly grow his own constituency.

This morning, Motorin watched the clothes and manners of the foreigners less than usual because of his focus on Dmitri's bride racket. He didn't possess all the details, but the scheme was genius. Yesterday he learned a key clue to Chekhov's interest in International Friends when his boss told him to pick up a kid at a dacha and take him to an ancient orphanage in the city's industrial north. Vladimir did not do it personally. He ordered two beefy employees to force the babushka to pack clothes for the boy while he observed and took pictures from his new Saab.

He wouldn't have cared about such a little task, but he recalled the boy's family name. His mother was the woman Chekhov paired with the red-haired American last winter, the one who prompted the visit with Andrei Borovick at the Education Ministry.

Russian woman with US man. Child left behind. Boy snatched. Vladimir recognized a delicious extortion when he saw one. Push the woman to marry the foreigner, take the brat, and the rich Yankee would pay a high price for the return of his wife's child. Nice.

Vladimir mused about the number of children the facility housed, which he intended to discover. He sipped his coffee and congratulated himself on his perseverance. Now that he comprehended his boss' secret, he planned to somehow capitalize on it.

Motorin checked his Swiss watch and patted the smuggled Walther Model 4 in his shoulder holster. The 7.65MM fit well under his tailored coats. Classier than the Russian-made Makarov T 34 9MM.

This morning he had old business to handle. Fydor Kalita, the electronic store owner, had asked Vladimir's replacement and underling for a rate reduction. That was handled months ago, but the shopkeeper had tried again with the new bag man.

Vladimir decided to settle this one last time. He would smile and greet the man like an old friend, ask about his daughters, joke about the young prostitutes.

Then he would slap Kalita on the back and blast a bullet into his ear.

* * *

Jake needed to mind the coffee today. Though early morning, he gulped his third cup, and his head thumped as he leaned back in his office chair. He closed his eyes and thought of Natalia's touch, her scent, and the sound of her sweet voice. She was part of him. Her soft, creamy skin made him wonder why people thought suntans were sexy. He sighed when he thought of her light gardenia perfume, only noticeable when close. Her music filled the house when she played, and her feel next to him in bed reminded him of a kitten.

But Natalia had withdrawn into silence the past two days.

He looked through his open doorway at the glow of lights from the CEO's office. *Might as well do this now.*

Raj's secretary had not yet arrived, so Jake rapped on his boss' door, an unnecessary formality. Jake had worked with SmartSystems' CEO for thirteen years. Raj Gupta began his career at an Indian outsource company and moved to the United States. He'd earned a Stanford Ph.D. in Artificial Intelligence. A slight, soft-spoken man, Raj founded SmartSystems. Most of their products were ideas from his exceptional mind. Though the company's software had been developed by Jake's engineering teams, without Raj's innovative thinking, SmartSystems would not exist.

They lived in different social circles but shared a solid relationship based on their productive years together. Raj was employee number one, and Jake the fourteenth. He stepped into the office, and Raj smiled. His white teeth shone against his dark skin. He asked in Tamil-accented English, "So, how is married life?"

Jake winced, and his boss' smile faded. Jake shut the door, sat, and told the story.

Raj listened without interruption, his forehead plowed in furrows. When Jake finished, Raj paused in thought. "What do you plan to do?" he asked.

"I don't know yet. I guess I have to involve the authorities to save Alexandr and somehow not end up dead."

Raj steepled his fingers, took a prolonged breath, and did a rapid head wobble. "Jake, whatever you need, the company will support you. If that means a leave of absence to sort things out, consider it done."

"I can't ask you for that."

"You're not asking. I'm offering. Jake, you have brought SmartSystems ideas to life. Without your leadership of the engineering teams, we wouldn't have made it."

"But I would feel like I'm letting you down," Jake scowled.

"It's clear you have an extraordinary situation to deal with." Raj bobbled his head again. "You have been very valuable to the company, and I'm sure once this is straightened out, you will be again. But you must resolve this."

"Thank you, Raj. I can't express what your support means to me. Of course, I have to figure out how to survive."

* * *

Raj's words and offer of a leave of absence echoed in Jake's ears as he walked to his office. In Silicon Valley's high-pressure and ruthless environment, he was comforted knowing Raj valued his importance to the company. Perhaps he would need a temporary absence, possibly he wouldn't, but he appreciated the CEO's support beyond measure.

CHAPTER 23

Back at his desk, Jake opened his calendar. No imperative meetings today, so he reworked his schedule. "Oh, my gosh." He remembered the gangster had told Natalia to call a phone at four on Thursdays. He bolted upright in his chair and thought hard. He knew only one local policeman. He dialed the number and bit the inside of his lip.

"Milpitas Police Department."

"Lonnie Phelps, please."

"One moment, I'll connect you."

Jake tapped his fingers and listened to on-hold music.

"Detective Phelps, here."

"Uh, this is Jake Wilder. You may not remember me, but I helped with Youth Baseball three years ago."

"Sure, I do. Want to help out again? I'm short-handed, as usual."

"Well, I have a problem."

The man's tenor switched to a professional tone. "What's up?"

"Can I come over?"

* * *

Jake drove to the old stucco Milpitas City Hall at the corner of Calaveras and Milpitas Boulevards. He found a space in the crowded lot and walked into the police entrance. He identified himself at the receptionist's bulletproof window and worried how this meeting would turn out. "Detective Phelps is expecting me."

The receptionist called Phelps and advised Jake to wait in

one of the entry chairs.

He first met Lonnie back when several of Jake's friends had kids in the Youth Baseball League. Phelps ran the local program. He handled irate parents and whining players with aplomb. The sandy-haired man in his mid-thirties was dedicated to young people and baseball. No one pushed him around, and everyone respected him because he listened.

Moments later, the heavy door out of the tiny reception area clunked and opened.

Phelps smiled. "Jake, I'm intrigued by your call. Come back and tell me what's going on."

The detective led Jake to a cluttered office and took the chair behind the desk. He leaned forward and folded his hands. "What's the trouble?"

Jake began the tale, and by the third sentence, the detective held up his hand while he retrieved a notepad and pen. Phelps wrote several pages as Jake continued with the story.

"How's your wife doing?" Phelps asked.

"Natalia is terrified, though she tries to be brave. She has me and some friends but no one else here. It was difficult for her when I left this morning."

"You realize the only thing we can investigate is the man's assault on her. We can do nothing about a foreign kidnapping."

"I understand, but the man instructed her to phone a particular number at four PM once my life insurance beneficiary and will are changed."

Phelps referred to his notes and dialed. "Marge, I need an address for a 916 phone." He gave her the number. "As soon as you can."

The detective's eyes took on a far-off stare. "This is a rough one."

"No kidding."

The phone rang. The detective answered and wrote on his

pad. "Appreciate it, Marge, thanks."

Phelps glanced up at Jake. "It's a pay phone in Sacramento, corner of Second and K." He checked the time. "Let me verify something. If this works out, would you and your wife be willing to take a quick trip to Sacramento?"

Jake gave a tired sigh. "Of course."

* * *

"I happy you home early!" exclaimed Jake's worried wife as Natalia flung herself into his arms.

He held her. "You alright?" She nodded against his chest, and he stroked her blonde curls. "Things will be okay. A police friend will take us to Sacramento to find out about the phone you're supposed to call, and Sidor Borisov will visit your mom to learn all he can."

Natalia broke the embrace and went to the kitchen table. She scowled, and her hands shook. Jake joined her and rubbed Silky's side.

"We cannot trust policeman," she said. "The police always take Bratva bribes. We can never believe *politsiya*."

"Maybe in Russia, but it's different here. Sure, we have crooked cops, but most are honest. Lonnie is honorable, and we can't get Alexandr alone."

Natalia remained unconvinced when the white van parked in their driveway. She and Jake walked out and took the second-row seats. Sacks of baseball gear had been stacked in the back.

"This is my wife, Natalia. Natalia, this is Detective Phelps."

Natalia warily shook hands and spoke with little conviction, "Please to meet you."

"My pleasure, and call me Lonnie," he said as he backed out.

"Thank you for helping us," Jake said.

"It's what I do, but I have a selfish motive."

"What's that?" Jake asked.

Phelps smiled. "Once we clear this up, I want your support with the kids."

Jake nodded. "You got it."

"Heck, another couple of years, you may have a little guy in the program yourself!"

Jake patted Natalia's hand. "I look forward to that." She gave him a sad but loving smile.

Phelps fought the heavy gridlock on Highway 680 North before turning east on Interstate 80. Traffic was lighter as they drove across the Coast Range into the Sacramento Valley. The wild flowers were gone, and the grasses had turned their annual brown. Heat mirages glistened on the road ahead. As they drove toward the Sacramento River, they passed miles of flooded rice fields.

"I'm picking up a friend in Sacramento," Phelps said. "I think we need local support if we can get it. The more the better."

Natalia stared out the window at the unfamiliar landscape and squeezed Jakes hand. He lifted her hand and kissed it.

* * *

An hour later, they crossed the river into the state capital and exited the freeway on J Street. They went east to Eighth and turned left as Phelps made a call on the car's clunky console cellphone. When they pulled to the police department building's curb at Eighth and I, a black man with running shoes, baggy shorts, tank top, and canvas camera bag came out and climbed into the front seat. About six feet with broad shoulders, he sported cornrows and a diamond stud earring. Two gold chains dangled from his neck. A gold watchband and ring sparkled on his wrist and hand. *He's a narc,* Jake thought

Phelps and the man enthusiastically greeted each other. "This is Detective Bill Jackson. Bill, this is Jake and Natalia Wilder."

Jackson turned and shook their hands, and Natalia recoiled. Jake hoped the detective wouldn't take offense. He patted her leg to reassure her. "My wife is just over from Russia, and their press paints all blacks as bad people. I witnessed their racism myself when I visited."

Jackson crunched his chin and nodded. "We're cool."

"Thank you to help us," Natalia said.

Jackson's smile lit his face. "Hey, I want to know what this is about."

CHAPTER 24

Phelps drove the few blocks down I Street to Old Town and entered the multi-storied parking garage beneath the elevated Interstate 5. Jackson directed Phelps to park on the second level. "We should be able to see from here."

They stepped into a blast of hot summertime and peered over the railing down to the street. Jake would not have been surprised if the asphalt below bubbled in the afternoon heat.

Jackson pointed. "Up past the Pony Express statue is the phone." He retrieved a pair of binoculars from his bag. "Interesting."

"What?" Phelps asked.

"Take a peek."

Phelps adjusted the field glasses. "I wonder if there's a connection," he said and handed the binocs to Jake. The payphone stood on a corner in front of a shop that sold Russian dolls and lacquered trays. Jake added his own, "Interesting," and passed the binoculars to Natalia, who stared without comment.

"Now we wait," Jackson said.

Sacramento's temperature topped a hundred degrees. Natalia, Jake, and Phelps perspired in the shade, but the local detective seemed immune. Tourists strolled along the wooden sidewalks down below in shorts, light shirts, and sandals. Almost all pedestrians carried cold drinks or voraciously attacked their rapidly melting ice cream. Few cars cruised the historic district that had once been skid row. The primary attractions now were the California Railroad Museum, the riverboat moored to the dock, and the old-timey stores.

At three-fifty-two, a white Corolla parked at the Russian

store. Phelps peered through the binoculars, and Jackson used his camera with telephoto lens. A tall, beefy man extricated himself from the auto.

Natalia asked Phelps, "Please to let me see?"

She held the field glasses to her face, and her hands shook. "That is him. That is man."

Jake glared at the bastard who invaded his house and frightened Natalia. A man who wanted him dead.

Jackson's camera *clicked* as he snapped photos.

Phelps reached for the binoculars, but Jake beat him to them. Jake focused on the man who hobbled across the wooden sidewalk, and a chill ran through him despite the oppressive heat. "Dammit! He was at the airport when Natalia arrived. He wouldn't get out of our way. He's been stalking us from the start. Damn he's big. I can't believe Silky tore him up like that. He can hardly walk."

Jake relinquished the glasses to Phelps and hugged Natalia.

"I'm going for a stroll," Jackson said.

The detective took on his undercover role and strutted up the street. The time was three fifty-seven. He went straight to the phone and picked up the receiver.

* * *

Rublev felt nothing like the masculine persona he liked to project. God, he hurt. His left ankle was less painful, but his right remained angry and swollen, same as his shoulder. His scabbed-over dog bites, thorn punctures, and scratches compounded his misery as he soaked his clothes with sweat. *I miss Moscow's cold on days like this.* He was, however, happy with the sympathy the shop owner gave him when he limped in.

"Ivan Rublev! What happened to you?" the shopkeeper exclaimed.

"Three gang members robbed the old woman next door.

When I ran to stop them, they tried to run over me. I jumped into the bushes to escape."

"Such a brave man. You stay here. I will buy coffee and return."

Rublev watched the shopkeeper's sturdy figure scurry away and noticed the Negro at the phone. "Fuck-your-mother!"

He hobbled outside. "I expecting call!"

The man ignored him.

He drew himself up. "I have important four o'clock call!"

The black man on the phone turned. "Hey, man, be cool." He hung up and ambled away.

Rublev didn't know if he would hear from one of the women today or not, but he had to monitor the pay phone, though he worried his ankle wouldn't hold another minute. He glowered at the man who walked away. "Fucking Negroes. All criminals."

* * *

Jackson returned to the van a few minutes later with a grin of triumph on his face. "He looks like he mated with an unwilling mountain lion. Your dog did that?"

"Silky bite him to protect me," Natalia answered.

"Good dog." Jackson took out his phone. "I'll check his plate."

Jackson took a mobile phone from his bag, dialed, and held the brick-sized device against his shoulder as he scribbled on a piece of paper. "Rublev, Ivan. Twenty-five-sixteen Meadowview, apartment 14C. In the south part of town."

"Thanks, Bill," Phelps said, "but it's four-ten. I've got to head back to Milpitas. Send me copies of the pics."

"You got it, brother. I'll also do more digging on this mutt to confirm what he's up to."

Natalia smiled and extended her hand to Jackson. "Thank you, again, to help us."

* * *

Sidor Borisov walked out of the Moscow police substation, unlocked his old Lada, and sighed. He got little enjoyment from his job these days. Hundreds of senior comrades sold their rights to stay in their apartments to the Kazakh gangs. Sidor sympathized with the old peoples' motives. The crooks gave them cash now for the right to take their apartment after they died. The elderly stayed as long as they lived, often two or three days after signing the document. The Kazakh gangs fooled many, which created the dreadful task for Sidor and his team to identify the dead and track down the criminals.

Today he experienced gratification when he broke the nose of one of those Kazakhs and blackened the eyes of another.

Sidor drove out of the parking lot and turned toward home instead of joining his squad for vodka. He and Sveta were to visit the mother-in-law of the red-haired American. He didn't mind the excuse not to go drinking. His wife's kindness took the sharp edges off his life. She kept him from becoming as brutal as the criminals he hunted. She brought culture and humanity to his life.

He was not surprised at the account of the taken boy. Another Bratva depravity. *But what can I do about it?* Whatever he did, he had to be careful. He trusted his team—excellent men, all—but he held no illusions about mafia power and influence inside the *politsiya*. Living on a cop's salary was not possible, so income supplements from criminal sources kept the majority of law enforcement families alive and police brass in relative luxury. Neither applied to Sidor. As a lieutenant, he earned enough for him and Sveta to live. Of course, he often thought about the bribes offered by the hoodlums he caught, but he couldn't take their money and look Sveta in the eye. Concerning the kid, Alexandr Melnikov, he feared the bosses above him and their Mafia connections.

He would do this favor to repay the wonderful meal Wilder had bought them, their first restaurant dinner in years. He was grateful Sveta had enjoyed the evening. *She deserves better from life.* But he would not take bribes.

Gratitude was only one reason for visiting the grandmother. He understood Sveta's unfulfilled, heartbroken feelings because they had no children. Like most other things in their life, nothing could be done. And the babushka might provide information helpful to finding the child, but Sidor doubted it.

But for Sveta, I must try.

CHAPTER 25

Jake sat at his SmartSystems desk, leaned forward, and focused on his email inbox. He contemplated the day's schedule. Perhaps a hectic day would help the hours move faster. He could control his job, which eased his helplessness about Alexandr.

Sergey came to Jake's office and plopped into a chair. "I call Sidor Borisov. He and Sveta talk to Natalia's mother."

"Is Regina okay?"

"Bruise on face, but otherwise fine. Furious and unhappy." Sergey twisted his beard. "Two tough guys came. She wouldn't open door, but they say they burn down dacha and kill her and the son if she didn't."

Jake's face flushed. "Dammit!"

"The men took the child. She saw out the window when they left. Another man watched from a new car. She say such man asked neighbors about Natalia during your visit. Sorry Borisov did not have better info."

Jake clenched his fists. "Thank you, and please thank your friends for me."

Sergey nodded. "The Borisovs will pick up Regina tonight so Natalia can telephone her."

"Excellent!"

"Because of time zones, you will be here at the office," Sergey said.

"I don't need to be on the call, and it's important Natalia talks to her mom."

Before Jake could tell Sergey about yesterday's Sacramento trip, his phone chirped.

"Hi, Jake, this is Lonnie Phelps. How're you and your wife doing?"

"Better, thanks."

"Bill Jackson sent me the photos and a preliminary report on Rublev." Jake grabbed a pen and pad. "He's thirty-two. Russian here since last year on a permanent resident visa. Listed occupation is auto mechanic, but no work address shows up in the State's Employment Development Department computers.

"Anyway, Bill was able to get a search warrant for Rublev's apartment telephone records and pulled his call log. Rublev's calls from his apartment are all to a dial-up Internet service provider. He apparently uses public phones for his other communications."

Jake bolted straight in his chair. "Internet?"

"Does that mean something?" Phelps asked.

"That must be how he communicates with Russia. Their voice lines are awful. Internet mail is relatively reliable there and improving. Anything else?"

"We should bring in the Feds."

"Do I contact them?"

Phelps hesitated a moment. "So far this is unofficial. I'll require a signed statement for the assault at your house before I engage the FBI."

"Can we keep this quiet?"

"We have to."

"Thanks, Lonnie. How should Natalia file the complaint? I assume she needs to do it."

"Correct. I'll come over this evening after the kids' games. No one will suspect a baseball coach. Work for you?"

"Of course!"

Sergey raised his right eyebrow when the call ended, and Jake said, "Natalia and I went to Sacramento with a police friend. We saw the bastard who came to our house, and the cops identified him. Ivan Rublev."

"Internet?"

"The only calls on Rublev's home telephone are to an ISP. Makes sense. What better way to communicate internationally?"

Jake wasn't sure Sergey heard him. His senior engineer's mind seemed to fly to another place.

Jake's thoughts went to dreams of revenge.

When Jake arrived home, Natalia threw herself into his arms. "Oh, Jacob, I talk to Mama three hours. I scared for Alexandr, but I happy she okay."

"I'm glad. You should talk with her every few days. Perhaps at your girlfriend's? I understand the Borisovs and your mom live far from each other."

"*Da*, they do. My friend will help."

She squeezed him tightly, and he hugged her back, relieved she seemed more hopeful and not so depressed.

"I love you, Jacob, for everything you doing for Alexandr and me."

He kissed her softly. "I wouldn't be much of a husband if I didn't."

* * *

Two days passed, and Jake, Natalia, and Phelps sat at the dining room table with FBI Agent Cochrane. In his late twenties with dark hair and brown eyes set too far apart, the G-man radiated a better-than-everyone-else attitude.

"Mr. and Mrs. Wilder, I understand your angst over this situation, but there may be little The Bureau can do. We have no jurisdiction for the alleged kidnapping in Russia, and no federal crime has been committed here."

Jake's anger erupted. "Wait a minute! The recording

implies I will be murdered when my will and insurance beneficiaries are changed, and the *alleged* kidnapping happened. There is a conspiracy here, and my stepson and I are in danger. Why wouldn't the FBI help us?"

"Because the threat on your life is a local law enforcement matter."

"Shit! What am I supposed to do?"

"I don't know what to tell you, Mr. Wilder, other than coordinate with the Milpitas police."

After Agent Cochrane left, Jake stomped across the living room in fury. "Damn, damn, damn! I can't believe this!"

Natalia looked frightened and worried. Detective Phelps shook his head in apparent embarrassment.

"Is he right, Lonnie?"

"Tell you the truth, I'm shocked. I've worked with The Bureau numerous times and expected they would at least take a look because of the international aspect."

"Is it hopeless?" Natalia asked.

"I don't think so. The issue may be this particular person," Phelps answered.

"Dammit!" Jake exclaimed, "Someone wants me dead, and this idiot tells us it's a Milpitas problem! If Russian mobsters threaten extortion and the homicide of American men, the FBI *has* to take this."

"I'll make a call to a Fed I partnered with on a couple cases years ago. See what her view is."

"Appreciate that." Jake took a deep breath, shook his head, and turned to Natalia. "I'm sorry the agent was such a jerk. We'll pull The Bureau into this one way or another."

"Not your fault," she said. Her blue eyes told him she blamed herself for this mess.

"What will help is more evidence, the more the better," Phelps added as he rose to leave.

"How we get this?" Natalia asked.

Jake caressed her hand. "That, my love, is the question in front of the bigger one. How do we find Alexandr?"

CHAPTER 26

The following Wednesday, Jake again called his life insurance company. He had made Natalia his beneficiary after Hawaii and the previous week had apprised the carrier of the threat. He checked each day to ensure they had all they needed from him.

After the investigator recovered from her initial shock, she wanted to help.

"Hello, Standard Mutual, Jill Edwards speaking."

"Ms. Edwards, this is Jake Wilder again. Sorry to bug you, but I want to make sure my policy pays off promptly if I... pass."

"You realize that settling the claim would be difficult because your spouse is involved however contrary to her will."

"But my wife will need the cash for our son! The men who kidnapped him are dangerous."

"I understand your dilemma. I promised you I would help if we can, but we can't disburse benefits where we believe there is fraud."

"This isn't fraud. It's a murder plot, and my wife can't do anything about it."

"Good point, but this is a complicated problem."

"My house and lot have substantial worth. I'll sign them over to Standard Mutual as collateral against...possible payout."

She paused a moment. "Hmm. Unusual, but I admit we're dealing with bizarre circumstances here." Her voice became softer. "Let me discuss this with management."

"Thank you!"

"I've been an insurance investigator for twelve years and

thought I'd seen everything, but this is a new one. I'm going to Sacramento tomorrow to check out this Rublev character. I searched the industry actuarial databases for husband deaths in Northern California after a short marriage where the wife received the proceeds. Ninety-six claims were filed over the past two years. We insured three of them; other carriers covered the rest. The details are available, but my counterparts at the other companies need to supply them. I've sent e-mails to them.

"Only one we underwrote appears to fit; the others were clear accidents and medical issues. The suspicious case is a restaurant owner in Red Bluff who was stabbed and robbed at his business. His wife has a Russian-sounding name. I'm going up tomorrow but don't have much hope because the phone is disconnected.

"After Red Bluff, I'll loop through Sacramento to find out what I can about Rublev."

A stab of dread sliced through Jake as he strangled the receiver. He assumed there were other targets, but to learn about someone killed unsettled him to the extreme. He swallowed hard. "Thank you again for your help. If you come up with anything, can you let me know?"

"Happy to. The files contain confidential information I can't disclose, but I'll send you what I can. If federal authorities take over, of course we will give them everything."

After the call, Jake stared out his window and thought of Natalia, Alexandr, and other anonymous victims. At that instant, he didn't know if he was more angry or afraid. No, rage outweighed his fear.

* * *

Natalia couldn't lose herself in her music. The piano remained untouched. She paced the house and muttered about the danger she'd created for everyone. Silky followed her and stayed close. *Why was I so stupid? I love Jacob and would be happy to be here if it were not for Alexandr. I can never repay Jacob for what he is doing to help.*

She vowed she must find a way.

* * *

Sidor Borisov went into his kitchen and sat at the table. Though early, Moscow's summer sun shone through the plastic kitchen curtains. Sveta put his plate of eggs, sausage, potatoes, bread, and pickles before him. She filled his cup with strong tea. While she served up her own breakfast, he looked at the small vase on the table. Today, it contained a purple and white flower. He pondered where his wife found fresh flowers, even in winter, without spending money, but somehow, she did. He never asked because he didn't want to destroy the mystery. When he dealt with criminal scum he thought of a single bloom on his table, which kept him from "losing discipline," the cop euphemism for throwing a crook head-first down a stairwell.

Sveta joined him. "There is not much you can do about the child?"

He sighed. "*Nyet.* The grandmother gave us nothing helpful. The only clue came from Sergey Nazarov, who told me International Friends is linked to this. I have nothing else to go on." He paused and took her hand. "You understand the risk, my love. I cannot trust my own men on this."

Worry etched Sveta's face. "Be careful, but a little boy...." Her eyes took on an unfamiliar hardness. "Please do what you can. Such evil must stop. No one should take children from their mothers."

Sidor understood his wife's soulful ache and would help if only to lessen her pain. "I will do what I can."

Her smile returned. "Eat. Your food will be cold."

He touched her cheek, sipped his hot tea, and ate.

As he walked down the stairs to the street, Sidor thought about the purple and white flower.

* * *

A forest of smokestacks spewed soot-filled smoke into North Moscow's polluted haze. Apartments here were more decrepit and overcrowded with immigrants from remote villages and far-off confederation of independent states republics. Contaminated air, water and soil shortened their lives, but not as much as where they came from.

At least the area had jobs sweeping foundry floors or scrubbing chemical tanks, and food enough to keep a family alive. So what if few men survived to their fifties?

Vladimir Motorin speculated why the ancient orphanage had been built in such a location. He crunched his chin and nodded. Because the land was of little value and unwanted, like the children it housed.

A high concrete wall surrounded the place, and next to the pot-holed road lay a two-meter pipeline from one of the dozens of central heating plants across Moscow. The massive insulated pipes ran throughout the city for heat and bathing. Efficient system, when it worked. A rupture would deny hot water and warmth to thousands. The pipe made a right angle skyward at the orphanage entrance, spanned the few meters needed for vehicles to pass underneath, and dropped again to earth to continue its path.

Vladimir turned his Saab off the road, drove beneath the pipe, and entered through the iron gate to the grounds. Children of various ages from about four to thirteen, more than he imagined, played under the watchful eyes of four old babushkas. He parked in front of the dingy, soot-streaked concrete building and stepped into the foul air. Chemicals. Petroleum. Sewage.

This was a gamble. If Chekhov found out he visited here, he could have problems. He would say he followed up on the Melnikov kid to be thorough, but his real mission was to determine the scope of Chekhov's blackmail scheme. If as extensive as Vladimir guessed, how did his boss keep the husbands from saying anything after they paid the ransoms? Americans were notorious for seeking revenge when wronged.

Questions for other days. Today he intended to discover the profit potential for Chekhov's racket.

He straightened his tie and hoped his soft voice would convince whoever guarded Chekhov's child treasury to give him a tour.

* * *

Jake listened to Silky drink from her water dish downstairs while Natalia slept next to him, snuggled close. After a long, upsetting day and sleepless night, Jake stared at the ceiling. Despite passionate lovemaking with Natalia, his mind wouldn't calm for sleep.

He had considered one idea after another to deal with their impossible situation and always came to the same conclusion.

To rescue Alexandr, he himself must die.

Natalia stirred as the morning pushed away the gloom. He ran his hand down her body and felt more at ease. Now, he had a plan.

CHAPTER 27

What had been so straightforward and simple in the dim shadows before dawn now seemed irrational in the light of day and Natalia's questioning stare.

She stood in her robe and slippers next to Jake in the bathroom while he fidgeted with his unruly hair. "You pretend to die? Standard Mutual pays money I give mob boy for Alexandr? Where will money come from?"

"I'll borrow equity in the house, which will protect the carrier. To save our son, the criminals must think I'm dead so they can be paid."

"Can you do this?"

"Not without support from my boss, Standard Mutual, and Lonnie Phelps." He made a last check of his appearance in the mirror and concluded his red locks would not behave today. "I cannot think of any other possibility. This *has* to work."

She put her arms around him and pressed close. "You are fine man, Jacob. I love you."

"Seems I waited my whole life for you, Natalia. I never want to let you go, ever. And I want Alexandr."

"You be perfect father."

He smiled and gave her a tender kiss.

* * *

Jake had hoped for a morning meeting, but SmartSystems' CEO had a full calendar until mid-afternoon. By then, Jake had consumed countless cups of coffee to stay awake. He could not focus and caught himself twice when his anger boiled over with his team leaders. He was exhausted.

As three o'clock approached, Jake walked to the CEO's office. Sergey stood there and waited. He stopped twisting his beard and asked with unhidden worry, "You alright?"

"As much as I can be. This is ripping Natalia's heart out, though she tries not to show it. I am *so* angry."

The door opened, and Raj ushered his visitor to the front lobby. He motioned to Jake and Sergey to enter his office as he walked past with his departing visitor.

Raj came back, closed the door, and said in his accented English, "Sorry for the delay." His usual smile was absent as he asked in his gentlemanly voice, "How is Natalia? This must be hard for her."

"Yes, but she's doing okay. Appreciate your asking."

"Plans for what you're going to do?"

Jake shifted in his chair. Raj had to be worried about his lower performance. "I was thinking about taking the leave of absence you offered, but with a twist. I'm going to fake my death."

Raj's eyebrows shot up.

Sergey stopped beard-twisting.

"I think I can arrange things with my carrier," Jake said, "and I'll need help from the police. But if the kidnappers receive at least a million dollars, they *should* release Alexandr. I sure hope so. Then I'll come back to life."

Sergey and Raj sat in silence.

"If I'm 'dead,' I can't come to work. Sergey's the best person to take over for me."

Sergey scowled.

"Getting Alexandr will take time, so I have to stay hidden. Telecommuting would be an option, but we must be careful. The gangsters might be watching.

"I know I'm asking a lot, but this is the only idea I came up with."

Raj waved the notion away, "You helped build SmartSystems.

You brought us through some difficult times, especially in the beginning. Now you have difficulties. How will you pay these men?"

"I'll use my house as collateral with the insurance company if they agree."

Raj frowned. "But you must still repay the loan."

Jake nodded and fidgeted in his chair.

Raj appeared to sense his leader's discomfort and said, "SmartSystems might help some."

"I can't ask for that."

"You haven't. Again, I offered. The amount will not be as much as you need, I'm certain, but it will lessen your burden."

"At this point, I don't know how I'll pay anything back other than from my retirement."

Raj's smile returned. "Consider it an advance on your next couple of bonuses if it makes you feel better. You mean much to this company and to me. That's the truth. Getting quality applications released on-time is problematic, and few companies consistently do it well. We do because of you and your teams."

"Thanks," was all Jake could say.

The CEO leaned forward on his desk. "So when will you leave us?"

"Soon as I can make the arrangements."

"I wonder about their Internet use," Sergey said. "Why couldn't Rublev's Internet Service Provider monitor his access and email? Who's the ISP?"

Jake pounced on the idea. "I'll find out. Worth a try."

"Why not drop an exploit into his machine?" Raj said.

Jake and Sergey stared at Raj and both smiled. An exploit was a program, often malicious, downloaded from the Internet without the user's knowledge. Once in the target computer, the exploit could record all keystrokes and copy files off the

PC. Writing one to avoid triggering anti-virus software would be tricky.

Sergey nodded. "I can code hacker-ware. Did in Russia."

Jake felt the first genuine smile in days spread across his face. "I need to contact my detective friend."

* * *

Though the morning had crawled by, Jake's day accelerated. SmartSystems would let him take leave and go along with his faked death. He could hardly wait to tell Natalia.

Back in his office, he left a message for Phelps to telephone him and blasted through his neglected inbox. He had a lot to wrap up before his "demise." He thought about the people who would be hurt by the ruse, but they would understand when the story came out. He wondered who would be saddened with his resurrection. Not many, but the Russian asshole in Sacramento would be one of them.

* * *

Phelps' return call interrupted his thoughts. "Jake, I want to apologize again for the FBI jerk. I complained to some folks and got a sympathetic ear, but we need more evidence before they will act. I'll tell you this, once they're in, I'll enjoy informing Special Agent Cochrane's supervisor of his agent's ineptitude."

"You couldn't change the asshole. Anything else new?"

"Not yet. Bill Jackson is keeping tabs on Rublev when he gets a chance."

Jake couldn't hide the concern in his voice. "I pray nothing occurs until we have Alexandr."

"I understand, but if the guy breaks the law, we may not

have a choice. The resolution of your situation might take months."

"I'm working on something to speed things up."

"Oh?"

Jake explained and added, "What do you think?"

"Might work. Let me do some checking with the chief and the coroner."

"That would be great. When my stepson is with us, I don't care what happens to Rublev. Well, I do, but you know what I mean. Also, which Internet service does he use?"

"Hold on." The sound of rustled paper came over the line. "NetWorks in Santa Clara. Why?"

Jake told him about the computer hack idea. Phelps listened and said, "A court order would be required to make this legal. Who would write the, what'd you call it, spyware?"

"One of my people."

"NetWorks is in our county. I know a superior court judge well. Both his son and daughter went through Youth Baseball. I'll phone him and find out what he would need for a warrant."

"Again, thank you so much."

"No problem." Phelps laughed. "I'm so desperate for help with the kids, I'll do anything for extra hands."

"As soon as I'm resurrected, I'm yours."

Time to give Natalia the news.

CHAPTER 28

The telephone rang after dinner, and Jake saw Natalia's involuntary start. She was on edge but wore a brave face. He answered at the second ring. "Hello?"

"Mr. Wilder, Jill Edwards. Sorry to bother you at home."

"Don't hesitate, anytime," he told the insurance investigator.

"I went up to Red Bluff today and think the case there is similar to your circumstances. The homicide hasn't been solved, and the detectives have no leads.

"The insured's house and restaurant are vacant and for sale, so I called the listing agent. Turns out he was friends with the deceased, which I guess is to be expected in a small town. He confirmed the widow is Russian."

"Did she have children?"

"Not that anyone knew about. She went back to Russia after the funeral. She had nothing to keep her here, but I have her Moscow address for mailing the paperwork and proceeds for the properties when they sell.

"The real estate broker speaks highly of the spouse. His friend was a long-time widower, and she made him quite happy. They met through correspondence, same as you and your wife. By the way, he would like to meet with you. He is extremely upset about the murder."

"Of course. Can you tell me who he is?"

"No reason why not. The man is Stuart Baxter. The victim, Stephen Sands, and the wife is Yelena." She gave him Baxter's number.

"I went through Sacramento on my way back and caught

up with Detective Jackson as he staked out Rublev's apartment." She chuckled. "He was surprised I spotted him, but I've been on so many stakeouts myself I recognize the signs.

"Anyway, nothing new on Rublev. Jackson reports he stays at his apartment except to go to the liquor store and an Old Town pay phone. Jackson says Rublev still hobbles from your dog tearing into him. That must have been some fight."

Jake laughed. "No doubt. Silky is protective of Natalia."

"I told Jackson about the Red Bluff case. I think he'll be able to turn up more evidence than I can.

"Finally, I received information from four carriers confirming other cases. This criminal fraud might be extensive."

"You've been busy."

"Just doing my job, but I'm happy to help you and your family."

"Is there anything I can do?"

"Stay alive."

* * *

Vladimir Motorin skipped his trip to the café for pastries and imported coffee this morning. Pity. Chekhov's one-on-one meeting was more important. Motorin straightened his silk tie and waited for Chekhov to finish a task on his computer.

His tired-looking boss stopped typing, lit a cigarette, and focused his gaze on him. The more nocturnal the Bratva leader became, the more daylight activities the boss delegated to him.

"You are doing well. Your areas show excellent growth. I congratulate you," Chekhov said.

Motorin bowed his head and said in his gentle voice, "I am glad you are satisfied."

Chekhov grilled Motorin over the next half-hour on the status of each protection account and the performance of underlings. This update used to be a daily requirement, but now he briefed Chekhov weekly. Motorin valued the greater freedom and predicted his responsibilities would continue to expand.

After his report, Chekhov nodded and handed him a sheet of paper. "Here are two more children to pick up."

"It will be done tonight."

Perhaps he should cover himself for visiting the former orphanage, which had been a revelation. The disagreeable woman with wild black hair, huge red lips, and yellow teeth who ran the operation gave him a tour, and dozens of mosquito-bitten brats crowded the place. A gold mine! Chekhov did not spend much on their care. They were thin, and the kids did the chores themselves, not that he cared. What interested Motorin was the cash Chekhov earned and how he would obtain a slice. Yes, better for Chekhov to learn about the visit from him than from someone else. "So you are aware, I went to check on the Melnikov boy."

A sudden, sharp glint in Chekhov's narrowed eyes told him he erred. "I assumed you want him well cared for. The boy is fine. I apologize if I overstepped my responsibilities."

Chekhov gave a dismissive wave with his cigarette hand, and a curtain of smoke floated toward the ceiling. "I value your concern and initiative."

The words were not reassuring, since Chekhov spoke them with icy, unforgiving eyes.

* * *

Chekhov was more fatigued than usual and stamped out his Marlboro in the overflowing ashtray. Time for bed, past time. As he descended the stairs to the quiet casino, he thought about whether he should retire to Finland sooner than planned. His casino and prostitution businesses were booming, but competition in the protection racket had become fierce. But Motorin demonstrated how a more sophisticated approach captured new clients.

Best of all, Chekhov expected the brides with youngsters to generate enormous income. The select women wanting to leave Russia to live with foreign men grew to more than he could handle. He had added more staff to keep up with the applications and spent many nighttime hours sending and receiving messages to manage his representatives in America.

Yet, two things troubled him. One was the decline in communications from Ivan Rublev. Three of his special Moscow girls were communicating with men in Northern California, but he had received no updates about them from Rublev. Chekhov made a mental note to email him.

His second discomfort was Motorin. Chekhov trusted his lieutenant, but something about him going to the orphanage on his own did not seem right. True, he delegated much to his lieutenant and welcomed his ruthless ingenuity, but the bride operation was his secret money machine poised to make substantial profits. He would tolerate no risk to the scheme, which is why Motorin's initiative unsettled him.

Chekhov yawned. *Perhaps I am too tired.*

He shook his head and walked into the morning light, his bodyguard at his side. They both climbed into the back of the waiting Mercedes. Chekhov focused on deciding which of his many beds he would sleep.

CHAPTER 29

A smoggy summer haze spread across the Santa Clara Valley, but Natalia enjoyed a clear, early-morning view. The house sat high enough on the hill to be above the dirty air. She rested on her piano stool and sipped strong tea Jacob found from a catalog. She savored the flavor.

Silky came over and nudged her arm. Natalia set down her cup and rubbed the brown-mottled dog behind the ears. "Good *sobaka*." She felt a newfound optimism. "You and Alexandr will be perfect playmates."

She looked out over the valley and worried about her son. *Where is he? Is he safe?* Though she did not have the answers, at least today she had hope. She would wake Jacob soon or he would be late to office.

Natalia stroked the dog's head with one hand and picked up her tea with the other. After a sip, she allowed herself a smile. She and Jake had passed last evening discussing his plan. Her emotions had overflowed at how much he did for her and Alexandr. She made love to him until he dropped into exhausted slumber.

The clock chimed seven, and Silky followed her to the kitchen. She filled Silky's water dish, poured Jacob's coffee, and carried the cup upstairs to the bedroom where he slept in a jumble of sheets. Such a strange, wonderful man with his bright red hair, dark green eyes, and forgetfulness about removing shoes in the house. He was kind, gentle, and generous, but something had roused within him. Courage never tested until now. The bravado of young soldiers like her first husband was different. Jacob's mettle was deep and genuine.

Natalia put his mug on the nightstand, sat on the side of

the bed, and slipped the sheet down to scratch his back. He stirred and opened his eyes. A smile crossed his face before his eyes went wide and he bolted upright. "Oh, my gosh. I just remembered. We're married, so the K-1 Visa is satisfied, but there needs to be the final INS hearing."

When she gave him a questioning look, he said, "Until you receive your green card, you can't leave the country. Well, you can, but you can't come back. Darn, with everything going on, I spaced it."

"I cannot come back?"

"Not without permanent residency. Immigration might take months to schedule you." He grimaced. "I'm sorry, sweetheart."

"Is it now impossible? What if emergency happen?"

"I don't know." He realized the time, yet he didn't vault out of bed. He reached up and ran his fingers through her curls. "We'll think of something."

She gave him a brave smile. "We will. You must hurry now."

Jacob gave her a passionate kiss, grabbed his mug, and hurried to the bathroom for his shower. "Thanks for the coffee!"

Natalia made the bed and thought. There must be a way. If things were like Russia, rubles placed into the right hands solved everything. Simple. But perhaps money wouldn't buy the government services one required in America. She sighed. She had entrusted her husband with her life when she came here, so now she needed to do the same with Alexandr's. And Jacob's.

She did something she had not done in days. She went downstairs, made herself comfortable at the piano, and played with passion.

* * *

After arriving at the office, Jake could not focus on work. He started when his telephone rang. *Please not another meeting.*

"Mr. Wilder, Jill Edwards from Standard Mutual. I want to inform you management agrees on a policy process like you suggested."

"Thank you! That's a relief," he said, though he understood he would be gambling his financial future while the carrier was protected from loss. If the Russians monitored them closely, there was too much danger taking out a mortgage. Funds coming from Standard Mutual would be more convincing. "I'll tell my attorney to FedEx the documents to you that I've executed."

"Good. This should be straightforward. Also, we're getting hits from other carriers. We scheduled a summit here tomorrow to pool our efforts, and if we confirm more cases like yours, we'll bring in the FBI."

"Great!" He caught himself and said, "Oh, no, it isn't. That means more dead policy holders."

"Correct. I'll keep you informed. By the way, did you call Stuart Baxter?"

"Not yet."

"He very much would like to talk with you."

"I'll telephone him today."

"So what's your next move?"

"Well, I want you to return the completed paperwork right away. I'm going to fake my death."

Edwards was silent a moment. "I get it. If this works, we'll disburse the funds, you and your spouse get your son back, and the authorities can clean things up."

"I like the way you say it. Thank you."

"Again, just doing my job."

After the call, Jake telephoned his lawyer about the loan paperwork and called Lonnie.

"Detective Phelps."

"Lonnie, Jake. The insurance company found other possible cases, and they'll bring in the FBI once they have confirmation."

"I hope they do something this time."

"Me, too. Any news on my idea?"

"Yes. The chief gave his blessing. The city has no risk, and this might prevent a major crime."

Jake flinched. The crime would be his homicide.

Phelps continued, "The coroner is willing to go along but needs clearance from county counsel. Again, no liability for them as long as this is part of an active investigation. I assured him that is the case.

"By the way, do you still drive the pickup?"

"Yeah, why?"

"Just a thought."

"Where are you on obtaining court approval for NetWorks to report on Rublev's emails and computer searches and dropping the spyware into his PC?"

The detective chuckled. "You're an impatient guy. Hey, I understand. I talked to the judge this morning, and he will issue the warrant for the Internet traffic, messages, and spyware download. We're putting a wiretap on the Sacramento pay phone, too. I'm working on that affidavit now. How do we coordinate with your people? You're supposed to be dead soon."

"I'll give you my tech guy's number later today once I confirm some things. He's Russian and understands the whole story."

"Alright." Phelps paused. "In case I didn't tell you, good luck."

After the conversations with Edwards and Phelps, Jake's spirits lifted. He had more optimism than a few long days ago.

He swiveled in his chair and gazed at the summer morning. *Beautiful day.* Perhaps he now more appreciated each sunrise. Nothing like the prospect of imminent demise to sharpen one's perspective! Jake chuckled and thought about having a barbecue after Saturday's softball tournament. *Why not throw a party?*

Contemplating his end seemed bizarre. No job. No baseball. No hikes in the hills with Natalia and Silky. But those would resume once Alexandr was here. He turned his thoughts to what life would be like with a son and smiled to himself. *Heck of a way to have a child!*

CHAPTER 30

Jake had time to phone the Red Bluff broker. *Might as well find out what he wants.*

A pleasant-sounding receptionist said, "Baxter Real Estate. May I help you?"

"Yes, this is Jake Wilder down in Milpitas. I was asked by an investigator with Standard Mutual to reach out to Mr. Baxter."

A moment later a man with a rich, deep voice announced, "Stu, here. Mr. Wilder?"

"Yes, Jake."

"Thank you for calling. What Ms. Edwards suspects about my friend shook me up. She also explained your situation."

"He corresponded with his wife through an agency?"

"Yelena? Yes. She was beautiful with the sweetest disposition. I'd never seen Stephen so joyful. In fact, I didn't believe he *could* be so happy."

"Other than the trap we are in, I understand your friend's feelings."

"This may sound odd, but I would like to talk with you face-to-face. I didn't suspect his murder was more than a robbery gone bad." His voice drifted into sadness. "It would help me deal with this if we meet."

Jake thought a second. Why shouldn't he meet this stranger? Besides, he might have helpful info. "Sure, but it needs to be soon."

Baxter's voice conveyed relief. "Thank you. This means a lot to me. Would this evening be convenient?"

"That would be fine. Here's my home phone and address."

After they hung up, Jake pondered Baxter's request. Peculiar, but why not? He glanced at the time. "Shit," he said aloud and rushed across the hall.

Raj's secretary looked up at Jake. "Go on in. He's expecting you."

As he walked in, Raj and Sergey were in vigorous debate. Each man held a marker and scribbled on a whiteboard diagram. Jake studied the board. This was a schematic for spyware that would record Rublev's keystrokes and transmit a copy of his hard drive.

"Impressive," Jake said. "How will you get him to download the exploit?"

"I will add code to picture of *The Motherland Calls*, world's largest sculpture in Volgograd," Sergey said. "No Russian can resist looking at statue."

"How long will this take?" Jake asked.

Sergey gave his beard a twist. "One day to build, one to test."

Jake's smile stretched wider. "Perfect. The court authorizations should be signed today. When that's in place, I'll give Detective Phelps your contact information and have him call you."

Raj Gupta's expression became more solemn. "How are the other preparations? Can you act soon?"

"Everything's going well, except that with all the excitement, I forgot about the last Immigration interview. Natalia will have difficulty re-entering the US after getting Alexandr if she leaves without her green card. I don't know what to do."

"I may be able to expedite things," Raj responded. "I'll dictate a letter avowing the company needs to send you and your bride on an overseas work assignment. You have it couriered to the INS today." He beamed his glistening smile. "And where do you think we should assign the two of you? How about our London office?"

Jake heard the mirth in his voice. "Fantastic, Raj. You can tell them Antarctica for all I care!"

* * *

Ivan Rublev cursed the message from Chekhov. How would he check out the new targets while crippled with pain in his right ankle and left shoulder?

But what to say to Chekhov? He couldn't admit his foolish move against the Melnikova woman almost got him killed, so he emailed his apology for having contracted stomach flu. He should be recovered in a few days.

That should satisfy Chekhov and give him enough time to resume killing husbands and earning bonuses.

* * *

The parking places at International Friends' office on Rus Street were occupied, so Sidor Borisov parked on a street intersecting the alley behind the old brick building. He figured the mobster had something to hide and would use a back entrance instead of the front door.

Sidor did not know what to expect, but his only clue about International Friends was that the mob boy threatened Melnikova in the evening, not during the day. Not much to go on.

Night came late at this latitude. After sunset, he would have trouble looking inconspicuous, but the lingering light provided a foolproof cover. He opened the hood of his car, took his tools from the trunk, and tinkered with the small motor. Working on one's car along the road was as common as gypsy beggars in the Metro.

Sidor cleaned the spark plugs, wiped off leaking oil, and fiddled around while he thought about Sveta. He would prefer to be home with her.

A shiny Mercedes cruised up and turned into the alley-way. Sidor memorized the license before the car stopped in the shadows. Two men exited as he moved around to face away from them. He had seen more than anticipated and feared the power possessed by men with cars costing more than a life-time's wages.

He latched the hood, stowed his tools, and drove home. Yes, he had agreed to investigate, but this was too dangerous. Both for him and Sveta.

* * *

Pleasant sounds greeted Jake after he turned off the pickup and heard Natalia's music and Silky's bark. He hoped someday soon to hear Alexandr's voice as well.

What a day! His plans were coming together, and, best of all, the INS review would be in two days.

To retrieve his stepson, Jake might be separated from Natalia for some time. Once she had Alexandr, he prayed he would get them both back without complication. Perhaps they could travel to Poland, which was easy from Moscow. He would join them and go to the US embassy to secure Alexandr's entry to the US.

Silky barked again, and the music stopped. Jake remembered to kick off his shoes before he went into the kitchen. "Hi, girls!"

CHAPTER 31

Two hours later, a slim man in his mid-thirties stepped out of a new, dark-gray BMW and stood with a self-assured, erect bearing. Jake opened the front door with Silky at his side as the man approached. "I'm Stu Baxter." The man's voice was richer and deeper than on the phone. They shook hands.

"Please come in."

Silky gave the intruder a suspicious sniff and huffed.

Inside, Baxter said, "I'm sorry to intrude." He presented Jake with a bottle of wine. "A small 'thank you' for allowing me to come."

"Appreciate it."

"Nice home," Baxter commented in his real estate broker voice on the way to the living room. He suddenly hesitated when he saw Natalia.

Jake sensed a wound in Baxter's confident demeanor, and his pain was evident as he shook Natalia's hand and introduced himself to her.

"Pleased to meet, Stuart. You like coffee? Tea?"

"Thank you, no. I'm embarrassed for intruding. You have more pressing things to worry about."

Jake didn't comment on the obvious. "Please sit down." He and Natalia took the couch, and Baxter sat in the loveseat opposite them. Silky gave the man another sniff and accepted Baxter's scratch behind her ears. *Well, I guess he passed the Silky test.* "We're happy to have you here, but we don't understand how we can help you."

Baxter shifted in his seat. The man's expression shifted to despondent, his voice soft and slow. "Let me start at the beginning. You see, Stephen Sands and I were best friends since second grade. He saved my life once.

"My folks had a cabin at Lake Almanor, near Mt. Lassen. I still own it. Anyway, when he and I were ten, we were up at the lake, and I got a wild hair to go swimming one night, though we were forbidden to. The night was warm with a full moon, the most beautiful moon imaginable. I couldn't resist. He tried to stop me, but I ignored him.

"Well, to shorten the story, I fell off the rocks into the water and got the wind knocked out of me. I almost drowned. Stephen rescued me. He never brought it up afterwards, but that's the kind of guy he was. He'd do anything for you without hesitation or fuss. Stephen never made you feel you owed him.

"We were friends our whole lives. When I went away to college, I'd return, and we'd pick up where we left off as if I hadn't been away.

"So, life went on. Stephen and Julie wed and started their restaurant, which was always busy. But Julie got breast cancer. What she went through ripped his heart out. He loved her so much, and for once he was helpless. Julie's death changed him into a lost, sad man."

Baxter cracked a slight smile. "I tell you, we were all surprised eight years later when he announced he corresponded with Russian ladies. We all knew he was lonely but were amazed he did it. I guess he liked the back-and-forth with letters because he could say what he felt without small town social pressure.

"We thought he was nuts when he went to Moscow to spend time with three ladies, but he came back so alive. Believe me, no one thought he was crazy when Yelena arrived. Beautiful, intelligent, and she worked alongside him. I didn't know a man could find such happiness."

Baxter looked at Jake. "I see a lot of the same in you."

Jake nodded.

Baxter's smile faded, and his look and voice turned to granite. "Then Stephen was killed." The man clenched and unclenched his fists. "We thought it was a standard robbery. Yelena was inconsolable and fled back to Moscow after the burial.

"When the insurance investigator told me about probable extortion in your situation, I grew frantic and suspicious about what happened to Stephen. Ms. Edwards indicated the probability of targeted murder without explicitly saying those words. Her demeanor showed she thought that was exactly what happened. So, talking to the two of you is important to me."

"But I still don't understand how we can help you," Jake said.

Moisture gathered in Baxter's eyes. "I understand this sounds odd since you don't know me, but I wanted to see the two of you to verify my friend's relationship wasn't imaginary. Seeing you together shows me what they had was real.

"If there is anything I can do for you two, I will feel better about Stephen."

"Thank you, but I'm not sure what that would be," Jake said.

"I don't know, either."

Jake figured the man was who he appeared to be, a small-town businessman with a dead friend. Even Silky liked him. "There might be one thing."

"Name it, please."

"Well, you mentioned a cabin. Could I disappear there for a length of time?"

"It's yours!" Baxter frowned. "But if you're hiding, how will you get your son? I thought he's still in Russia."

Jake decided to describe the ruse despite his concern about a leak to the mobsters.

Baxter whistled. "Wow!"

"Staying concealed will be tricky, and I will need to be far enough away to avoid accidental sightings but not too far. The use of your place would be a godsend."

"Please count on it. I don't want anyone else to go through what Stephen and Yelena did."

"Me, neither," Jake added.

CHAPTER 32

Q uite a party, Jake!" Lonnie Phelps said. The detective winked while he juggled a full plate of food in one hand and a beer in the other.

"Thanks." Jake whispered. "For everything."

Phelps nodded and moved off to find his wife.

This is a lively get-together! Jake surveyed the boisterous group spread across his backyard. Most of his softball team huddled at the kegs and celebrated their second-place finish in today's tournament, to which Jake's strong right arm from third base contributed. Others from work gathered near the food tables and three barbecues. Natalia fussed over *everything*. Raj and Sergey debated something. Silky barked and played with the children who raced through the crowd. Everyone who mattered to him was there. Well, almost, but Jake hoped Alexandr would attend the next barbecue.

The warm sun and a light breeze off the bay made the vista down to Silicon Valley clear. Jake leaned against the ivy-covered fence, sipped his beer, and took in the view. He worried about Alexandr, and his mind drifted away from the party.

All was ready. The Immigration interview had gone well, and Natalia had been approved for a green card.

Raj, Sergey, and Detective Phelps would go to NetWorks Monday armed with the court order and Sergey's exploit. The Internet service provider would intercept Rublev's emails and searches and transmit the data to Phelps. The spyware would mirror Rublev's hard drive and keystrokes to a NetWorks server, and Phelps would access those files remotely. They soon should know as much about Rublev and his activities as the thug himself.

Yesterday, he and Natalia raided his favorite bookstore and loaded up on novels to occupy his imminent, house-bound demise. When he tired of reading, his new exercise bike would help him keep in shape.

Jake had to be careful. He had stashed his truck in Raj's garage because Phelps planned his "death" would be in a car crash. So she would not be alone, he would hide at home until Natalia went to Moscow to retrieve Alexandr. He would stay in Baxter's cabin after she departed.

Other parts of the plan were finalized as well, including a police tap on his house phone. Jake smiled to himself. Strange to think he had about twenty-four hours to live. The story would be that he would be cremated and there would be no memorial. He anticipated some friends would be upset about no funeral service, but he didn't want to put them through needless emotional pain. He also wanted to lessen Natalia's public mourning. Though flowers and donations would be discouraged, anyone so compelled could donate money to Youth Baseball. The preparations were in place. Tomorrow night he would "die."

Jake's mind returned to the moment to enjoy this gathering of his friends. He took a drink of beer and waded into the crowd.

* * *

Sunday passed quickly as Jake and Natalia finished cleaning up after the previous day's cookout. At ten o'clock, as they prepared for bed, the telephone rang.

"We're all set," Phelps said. "A picture and a police department statement will be in tomorrow's *Mercury News* about a wrecked pickup and a description of how you ran off a road up in the hills. A friend on the paper helped me on this after getting permission from her editor, but she demands an exclusive when the whole story can be told."

"It's hers."

"Finding a file photo somewhere with a truck mangled enough to be unrecognizable took a while. I've called the coroner, too.

"As of now, Jake, you're officially dead."

* * *

The news story and photo of the mangled truck gave Jake pause. When he showed Natalia the picture, she gulped. The wreck was barely unrecognizable as a pickup. They knew someone had perished in the accident. Odd, Jake reflected, that another's demise might help him live.

The police statement lacked details, which offered a thin trail for Rublev and whoever else might be watching. The combination of the newspaper report and the coroner's death certificate should provide the plausibility of Jake's passing that they needed.

* * *

The number of sympathy cards and flowers to Natalia over the next three days astonished Jake. For the phone calls, she handled them well. She sincerely thanked each caller.

Several funeral homes called and asked if she had made internment arrangements. Natalia claimed ignorance of the English language. She firmly shot down the buzzards who circled his carcass.

This was all so strange to Jake. Everything he now did was with the thought he could be dead and missing life's experiences. His coffee's aroma seemed richer. The sun through the window felt warmer. Natalia's touch was more sensuous.

She finished yet another call and fixed herself tea.

He gave her a hug from behind. "You doing alright?"

She turned to face him. "All okay. Thank you, Jacob."

"This is weird," he said. "You'll probably grow tired of me being with you at the house the next day or so."

She nodded and smiled. "Of course!"

The telephone interrupted their laughter.

Natalia picked up the receiver, and her look was etched in worry as she gave Jake the phone. "Detective Phelps," she said.

"How did everything go at NetWorks?" Jake asked.

"It took longer than expected. Their attorney had to give his blessing, though they had to comply. They were not adversarial, just cautious.

"Sergey spent two hours explaining his spyware program. The company is not involved in capturing Rublev's keystrokes and disk image, but they wanted to review the code since it would be delivered through their network. I think he impressed them. Don't be surprised if your friend gets a job offer out of this."

"Well, I'll do whatever's required to keep Sergey, but I wouldn't blame them for trying."

"One thing we have is Rublev's browser history. He makes daily searches of Northern California counties' vital statistics sites."

"What about communication to Russia?"

Lonnie laughed. "You're impatient for a dead guy. He sends and receives emails from dc@busserv.mos.rus. We're not sure yet how to track the domain further, but we now have his Russian connection."

"Fantastic!"

"A start. We should discover more as NetWorks sends us Rublev's activities.

"And I called Bill Jackson in Sacramento to bring him up

to speed. Rublev still doesn't go out much except to buy groceries and booze." Phelps chuckled. "Bill says Rublev would save a lot of money if he bought his vodka by the barrel. And Red Bluff Police asked for Rublev's photograph. They have a case there where he may be involved."

"Yeah, I haven't had time to tell you." Jake explained Stephen Sands' death and Stu Baxter's visit.

"Interesting," Phelps said. "Oh, and I wanted to tell you the FBI is curious. A bulletin came in today asking for information on similar cases. I'll brief them on what we're up to."

"Thanks again, Lonnie. I guess all we do now is wait until Natalia phones Rublev on Thursday."

"I'm sure the time will crawl by," Lonnie said.

Jake looked over to Natalia, and she gave him a smile. "I think I'll stay busy."

CHAPTER 33

After three weeks, Ivan Rublev's bruises and lacerations had faded. His shoulder and ankle had improved almost back to normal. He thought he would be back to full strength in a day or two. He planned a drive that day to Old Town and call on his lady-friend at the doll shop. He believed his conquest of the store owner was close.

He drank from a bottle of vodka as he saw an email that included an image of The Motherland Calls, the massive Volgograd statue that celebrates Russian nationalism. The monument was his favorite statue. He did not know who forwarded it, but he loved the enormous sculpture.

He made his usual government online searches for targets who had married. His PC seemed slower this morning. The dial-up Internet was unpredictable sometimes. An hour later, he reviewed the Santa Clara County vital statistics site. He tabbed down the lists of births, deaths, marriages, and divorces.

A swallow stuck in his throat, he choked, and burning vodka geysered into his nose. Jacob Wilder was killed Sunday night! *How do I check for sure?* He searched the San Jose *Mercury News'* website. An article from yesterday's paper stated, "Jacob Wilder of Milpitas dies in car crash."

The news account did not mention the wife, so she must have not been with him.

What good fortune! And without any work!

Ivan Rublev typed his boss, Chekhov, a message that claimed another kill.

* * *

The yellow flower on Sidor Borisov's breakfast table that morning had done nothing to soften his fear, nor did Sveta's frustrated pleas. He had kept his promise to research what he could about the Melnikov kid. He found nothing, but she pushed him to do more.

Now, as he led his squad on a raid against a small Kazakh gang that had killed six old people for their apartments, he pondered what more he should do. *Da*, he wanted to help locate Melnikova's son, but not at the cost of his and Sveta's lives. Punishing ignorant Kazakhs was one thing, but taking on a mobster as powerful as Chekhov was insane. Such men would not just murder you, they would first butcher your family while you watched. Then they'd torture you until the end.

Borisov had taken a major risk to look up the license number of the Mercedes at International Friends. When the information that the car belonged to the New Russia Casino arrived, Sidor realized he may have made a fatal mistake. His inquiry might somehow be passed to the Bratva leader or one of the mobster's employees.

He knew the passenger in the Mercedes. Every policeman had heard of Dmitri Chekhov, and they either tried to be the gangster's friend or stayed out of the man's way. Sidor fit in the latter, smaller group.

Had he placed Sveta and himself in Chekhov's vicious path? If so, what the Kazakh gangs did to the old people was nothing compared to what Chekhov would do to them.

* * *

Chekhov lit the first satisfying Marlboro of his business day and powered up his computer. A long list of new messages filled his inbox. Given the recent decline in Ivan Rublev's reports, Chekhov was surprised by an email from the man. The word "weather" in the title told him he was about to make another pile of cash, so he checked Rublev's message first. *Jacob Wilder. That was fast!*

He sent a congratulatory reply to Rublev and glanced at his watch. If he left now, he could be back before the casino opened for the night. The sooner the mother spoke with her brat and carried out his final demands, he would receive his money. He dialed the orphanage. "I want Melnikov ready for a call."

Chekhov arrived at the orphanage and waited in the room from which he called the anxious, frightened mothers he targeted.

* * *

The headmistress shoved Alexandr into the small space. The child winced as the woman with yellow teeth and red lips sneered. "Here is the worm. He stole salted cucumbers and bread again. I gave him the belt."

Chekhov inspected the boy to make sure his arms, face, and hands were not marked. The woman sometimes became aggressive with her discipline.

But no problem here, at least so far. The whelp remained visibly undamaged. "Alexandr Melnikov, you have disappointed me and your mother. If you want to be with her again, do not break the rules."

The blond, blue-eyed imp glared at him and said nothing. Chekhov dismissed the woman and telephoned the mother. The circuit completed after six tries. "Natalia Melnikova Wilder, I extend my deep sympathy, but do not despair. Soon you will be reunited with your handsome son. He is in good health, but he has been punished for misbehavior. I will not tolerate trouble. You can speak with him, but first, pay attention. You will be given precise instructions. Execute them exactly, and you will have him back. Here he is."

"Mama? *Da*, I am well. Are you well? When will we be together?" The kid listened a moment and confirmed, "I will behave, Mama." He glowered at Chekhov. "I not afraid. I miss you, Mama."

The child sounded neither weak nor scared, which baffled Chekhov. He snatched the handset, blew smoke into the child's face, and terminated the call.

* * *

Jake had just witnessed a first-hand example of a mother's love. When Natalia talked on the telephone, her face betrayed her delight. The only person who would give her such joy was Alexandr.

He felt her elation as he stood next to her in the kitchen. He stroked her arm and smiled at her.

After several minutes, Natalia stopped talking, and tears welled in her eyes. She replaced the handset and hugged him. "The connection cut, but Alexandr is well, I think. He cause problems, but his voice tells me he okay."

"Wonderful!"

"*Da*." She stared up at him. "Your plan is working. The man say me to wait for what to do. They believe you dead."

Jake shuddered and nodded. "I have to tell Phelps."

He phoned the detective while she washed the few accumulated dishes. "Natalia just got a call from Russia and spoke with Alexandr," Jake said.

"Wow, that didn't take long."

"No, it didn't. Anything on Rublev?"

"The ISP had a snafu getting me access to the data, but I got it about thirty minutes ago. Sergey's spyware uploaded a lot of stuff, most in Russian. He's on his way over to translate.

"Anyway, I'm going to inform the FBI we found several American names scattered through the files and emails. Some may be other victims. Hold on, let me check something."

Jake broke into a sweat as he thought about others who might be mobster targets.

After a moment, Phelps said, "Yep, here you are. A message to dc@busserv.mos.rus went out this morning and your name is in the text. A reply from the same address just arrived. Did they tell Natalia anything?"

"Only to wait for instructions. What if Rublev comes to the house?"

"Call me. I'll have an unmarked car make a couple passes through your neighborhood, but we don't want to spook him."

No, but the bastard is a murderer.

CHAPTER 34

Natalia played a mournful tune on the piano while Jacob pretended to be dead. The day seemed an adventure. They mislead the Bratva. She hoped and prayed for Alexandr's return and that Jacob's hiatus from the living would be short. She knew he had to go to Lake Almanor to Stuart's cabin tomorrow but was glad he hid at home today.

Her talk with Alexandr had been wonderful and confirmed he was alive. No reason to worry until the Bratva had their cash. *I hope million of Jakob's money is enough to free Alexandr.* She had to trust the villains would release him. He was unhurt now, but she worried what they would do if they discovered Jacob still lived.

Natalia had questioned why Jacob did not own a gun. Before coming to America, she thought everyone there owned guns, but he did not.

Jacob appeared subdued from the conspiratorial pleasure they shared as he absently thumbed through a new novel. Silky appeared unconcerned as she stretched in the patch of sunlight that crept across the living room floor.

Natalia had received two additional calls since the one from Russia, one from Veronika Nazarov, and another from a telemarketer.

Jacob gave up on his book and sat on the floor next to Silky. He rubbed her stomach. Natalia smiled as the dog's hind legs thrashed the air.

Her sour mood faded, but her mind was in Moscow with Alexandr and Mama. She missed them more than she had American words to describe, but Jacob understood. What a mess she had created when she kept Alexandr secret, but

Jacob's plan would hopefully work. Alexandr would be safe here, but the financial cost would be enormous, which caused her much guilt.

She watched Jacob play with Silky and imagined him and Alexandr together like father and son. She smiled.

The phone rang. She hesitated to answer and was tempted to let the phone machine record the message, but she didn't dare. Nothing good would come from ignoring a Bratva contact attempt if that was what the call was.

She went to the kitchen phone. "Hallo?"

"Are you happy you talked to your son?" said a voice she recognized and dreaded.

"*Da.*"

Jacob was by her side in an instant. He gave her a questioning look, and she nodded.

"Is there anyone there with you?" the man asked.

A shiver ran through her. "*Nyet.*"

"Good. I must give you information so you can retrieve your son." The man's voice hardened, "Where is the sobaka?"

"Here."

The voice moved from hard to vicious. "Lock the animal up, or I will slice its throat."

Natalia looked down at Silky, whose short stub of a tail wagged. "I'll put her away."

"I will arrive in minutes. Be happy. You will reunite with your son if you carry out our directions."

The line went dead.

Natalia looked at her anxious husband. "Rublev. He say he come here now. He said me to lock up Silky, or he will kill her."

Jacob's expression switched to anger. "If we didn't have to rescue Alexandr, I'd kill him." He got control of himself. "Okay. Silky and I will go to the garage. I'll call Phelps on my cell."

He pulled her to him and hugged her. "Don't worry."

Natalia was afraid and prayed they would get through this together. Her husband's green eyes blazed with intensity.

"I love you, Jacob," she whispered.

"I love you, too, beautiful."

He went toward the garage. "Come on, girl," and the dog followed.

* * *

Jake had tried to appear confident to reassure Natalia, but the butterflies in his gut made that impossible. Once in the garage, his exterior confidence evaporated. He called Phelps and told him Rublev was on his way to the house.

"Where are you?" Phelps asked.

"The garage with Silky. Rublev told Natalia he would kill my dog if she was in the house. Natalia's on her own."

"Yeah, but not much we can do about it. You know that as well as I do. Listen, I'm sending a unit, and I'm on my way, but all we can do is watch the house. If Rublev sees us, you might never get Alexandr."

"You're right. But what if there's trouble?"

"Call 9-1-1. We'll be half a block away. I know this is scary, but it's necessary. Until you have Alexandr, you must follow their rules."

"Okay," but Jake didn't feel any better about the situation.

* * *

Natalia willed herself not to show her fright. She remembered the menacing glint in Rublev's eyes, and he probably murdered Mr. Baxter's friend. Natalia didn't want to meet this man, but she had no choice. She forced her mind to think about Alexandr and her desire to hold him in her arms.

The doorbell chimed.

Natalia's heartbeat thumped in her ears. She slowly moved her feet forward, grasped the knob, and opened the door.

Rublev towered over her as he walked in. His eyes darted around the room. "The *sobaka*?"

She noticed his unpleasant smell of body odor and booze. "In garage."

His eyes settled on her.

She tried to be self-confident and forceful, but he was so tall and strong.

"You still alone?"

"*Da*. What must I do?"

"*We* have things to discuss first."

Natalia's voice quivered. "What things?"

He snatched her wrist, pulled her to him, and hoisted her over his shoulder.

"*Nyet! Nyet! Nyet!*" she shrieked and pounded her fists on his back.

Rublev roared with laughter.

Silky barked as Rublev carried her upstairs. Natalia knew what Rublev wanted. She had to reunite with Alexandr but could not let this happen. In the crystal clarity of her fear, she knew Jacob would not allow it, either.

She struck and scratched Rublev and feared for Alexandr, Jacob and herself.

CHAPTER 35

Jake froze at the first scream. Natalia's startled, "*Nyet!*" turned his blood cold.

Then hot.

He stopped himself as he was about to storm into the house. He remembered Rublev's immense size. The Russian could strangle him with his bare hands.

Jake scanned the garage and ran to his sack of softball equipment. He found a Louisville Slugger aluminum bat and wavered. If he charged in or called 9-1-1, Alexandr might be lost forever, and Rublev might kill Silky if she got into the house. Jake eased through the door into the kitchen, leaving his agitated dog behind.

Sounds of a struggle in the master bedroom spurred him to rush up the stairs. At the top, he heard Natalia's tearful pleas and the sound of shredding fabric.

Time slowed. Jake crept to the door and peeked in. Natalia thrashed on the bed, her dress ripped apart. Rublev leaned over her, his trousers bundled at his ankles, his hairy ass scarred from Silky's earlier bites. Jake knew their chance to discover Alexandr's location was now as destroyed as Natalia's clothes. His sight went blurry around the edges.

He dashed into the room.

Natalia was pinned. She squirmed, punched Rublev with her small fists, and shouted in Russian.

Rublev had torn off everything she wore. He spewed angry Russian.

Jake's vision narrowed from pure hatred. *Why didn't I let Silky in? Stupid.* The only shot he could make was to Rublev's back. Jake cranked the bat back and visualized hitting the bastard's kidney to deep center field. He swung with all the energy he had.

Thump!

Rublev shrieked but didn't crumple to the carpet.

What the hell? Jake thought.

With startling speed, Rublev spun with a backhand. Jake jumped back and felt a rush of air as Rublev's fist flew by his face. Rublev's hand struck the bat and wrenched it out of Jake's grip. The bat landed on the floor and rolled to the wall.

Rublev's jaw fell, and his eyes locked on Jake. Surprise and confusion spread on the mobster's face. "Where the fuck did you come from?"

Jake said nothing and stumbled back out of range when Rublev punched again. *Shit, this is a fight to the death.*

Rublev hurled vodka-smelling profanities in animal rage.

Jake yelled, "Natalia, run! Dial 9-1-1! Release Silky!"

Rublev loomed between Natalia and the door, his back to her.

From the bed, Natalia shoved Rublev in the butt with both feet.

The Russian lost his balance in the tangle of jeans wrapped around his ankles. He crashed to the floor.

Jacob again yelled, "Run, Natalia!"

Instead, she scrambled off the opposite side of the bed and grabbed the Louisville Slugger. She tossed it to Jake while Rublev struggled with his pants.

Jake caught it and tightened his grip on the handle.

Natalia made a break for the door and safety.

Jake ran forward and clobbered the Russian with all his might. Thump! Thwack! Thwack! "Take that, you bastard!" Jake shouted.

Rublev squealed and backed away.

A sick feeling coursed through Jake. He'd delivered his hardest shots, yet the man seemed unaffected.

"You die today," Rublev sneered.

Jake maneuvered for another blow, but Rublev was too fast. The mobster pivoted and kicked. Jake darted back. Rublev's boot caught him in the thigh. Jake fell and crashed into the dresser. Pictures clattered to the floor as Jake bounced away. He raised the bat.

Rublev was up and so were his trousers, held in his left hand.

Jake heard a *snick* from Rublev's right hand.

The Russian mobster brandished a switchblade and grinned. "A trick! All a trick, you red-haired cur." He turned to Natalia and roared, "Do not interfere, bitch, or your son will die!"

Natalia seized the nightstand phone and pressed 9-1-1. "Help!"

Jake stood and gulped for breath. His heart hammered.

Rublev jabbed with the knife and grinned when Jake stumbled. "I'm going to kill you quick so I have plenty of time to fuck your wife. Then I will carve up her face."

"Get Silky, Natalia!" Jake roared.

Natalia, naked, raced behind Rublev. He turned, let go of his jeans, and grabbed her arm.

Rublev swung his right hand at Natalia.

"No!" Jake screamed as the shiny blade sliced through the air.

The sickening sound of impact brought vomit into Jake's mouth.

Natalia yelped, doubled over, and fell unconscious.

Jake's vision constricted further. "Fucker!" he shouted. Before Rublev turned back, Jake slammed the bat down on the Russian's shoulder. His back. His shoulder again. *Thump! Thwack! Thump!*

The Russian dropped the knife and charged.

Jake aimed for Rublev's ugly head and swung.

Thunk!

Blood sprayed. Teeth clattered off the wall. Rublev's bloody jaw hung to one side. The stunned Russian advanced with faltering steps.

"You fucker!" Jake cocked the bat all the way back and stepped into his swing with everything he had.

* * *

The *thwack!* and *pop!* when the Louisville Slugger smashed into the side of Rublev's head merged into one sound. Rublev's body spun, fell like a tree, slammed against the corner of the bed, and shoved it off-kilter. Somewhere in the angry blur of Jake's mind, he registered Silky's barks and the front door crash open.

He struggled for air, let go of the Louisville Slugger, and ran to Natalia's crumpled body.

She moaned as he rolled her over, but no blood!

"How?" Jake muttered.

He looked quickly at the knife on the carpet. Rublev must have punched her with his fist instead of the point of the blade. Realization dawned. If Natalia died, the criminals would never receive the money. *The asshole* couldn't *kill her.* The knife was for him.

Jake's world came back into focus as he struggled to catch his breath.

CHAPTER 36

Footsteps hammered on the stairs. Jake removed his shirt and covered Natalia's nakedness before Phelps and another detective burst into the room, guns drawn.

Jake gasped, "He hurt her."

The other officer went to Rublev's bloody, twisted body, gun first, touched Rublev's neck for a pulse, and shook his head.

Phelps reached down and touched Natalia's neck with his fingertips. "She's alive, but her pulse is weak." He scooped up the phone and told the dispatcher, who was still on the line, "This is Detective Phelps. Send an ambulance, Code 3. I want Homicide and someone from the coroner's office, too." He replaced the receiver and surveyed the scene.

Jake held Natalia and moaned in relief she wasn't dead. His eyes were blurred by tears that dripped onto her. "What do we do now?"

"I hear the sirens," Phelps said. "Give me a second to think. Yeah, you responded in self-defense, but you're supposed to be dead. This will take more cooperation from the coroner and district attorney than might be possible. We have to find a way to handle this."

Phelps called his chief and explained what had happened and what he thought should be done. Several minutes of back-and-forth conversation followed until Phelps said, "Thanks, Chief, that's what we'll do."

He went to Jake, who seemed lost in grief, and said, "This will be hard, but you need to stay hidden. You can't go to the hospital with Natalia."

"Shit, I want to be with her but understand. They still

have Alexandr. But Natalia..."

"I'll call the Nazarovs to be with her. There is nothing you can do now, but you might still be able to retrieve Alexandr if you stay out of the picture."

Four uniformed officers entered the room. Phelps ordered, "Set up a perimeter around the house. Only the EMTs, Homicide, and the coroner are allowed in. *Nobody* else unless I approve it. No one." He turned to Jake. "This whole thing might blow up in our faces, but we'll worry about that later. I want you out of sight before the paramedics arrive."

Jake cradled Natalia in his arms and kissed her forehead. He couldn't think of words to speak.

* * *

Jake paced across his home office with the door closed. His wrists were sore from when Rublev swatted the bat out of his hands, his thigh throbbed where the Russian kicked him, and his shoulder ached from the slam against the dresser. The ache in his heart was far greater than his physical pain. A confused Silky watched him.

The paramedics had rushed Natalia out of the house some time ago, and the detectives still went about their jobs.

If only I'd done something different. But what other than release Silky and call 9-1-1? You're so stupid, Jake. But let Rublev rape her? Never! Jake believed his only option was the one he took. He feared for what would happen to Natalia and Alexandr and, now, himself, too.

Phelps came in with a worried frown. "Natalia's in surgery and will be for a while. She must've taken quite a punch because her spleen ruptured. She's bled a lot internally and requires more units of blood."

Jake tumbled into a well of sadness. Others held Natalia's life in their hands. "What can I do?"

"Answer the homicide detectives' questions truthfully. You're not a suspect. What happened is obvious, and I'm damned glad you did what you did, but we have to keep the record straight."

"Alright... I understand."

* * *

Jake sat in his home office and gazed across the bay. Silky lay at his feet. He wondered if she missed Natalia as much as he did. The doctors saved her spleen, and she was in post-op. He ached to be with her, to hold her hand, but Phelps was correct. He had to stay dead. No way to know what would come next, but if the Russians discovered he lived, they'd murder Alexandr for sure.

Sergey walked in and handed him a tumbler of scotch. "You need this." Sergey took a sip from his own glass. "I do, too."

"Thanks, Sergey." The ice clinked against the crystal as Jake swirled his drink. He swallowed. The amber liquid burned with a welcome warmth.

"Natalia will recover," Sergey said. "She is fortunate." Sergey's face became more serious as he punished his beard. "You both lucky."

Jake nodded, resigned.

Sergey paused before he asked, "What about Alexandr?"

Jake let out an exasperated breath. "My last plan didn't work too well. I can think of only one thing."

Sergey gave him a curious stare. "What?"

"I have to find Alexandr myself before the secret gets out."

* * *

Jake called Stuart Baxter two days later. "Stu, are you someplace you can talk?"

"Hold a sec. I'll shut my door." After a moment, Baxter came back on the line. "You sound angry."

"I am." Jake told Baxter about the attack on Natalia and the Russian's death. "We barely escaped alive."

"Damn. I'm so sorry. Will your wife be okay?"

"The doctor says she will, but I haven't visited her."

"You still playing dead?"

"Not much choice. We don't know how many there are besides Rublev. Natalia must wait in case they contact her. The insurance company cut the bank draft, which helps if needed. What I won't need, though, is your cabin, but thank you for the offer."

"No problem, but what do you plan to do?"

"There's nothing I can do here except hide, so I'm going to Russia to find Alexandr."

"That's risky." Jake thought the broker would say, 'stupid.' "Shouldn't the feds run with this?"

"Yeah, but Alexandr's in Russia. Not a hell of a lot they can do."

Baxter's voice took a deeper timbre. "I'm sorry for what happened, but you were lucky. My advice is don't push it. Moscow is dangerous." More softly, he said, "I owe you one for Rublev. Anything I can do?"

"Nothing I can think of, but I wanted to thank you again for your offer."

"Appreciate the call. One other thing. What hospital is your wife in? I would like to send flowers."

Jake gave Baxter the information. "Thanks, Stu. Stephen Sands had a great friend in you."

"Not how I look at it. I couldn't save him like he saved me."

CHAPTER 37

Sidor Borisov and his squad consumed a long, hard day as they rounded up gypsies and pickpockets in the Metro, one of the grittier duties they sometimes drew. New criminals took the place of those arrested before his men were out of sight. He often thought his team was like a hand passing through water for all the impact they achieved. A momentary ripple might move through the crowd, but nothing that lasted. Still, unless they showed a presence, total anarchy would reign.

They had made thirty-four arrests by the end of their shift. They bought vodka, bread, and sausage and met in a park by the river where they drank and ate around a bonfire as the summer sun disappeared. One officer strummed a guitar, and they sang until they were hoarse.

Now, Sidor wobbled as he climbed the stairs to his apartment. He normally wanted to be home with Sveta, but, because of what he had discovered from the Mercedes' license, he held a nagging uneasiness. Chekhov was a man to stay far away from, but she still pushed him to rescue the kidnapped boy.

As he searched for the correct keys, his door opened. Sveta pulled him inside. He steadied himself. "What, woman?"

"Veronika called. A man came to Natalia about her son and tried to rape her. Jacob killed him. She in hospital."

He was suddenly sober. "She hurt bad?"

"*Da.*"

Sidor stroked his mustache. Sveta projected a determined expression with her jaw set that, under the circumstances, he did not want to see. "What?"

"The 'what' is you to telephone Sergey Nazarov to tell him what you learned."

"But these mob boys..."

"Why do you worry? This will not harm us if you tell our friend. Either you do this, or I will." She thrust a paper into his hand. "The number. You must call now."

Sveta was right, but he decided not to phone from home. Impossible to be too careful. "I will go to the Post Office."

Her round face softened, and her kind mien absent through much of this saga returned.

She said, "*Spasibo*," and shoved him out the door.

* * *

The room's greens and grays became clear after Natalia's drug-induced sleep. She ached below her ribcage. Above her, liquid dripped from a plastic bag into a tube connected to a vein in her wrist. Bouquets of flowers crowded the small table under the window.

She sobbed. Alexandr was probably lost. She remembered the terrible fight and feared the mob boy had murdered Jacob after she blacked out. Veronika assured her he lived during her few, fleeting moments of consciousness, but she would not be convinced until she held his hand.

A nurse entered. "I thought I heard something. I'll ask the doctor if we can move up your pain medication schedule."

"I fine. My husband?"

"Let me tell your friend you're awake." The woman seemed sad. Natalia could not tell if her demeanor was because Jacob died or because she had been told he was dead as part of the ruse.

Natalia surveyed the room through bleary eyes and fought to control her tears. The hospital was so clean and the staff attentive. She thought someone mentioned they would replace the needle in her arm to prevent infection, a luxury not available in Russia. You would be fortunate to receive a new one to begin with! And only the wealthy had money for nurses who were not surly or performed more than perfunctory checks. Such attention as this cost extra. *A fortune squandered because I created this disaster.* She needed her husband's reassurance.

Veronika walked in and gave her a solemn smile. "You are looking better but still pale. You were unconscious much of the past two days. How do you feel?"

"Where Jacob?"

"Home, hiding. Your husband protected you. He sent you this note."

Deep relief washed through Natalia. *He lives!* Her hands shook as she gave the envelope back. "Please read."

Veronika closed the door and read, "My darling Natalia, I am sorry I can't be at your side. My heart broke when Rublev hit you. It's a blessing you will recover. Please phone when you are able. The machine will answer. When I know it's you, I will pick up the phone. Forgive me for not being with you. All my love, Jacob."

"I would like to telephone now."

Veronika smiled, dialed, and told Sergey Natalia was calling. She passed the handset to Natalia.

"Jacob?"

"Sweetheart?"

"Oh, you good to hear."

"You sound tired and weak."

"I alright. Tell me what happened."

Jacob's voice was heavy with emotion as he told her. "I could not let that monster attack you."

"*Da*, but what will we do?" Silence on the line. "Jacob?"

"Veronika will stay with you when you come home. I am going to Russia to get Alexandr."

"When?" she said with strength that surprised her.

"As soon as I purchase the tickets and everything else I

need. Three or four days at the most. You will be home before I go."

Now Natalia fell silent. She understood. He had risked his life to protect her and would risk it again for her son. She whispered. "I love you, Jacob."

"Love you, too, beautiful."

They said their good-byes, and she sank back into the pillow, spent. But she had hope, however fragile. *Can my husband save Alexandr?*

Natalia shut her eyes and prayed she would hold them both again.

CHAPTER 38

Jake felt trapped in his own home with the blinds and curtains drawn as he waited for the FBI agents to arrive. Sergey and Phelps sat with him in the living room. Sergey twisted his beard while the detective reviewed his case notes.

Jake wrung his hands and glanced at the documents on the coffee table.

The doorbell chimed. Silky barked, and Sergey went to the door. A moment later, he escorted in three men.

The older man extended his hand. "I'm Supervisory Special Agent Lancaster. With me are agents Hilbern and Moore."

Lancaster appeared to be an FBI veteran a little out-of-shape. The hint of a paunch hung over his belt. His attitude communicated he gave commands and expected them to be followed.

Hilbern, with his unruly blond hair and gawky frame, looked more like an accountant than a fed. He lacked the toughness Jake expected.

Moore was olive-skinned and of unrecognizable ethnic origin. Six-one and fit, with dark eyes and five o'clock shadow, his haircut was perfect, every black hair in place.

"I'm Jake Wilder. This is Sergey Nazarov and Detective Phelps of the Milpitas Police Department. Please sit down."

"Thank you, Mr. Wilder," Lancaster said. "First, I want to tell you we are sorry about what happened to your wife."

While Lancaster talked, Hilbern took notes. Agent Moore sat impassive at the end of the couch.

Jake couldn't stop himself. "If you guys had shown an interest when we first called you, my wife wouldn't be in the hospital."

"I can empathize with your feelings, but that is speculation," Lancaster said. "And I apologize. The agent you spoke to was reassigned."

"He's an arrogant jerk," Jake said.

Lancaster attempted a smile. "The important thing now is the city police formally requested our assistance, and we're in this with all the resources at our disposal. We're working with Standard Mutual and several other companies. This is a major crime involving scores of actual and potential victims."

Jake interjected, "So what you're saying is because this is larger than one woman and little boy, you'll find time to investigate."

Lancaster raised his palms as a peace gesture. "Please, Mr. Wilder, we're here to help."

Jake spoke in a tone he hoped conveyed the challenge he intended. "What are you going to do?"

With weight, Lancaster said, "Well, we've notified our Moscow resident agent, who is investigating at that end."

Jake sensed Lancaster was trying to put the most positive spin on things but was also committed to providing support. "What will your people do?"

"Well, we are attached to the embassy's legal attaché's office, and they will make inquiries with the Russian authorities."

"Is that all?"

Lancaster shifted in his chair. "We have authority in the US but none in foreign countries. We must operate within their systems. But our relationship with the new Russian government is cooperative. We *can* make a difference."

Despite Jake's desire to vent more anger, he realized he would accomplish nothing. "So what do you want from me?"

"We need to interview you and your wife about the entire chain of the case," Lancaster answered. "Standard Mutual informed us that you accumulated considerable material on

Rublev." Lancaster eyed the papers. Hilbern absently patted his hair between scribbled sentences in his notebook. Moore listened attentively.

Jake nudged his stack of papers. "Here's everything. The Milpitas police records, call transcripts, Rublev's Internet mail from the Internet service provider, and translations of the data on the target computer."

Lancaster seemed pleased.

Moore pointed to the documents. "How was the network traffic gathered?"

"By the book," Phelps said. "These two men provided the solution, and I obtained a court order for the ISP, NetWorks, to forward me email copies and Rublev's browser history. The real magic is in the computer's files. After Jake and Sergey explained the spyware, a judge authorized a warrant for my department to access the information." Phelps motioned to Sergey with a nod.

The software engineer cleared his throat. "Not too hard. I also included code to retain deleted data where they cannot be seen. His PC now transmits mirror-image to police." Sergey grinned. "Nice, don't you think?"

Moore browsed through a dozen or so pages. "Clever, indeed."

For the next half-hour, Moore read through the reports with interspersed questions and compliments. "This is excellent." He addressed Sergey in Russian, which at first astonished Jake, but of course they would assign someone with appropriate language skills.

"This will help the investigation," Moore said, "and finding out who dc@busserv.mos.rus is will be crucial."

Jake paused a moment before he played the card dealt him by Sidor Borisov. "Rublev worked for a man named Dmitri Chekhov. He's a notorious mafia boss and the secret owner of International Friends. Extortion. Smuggling. Prostitution. Not a pleasant man. He works out of his office at Moscow's New Russia Casino."

Lancaster looked startled. "How do you know?"

"A local policeman told us."

"But no leads on Alexandr?" Moore asked.

Jake appreciated both the agent's focus on the heart of the situation and his humanizing Alexandr by using his name. "No, nothing."

Moore nodded. "This is not a priority for you, I get it, but one of our tasks is to safeguard other American victims. Our emphasis is the bigger picture."

Jake knew others suffered through similar agony, but fear for his family drove him every waking hour. His priority remained selfish and urgent.

"Do you think you can drop your spyware into Chekhov's PC?" Moore asked Sergey.

"Possible but difficult. His Internet service provider would be trusted source and would block the exploit."

"So we've helped you. How will you help us?" Jake asked.

Lancaster leaned forward. "I promise The Bureau will do everything we can to locate your stepson."

"Not enough."

Lancaster's face turned from sincerity to surprise. He wasn't a man who took orders from civilians. Jake perceived a wry glint in Moore's eyes. Lancaster regained his composure. "What do you mean?"

Phelps jumped in. "The City of Milpitas does not have the manpower for Mrs. Wilder's around-the-clock protection. We would like the FBI to handle that."

Moore stared at Jake. "And you?"

"I'm going to Moscow for our son."

"We can't allow vigilantes running around Russia," Lancaster admonished.

"I'm not a vigilante and won't break the law. And I value

your concern and assure you my intention is not to cause difficulties of any kind. But if I rescue my stepson, I might need help getting him and my mother-in-law to the United States."

Lancaster thought for a moment and nodded. "We'll do what we can for you and your wife, but, if you violate their laws, you may not be able to come home for a long time."

"I understand, but I have to find my boy."

CHAPTER 39

The past three days had been lonely, confined torture for Jake. He paced through the upstairs bedrooms and empathized with caged animals.

Natalia would arrive from the hospital today and be cared for by Veronika and a home-care nurse. The caregiver had been sternly admonished by the FBI not to discuss Jake's presence with *anyone* or face arrest and prosecution.

Natalia's calls with Jake relayed greater strength in her voice, which made their separation more bearable to Jake. Today, he would see and touch her, which meant so much to him because he would leave tomorrow morning.

The telephone rang, which startled him. He picked up when the answering machine broadcast Phelps' voice, "You there?"

"I'm here."

"I wanted to tell you Bill Jackson in Sacramento called me. The feds invited him along when they searched Rublev's place. He indicated Rublev probably committed fourteen murders. He kept a ledger with initials and collection amounts between ten- and thirty-thousand dollars. The last entry was J.W."

"Shit, I guess. How about 'S.S.'?"

"Yeah. The Bureau contacted Red Bluff. That case indeed may refer to Stephen Sands."

Jake shook his head and sighed. "All those people. Do they think others work with him?"

"Not sure, but agents are keeping his place under twenty-four-seven surveillance."

"I appreciate your letting me know," Jake said, "but I wonder if I'm reassured or not. We're still in danger and don't know Alexandr's location."

"Yeah, and Rublev is one of several possible killers the FBI is checking into." Phelps hesitated. "They found a trophy book."

"A what?"

"A binder with photos of the wives, including Natalia. The pictures had dates under each except hers. Given what he tried to do to her, the Feds think he sexually assaulted all the women."

"This is monstrous," Jake said.

"Beyond imagination. I'm sorry about Natalia and relieved she'll be okay. Our prayers are with her. And I worry about you. Please stay safe. Oh, I have to go, Jake, sorry. See you in the morning. I'll call if we turn up anything new."

Jake stared at the handset for a moment after the line went dead and dialed another number.

"Stu here."

"This is Jake..."

"How's Natalia?"

"She'll be home in about an hour."

"Great news," but Baxter's deep voice tapered off.

"You alright?" asked Jake.

"So-so. The local police believe Rublev killed Stephen, so they're closing their investigation."

"So you know, he kept records. S.S. is on the list."

"And the chief told me Rublev probably raped Yelena." Baxter's grief came over the wire. "Thanks. I owe you for killing the sonofabitch." He took a breath. "When do you leave?"

"Tomorrow morning. I'm not flying to Moscow, just in case the Bratva finds out. I'll land in St. Petersburg and take the night train to Moscow."

"I think I'm going to go over, too."

"You are? Why?"

"Closure. Stephen was my best friend, and through him,

Yelena, too. I have her address to send the proceeds after the properties sell, and I have thought about meeting her to tell her Stephen would understand. Something I must do."

Jake considered his own plans and couldn't tell the man not to go. "I hope things work out."

"I'll come down to see you off. I want to shake your hand for Rublev."

"Thanks, Stu."

After speaking to Baxter, Jake looked out the picture window at the sparkling San Francisco Bay.

Silky barked, and Natalia, Veronika, and Sergey came up the walkway. Natalia was supported between them, and their progress was slow. *She's so pale and thin! I wish I could kill the sonofabitch again!* He fought the urge to run out and carry her into the house.

They reached the door and slowly moved inside.

Jake stayed out of view and waited until Sergey closed the front door. Jake walked into the foyer and opened his arms. "Hi, sweetheart."

Her hug was stronger than he expected. "Hallo, Jacob."

They kissed and Jake whispered, "I love you. Welcome home."

"Love you, too."

He assisted her to the couch. Silky almost attacked her with licks. Jake restrained the dog by her collar, not that he blamed her. Natalia patted Silky's head.

"You can rest here while you talk to your mom. Then I'll help you upstairs. Be cautious on the telephone. We don't think Chekhov knows about Sidor and would not listen in on the Borisovs' calls. Still, be careful what you say."

"*Da.*"

After several tries, the connection went through. Waves of happiness and woe washed over Natalia's face.

Veronika looked weary but would stay to care for Natalia.

She would take a spare bedroom when Jake had gone. Sergey would manage their kids and work. That was a lot to ask of them, and he was grateful for their help.

Jake was thankful, too, for The Bureau's willingness to protect Natalia. He had not expected his request to be granted, but Supervisory Special Agent Lancaster appeared to believe a debt needed repayment for exposing the conspiracy. "You provided the Bureau with actionable information. Agents will come to stay this afternoon to make sure Natalia is safe," Lancaster had said

The FBI commitment provided Jake a modicum of peace of mind.

Jake fixed Natalia her strong tea, and she gave him a slight, forced smile. She grew weaker as she talked with Regina, her mom. They spoke for an hour, and Natalia was laced with sadness as she hung up. "Mama is sorry for all but say thank you."

"You ready to rest?" Jake asked.

"*Da.*"

He carried her to their bedroom, put her on their bed, and helped her undress. "My God!" he exclaimed when he saw the livid scar across her midsection. She flinched, apparently ashamed her body was now permanently scarred. Jake wished he could pull back his words as she slipped into her nightgown. "I'm so happy you are healing. That's the important thing."

"No. Imperative is to get Alexandr."

CHAPTER 40

D mitri Chekhov sat behind his casino desk exhausted and angry. He had been awakened at noon and informed another gang had taken down one of his bag men. He would make them pay. When someone pushed, you hit back without mercy. If you didn't, they would roll over you.

No one had tried to muscle in on him for some time, but as new business opportunities declined, the mobs turned on each other. He stamped out another Marlboro as the last of his five lieutenants arrived.

"One of our people was robbed by two men from the fuck-your-mother Georgian, Pavel Istomin," Chekhov said. "The follower was too far away to help. Our man took a bullet but shot one of the two attackers in the face. The second thief shot our guy twice more and fled with the money."

His leaders all nodded. One asked, "We sure Istomin is behind this? He runs the rackets in southeast Moscow, and he's always stuck to his territory."

Chekhov slammed his fist on his desk. "You fucking dare to question me? The follower identified the bastards."

"We must take out some of Istomin's crew," another lieutenant said.

"Or strike at the man himself," another offered.

Chekhov did not respond. He understood the imperative to retaliate, but what they proposed would be an escalation. He wanted to prolong the relative peace. The longer the inevitable mob war was postponed, the more wealth he would walk away with to Finland.

Vladimir Motorin straightened the crease on his slacks. "I say we focus on the idiots who did this and ignore Istomin for now. I think this was a test, a probe to gauge us."

Chekhov liked the man's thinking. "So, what do you propose?"

"One attacker saved us the trouble by dying on the sidewalk. The other must be found and executed along with his family. The dead attacker's relatives, too. Everyone will hesitate before they hit Dmitri Chekhov. All I require is six or seven men."

"Take ten," Chekhov directed.

"What about the money?" someone asked.

Motorin shrugged. "Burn down one of Istomin's protected businesses. He would lose about as much as we did. Things would be even. If he pushes back, we respond with a heavier hammer."

The boss nodded. "Make it happen, Vladimir. Show them the cost of pushing Dmitri Chekhov!"

* * *

Chekhov's aggravation simmered as he awaited the results of Motorin's retaliatory strike. The closed casino and sleeping girls down the hall were quiet, but he would not go to one of his homes until Motorin reported in.

His exasperation deepened when he received a message that a policeman had inquired about him, or, more accurately, about his car. What would some officer want with him? Was the cop stupid?

And the fuck-your-mother Ivan Rublev had not responded to messages for a week. What was going on with the *mudak*? He should have sent the insurance payout from Jacob Wilder's widow to the bank in Germany, but Chekhov had not been notified of the deposit. Did Rublev keep the cash? Unlikely. The man loved his mother and father. A double-cross would mean their gruesome executions. Had Rublev somehow fucked up?

Someone rapped on his door. "Enter," he commanded.

Vladimir Motorin came in and looked fatigued but purposeful. Blood spots marred his expensive suit. "Your task go well?" Chekhov asked.

"*Da.* All is done. The second man ate my gun after he watched his parents, children, and wife die. Our men enjoyed his bitch and oldest daughters. They strangled them."

"*Spasibo.*"

"This should end the skirmish."

"Yes, but only for now. The Georgian asshole, Istomin, will push again someday. It's his nature." Chekhov thought for a moment. "There is something else I want you to handle. A *politsiya* lieutenant named Sidor Borisov has made inquiries about my car. Dig into it. I want to know everything about him."

Motorin uncrossed his legs. "Any other requirements?"

"No, but you are tired." He motioned toward the hallway with his head. "Wake up one or two of the girls. You deserve the recreation. Take your pick. They're all exceptional."

Motorin surprised him by saying, "I will."

Chekhov grinned. Vladimir Motorin might be human after all.

* * *

The sunlight through the curtains glowed brighter after Vladimir Motorin finished with young Galina in her small room. The teenager smiled at him from the bed as he dressed. In his soft, kind manner of speech he said, "Thank you. I enjoyed your company and will compliment you to Dmitri."

Her smile widened and showed perfect teeth.

The casino and bedrooms were quiet as he strode down the

long hall to Chekhov's office. He quietly tapped on the door. No answer. Chekhov was likely at one of his many homes.

On impulse, he tried the door. Unlocked. Did Chekhov assume he was secure here, overconfident, or a moron?

He entered, and stale cigarette odor assaulted his sinuses. There was not much in the room. Desk with a few papers. High, black-leather chair. Filing cabinets. Staff chairs. A couch along one wall. He focused on the PC the boss used these days. He pressed the power button, and the device beeped, whirred, and clicked. A desktop picture of Red Square appeared. Down one side of the screen were a dozen folders with labels under them. One was Mail.

Of course! Chekhov communicated overseas about the Russian-bride scheme via the Internet. Ingenious! Vladimir was tempted to read some of the emails but dared not for fear of leaving some clue he had spied on his boss.

He powered off the machine, shut the door behind him, and left, his tiredness and blood-spotted suit forgotten. *I have to learn about computers.*

But for now, the policeman, Borisov, was his priority.

CHAPTER 41

Jake sat on their bed and held Natalia's hand. They had talked and recognized the risks, but both believed this was their only option other than to wait for Rublev's backup to contact Natalia.

Preparations had filled the prior afternoon. Sergey handled the shopping, and Jake's two suitcases bulged with what he thought he might need. Buying what he required in Moscow would risk drawing unwanted attention. Perhaps fatal notice.

Jake had discussed telephone hygiene with the FBI. They recorded any calls on his house line. In Russia, Natasha's mother did not have a telephone, and Jake assumed the mob boys would not know about the Borisovs. Still, they could not be too careful because the phones might be tapped. Part of Sergey's task was to acquire two satellite phones under the engineer's name. Natalia and Jake would communicate with each other over satphones. He might not be able to take the telephone everywhere, but his communications with Natalia could not be monitored.

"I wish I go, too," Natalia said.

He gazed into her eyes. He would miss her, but this was something he had to do alone. "It's safer for you here. I'll call when I can."

"You will be excellent papa to Alexandr. Thank you."

"You've given me much to be thankful for, too." He hugged her gently. "More than I can say."

Jake gave her a last kiss and ushered Silky downstairs. In the living room, he greeted everyone. "Sorry to keep you waiting. Agent Moore, thanks for coming, and please extend my appreciation, again, to Supervisory Special Agent Lancaster

186

for Natalia's protection." The first shift of four rotating agents looked on.

"No problem, Mr. Wilder. From your information, we've identified five other probable killers and additional victims. I must tell you again this is a bad idea. We have no authority in Russia. You'll be on your own. Frankly, if you go, most likely you'll return in a box or simply disappear."

Jake nodded. "Thanks for your concern."

Moore nodded with a resigned expression. "You have my number. Let me know if you find anything."

"I expect the same from you," Jake said. He turned toward the Nazarovs. "I owe you both more than I can repay."

"Come back soon so I won't be boss anymore," Sergey said. "Too many meetings!" He gave Jake a diskette. "If you get access to Chekhov's computer, boot off this. I assume he doesn't use Apple. This works on regular PC."

"What is this?"

"New version of spyware we put on Rublev's machine."

"Outstanding." The odds of getting near the Bratva's machine were infinitesimal, but Jake slipped the disk into his pocket and went to Raj.

Concern showed in the CEO's dark eyes. "Be careful and hurry back. This might also be useful."

Jake accepted the thin, leather shoulder satchel. "Wow. What is it?"

"A subnotebook and a cellphone. A jack connects the cell to the machine. You can call anywhere in the world and log onto the web."

"I'm overwhelmed." The smaller phone might come in handy in addition to accessing the Internet.

"Go get your boy. Your job will be waiting."

Stuart Baxter, who had driven down from Red Bluff, came next. "I'll get there Saturday. If you need me, I'm staying at the Hotel Mariupol," he said.

"I'll contact you first chance. I hope you locate Yelena Sands."

"Me, too."

Jake shook hands with the man and woman agents who would guard Natalia until the next shift arrived.

"We better go," Phelps said.

To a chorus of "Good luck!" Jake took his luggage to the garage and loaded it into Phelps' van. He scratched Silky behind the ears one last time and nudged her into the house. He concealed himself in the back of the van.

The overhead door opened, and Phelps drove to San Francisco International.

Jake prayed he would see Natalia, Silky, and Milpitas again.

* * *

This Russian trip was so different from his first. Jake felt no excitement when he switched planes in the vast Frankfurt am Main Airport, and he had no sense of adventure as the Lufthansa jet cruised toward St. Petersburg. The summer landscape below was green and lush compared to January's bleakness, which would have better fit his mood.

He had no plan on how he would locate Alexandr among Moscow's nine million people. *Am I a fool?* Probably, but he had to make every effort. He refused to go through life regretting he didn't try to rescue his stepson.

The flight attendant handed him the two forms for declaring his valuables, one for entry into the country and one for his exit. Russia didn't care about the money you brought in as long as you left with less. He thought about the thirty thousand dollars in travel pouches around his neck, ankle, and waist, plus his belt with an inside zipper. Each hundred-dollar-bill was relatively new and printed after 1986. Russians would not accept old or worn dollars.

Jake completed the form and listed his satphone, cell-phone, computer, and the thirty thousand dollars.

The Lufthansa airliner pitched downward, and St. Petersburg's cityscape came into hazy view. Hundreds of smokestacks hurled ash and steam into the air and reduced visibility to less than a mile. Jake contemplated the dreary warren of government buildings, apartment towers, and factories below. The city was supposed to be beautiful but wasn't because of Jake's state of mind. *I don't know how I'm going to find you, Alexandr, but I'm sure going to try.*

The plane landed with a bump and the roar of reverse thrusters. They taxied to the gate. He gazed out the window at the Pulkovo Airport terminal streaked with soot and filthy windows. *Well, I'm here.*

Jake jostled with the other passengers down to the terminal's depressing first level and took his place in line at Immigration Control. A middle-aged female officer with cigarette-stained teeth examined his papers with hard eyes. One problem he expected: he looked different from his passport and visa photos. His hair was now shorter than any time in his life thanks to Veronika and her shears. His bright ginger locks would be too obvious here, so he had his hair cropped to better blend in. He also wore a hat. With a scowl, the woman stamped his documents and released the stanchion. Jake wasn't sure if the sweat rolling down the back of his neck came from the stuffy heat or his nervousness.

He pushed through the door to the single baggage carousel. The lights were dim, and all the doors but one leading to the arrival area were chained and padlocked as in Moscow. Outside he hailed a cab to take him to the train terminal for the overnight trip to Moscow. On the ride, Jake noticed smiling pedestrians, and planters along the street were full of colorful pansies. All the trees had leaves.

CHAPTER 42

At the train station, Jake purchased a first-class ticket to Moscow. After he boarded, he located his compartment and felt like he walked into a sad shadow of what had been luxurious in years past. Once-elegant, burgundy crushed velvet seats were worn thin from extended use. Some of the tassels on the curtain were missing, the remaining ones were faded and dusty.

The railcar couplings made a loud metal snap as the train jolted forward. The best Jake could do was doze because his car lurched at every switch.

In Moscow, Jake spotted interpreter Tatyana and driver Victor from his previous visit. Jake had Sergey request them through his travel advisor when he arranged for his Moscow accommodations. Jake believed they were ignorant of Chekhov's scheme. At least he prayed they were. Engaging the pair might be a deadly mistake, but he knew them and hoped they would do what he asked of them. The thought of dealing with strangers was more upsetting than the possible risk Tatyana and Victor might entail

Victor had not changed from January, and his gray, ragged hair poked out around the edge of the same corduroy cap.

Tatyana took a last drag of her smoke and tossed it to the floor. She was a few pounds heavier and wore a quizzical, skeptical expression. "I surprised to see you, Jacob Wilder."

"I didn't expect to be here myself." He volunteered nothing more.

"You didn't marry after first time?" Tatyana asked.

Jake smiled. "Yes, I did. I'm here on business this time."

She lit another cigarette. "You come for entire month?"

"As long as required. I want you two available if I call you, day or night. I'll double both your fees." This brought a rare smile to Victor's stern face, which confirmed the man knew English.

Tatyana squinted through her glasses, exhaled smoke, and sized Jake up. She shrugged in acceptance and turned toward the door. This time, Victor carried the luggage. The ex-soldier's pride seemed softened by the salary increase.

After the potholed, uncomfortable drive in the squeaky Lada, Victor stopped in front of a newer building, and they trudged up the staircase. Jake and Tatyana entered the fourth-floor apartment, followed by Victor with the suitcases. This place was more spacious than the one he rented in January. The kitchen table accommodated four instead of two, and the bedroom was double the size.

"Do you want to rest?" Tatyana said. "I will arrange dinner for later."

"Please be back in an hour. I'll be ready. But first, write down this address." He offered her a pen and paper.

She complied and left with a shrug.

Jake unpacked and pulled out the satphone. He called, and the connection was instant.

Natalia's voice was anxious. She said, "Hallo?"

"Hi, beautiful. I'm here."

"Good."

"No problems for me. The important thing is how you are."

"I fine but fret."

He worried, too. "Things okay with the FBI folks?"

"They are not like policemen from my country. Here they courteous."

"I thought they would be. I'm happy you are comfortable with them. Here's my address. I want them to know where I am. Ready? UL. Chertanovskaya 21-2-33."

"I love you, Jacob."

"Love you, too. Stay hopeful. Alexandr will be okay. I promise I'll do whatever it takes to get him."

Next, he called Sidor Borisov to set the time to meet. He opened his computer, plugged in the cellphone, and selected the "Internet" icon on the computer's screen. In moments he read his email. He had received encouraging good-luck messages from Sergey, Agent Moore, and Raj. He answered them and gave them his location.

Jake powered down the PC, hid it behind the China cabinet, and checked the time. Tatyana and Victor should be waiting downstairs.

When he climbed into the Lada, he again observed Victor displayed more personality. The Russian's smile seemed sincere when he asked, "Where to?"

"The largest flea market."

They lurched forward through the maze of ten-story structures. Though this was a nice area, dogs still barked and rooks still cawed in their competition for garbage on the roadside piles. But fewer old people competed with them than at his January accommodations. This was a better neighborhood.

He exchanged dollars for rubles at a kiosk on the way. They drove toward the center of the city and turned north at the Jauza River. Traffic ran one-way on the boulevards on each bank of the concrete-lined waterway. Downstream led to the confluence with the Moscow River and the Kremlin. Upstream went out to the city's edge. Entrepreneurs along the avenues worked lively car wash businesses every quarter of a mile or so. Men stood ready with rags and a bucket on a rope. They lowered their buckets into the dirty river for water and toiled over cars impossible to keep clean on the dusty streets. Small fuel trucks also abounded. They offered cheaper prices but less accurate measures than regular gas stations. Capitalism had taken hold.

The drive to their destination took an hour. Victor located

a parking place far from the fenced field, Tatyana started to climb out, but Jake told her, "No, I'm going alone. I won't be long."

She flicked her cigarette out the open window and protested, "No! Too dangerous. I must go with you."

"I don't mean to be rude, but I can do some things myself."

He didn't wait for her to argue. He climbed out of the car and joined the throng that streamed to the sprawling area jammed with rows of kiosks and small tents. *At least the air is cleaner here than most places in the city.*

Many people glanced at him, but, as normal, few stared. He could not escape his American persona. Tall. Erect. Decent clothes. But this time Jake didn't feel ill-at-ease or apprehensive. Neither was he intimidated. In fact, his confident bearing was itself a type of self-defense. If someone wanted to mess with him, his stare conveyed they would pay a price.

Admission fee paid, Jake plunged into the noisy crowd that milled in the alleys of canvas-covered stalls on the grass and dirt. The hand-painted dolls, carved chess sets, and stenciled T-shirts held no interest for him. He purchased four sacks Russians carried when they shopped. He rummaged through the offerings of booths selling new and used clothing. He bought several combinations of pants, shirts, and hats like those worn by common people here. He also invested a buck in a pair of Soviet shoes with their flimsy cardboard soles.

By the time two bags were full, he had a following. Two rough-looking guys and two teenagers trailed him. Jake stared them down. The kids shrunk back, but the two adults stayed with him.

Jake wound his way to the back where the ground rose higher and more expensive goods were sold. He bought two knives, the hammer and sickle embossed on their handles. He glowered at his followers as he stuffed one knife into his waistband. Military binoculars cost him twenty dollars, and he was about to leave when another item caught his eye. The nervous, twenty-something hawker with greasy black hair danced back and forth and uttered unintelligible Russian. Jake took his time, inspected the device, and tested it against his cupped hand. "How much?"

The vendor had tagged him as American and understood. He responded, "Four hundred dollar."

Jake held up a finger and countered, "One."

The man shook his head, so Jake turned away. He hadn't gone far when the man stepped in front of him and pressed the night vision goggles into his hand. "Okay, one hundred, American!"

Jake peeled off a new C-note and put the goggles in a sack. He carried his purchases in his left hand, rested his right hand on the blade in his belt, and strolled back to the faded yellow Lada.

The supermarket was the next stop.

He anticipated this would be an interesting night.

CHAPTER 43

Jake felt refreshed after two hours rest. A boiling shower made him feel even better.

After Victor and Tatyana picked him up at the appointed time, they stopped to buy two bouquets of roses from a street vendor. When they arrived at his destination, Jake got out of the car into the evening breeze. He told Tatyana, "Be back in four hours."

He looked up at the yellow concrete building and went inside.

Butterflies fluttered in his stomach as he approached Sidor's apartment. The door opened after he knocked. Sveta Borisova greeted him with joy and concern. "Hallo!"

Jake handed her a bouquet. "Hello. These flowers are a small thank you for all you have done."

Jake entered, remembered to kick off his shoes, and accepted spare slippers from Sveta. Sidor reached around his wife with a firm handshake. "Welcome to our home."

"Thank you, my friend."

Jake looked around the modest but spotless flat. The back wall of the living room had a bookcase packed with volumes, but his eyes were drawn to the woman who stood perhaps five-feet-four with graying blonde hair and eyes like those he admired in his dreams and in his days. She came forward. "I Regina."

They hugged. "I'm Jake. I am so happy to meet you."

Sidor stood beside him and translated. Natalia's mother smiled, but her eyes held apprehension. He presented her the other bouquet, and her smile grew wider.

"I glad you not dead," she said. "I understand secret."

"Me too! And, yes, we must pretend I died."

Regina nodded and hugged him again. "*Spasibo* for all."

Jake proceeded to distribute the gifts. Santa Claus in July. Cosmetics, perfume, and a thick letter from Natalia for Regina. Toiletries and scented soap for Sveta. Sidor's jaw dropped when Jake presented him with a new Rawlins first baseman's mitt and baseballs.

"If I had such a glove in Cuba, we would never lose. *Spasibo*."

"You are welcome."

Jake gave the groceries to Sveta. Canned meat. Cartons of juice. Chocolates. A six-pack of beer.

Sidor said something in Russian and shot Sveta a hopeful glance. They exchanged words, and she made a shooing gesture. Sidor smiled and said, "Come while we have light. Bring your mitt. The women will prepare supper."

Jake was quite uncomfortable going outside in case he might be spotted, but he followed Sidor into the surprisingly fragrant evening. Sidor threw, and Jake caught the ball with the familiar and reassuring *slap* and sting. He fired it back and pictured the hot dust from Cuban diamonds that swirled around Sidor. Soon, they found a steady rhythm in the fading light.

"Sergey Nazarov told me you killed mob boy with bat."

"Yes."

Sidor nodded his approval, reached back, and fired the ball hard. "I am happy you are alive and here, but I fear about your quest."

"Me, too, but a father must do what he has to do," which sounded strange to Jake's own ears. Jake Wilder, software VP, so smitten by his Russian bride he would crawl through hell to save her son. *Their* son.

Sveta called from above. Dinnertime.

The spread was huge. Chilled Russian meat salad, which was Jake's favorite. Buttered bread. Pickled vegetables. Potatoes.

Garlic chicken. But the mood was not festive despite the red flower and bouquet on the table.

Jake became more serious and asked Regina, "When I have Alexandr, will you come to live with us?"Sidor translated.

"I would be a burden to you. I am too old to work."

He reached across and took his mother-in-law's hand. "These people will kill you when I take Alexandr from them. You must come with me. Natalia needs her mother and Alexandr his grandmother, and you will not be a burden. In fact, you should leave while I search."

Through a long conversation, Jake's friends did their best to convince her to go.

Sidor translated her final answer. "She says yes but will stay until you have Alexandr. You might need her help."

"I am happy you will come to live with us."

She smiled, though worry remained in her eyes.

"I will go to the US Embassy legal attaché's office tomorrow," Jake said. "You need to obtain your Russian passport as soon as you can. When you receive it, I will take you to the embassy to help with the US Visa. Here is the money you will need." He obeyed the custom of not handing cash to a woman and placed the bills on the table. The only women who took money from the hands of men here were prostitutes.

The discussion turned to Dmitri Chekhov. Sidor had learned nothing new, only reconfirmation of Chekhov's brutal reputation, which was a black shadow over an otherwise superb meal.

After they finished, Sveta shooed Jake and Sidor out of the kitchen.

Sidor motioned Jake to follow, and the pair went to the small, tidy bedroom. Sidor opened a bureau drawer and pulled out a semi-automatic handgun and box of shells. The Russian whispered, "You might need this. A Makarov 9MM. Not as effective as a 9MM Luger, but better than a .380 ACP."

Jake did not understand what he had been told, but the old pistol with cracked plastic grip was cold and heavy in his hand. "Thank you."

"If you have difficulties, I cannot assist you," Sidor added. "Would endanger Sveta's life and mine."

"I know. You've helped much already."

Jake put the gun and ammunition in a bag under his mitt. The ladies emerged with chocolates and hot tea.

Jake knew one ancient firearm would not protect him against the Bratva leader who had his son.

* * *

The whine of mosquitoes around his ears woke Jake after an inadequate night's sleep. He stumbled to the kitchen, put water on the stove, and hoped a hot shower would wash away his lingering jet lag.

Under the steaming spray, Jake thought about Regina and wished she had agreed to go to the US now. She would be safer, and Natalia would feel better if her mother was with her. But at least he achieved a partial victory. She had decided to leave for America whenever they rescued Alexandr. Jake prayed they would.

The shower, a long and encouraging conversation with Natalia, and a cup of instant expresso refreshed him. He checked his emails. The only new message came from FBI Agent Moore noting receipt of Jake's Moscow address. The Fed offered words of encouragement but no new information.

Jake plugged in his travel iron and pressed the wrinkles out of a white shirt. He intended to appear professional when he visited the Embassy.

After he dressed, Jake grabbed the Makarov. The old pistol appeared serviceable. He pulled the slide to check the empty chamber. He released the safety, aimed at a spot on the wall, and squeezed the trigger. The hammer came down with a startling *snap*! Jake repeated dry firing several times and concentrated to steady the gun.

On one level, he wanted nothing more than to murder Dmitri Chekhov. On another, Jake feared the consequences of his quest. He clenched his jaw and resolved to see things through no matter the risk.

Jake loaded the clip and inserted it. *Click.* He placed the pistol in a sack and added one of the Russian knives. He'd take the bundle with him wherever he could.

CHAPTER 44

J ake pushed the bag holding the gun and knife to the floor in the back of the Lada. A weapon would not be allowed where he would go.

The security checkpoints at the US Embassy took almost a half hour before Jake was ushered into the legal attaché's small office at the back of the first story.

A trim, middle-aged man with graying temples and creased forehead stood from behind his desk. "Mr. Wilder, good to meet you. I'm Ted Vandagriff." The man in a conservative gray suit shook Jake's hand. "I reviewed your file. You and your wife have had a rough time." Vandagriff frowned and sighed. "I am aware you've been briefed, but you must understand, I operate only in conjunction with the local authorities. If you think about it, that's no different from any foreign embassy in The States. They have to work with us. So, there's little I can do directly."

"But indirectly?"

Vandagriff squirmed in his chair. He handed Jake a folder. "Here's what I've put together, which isn't much."

Jake opened the file to two printed pages and a photo of a well-dressed man getting into a Mercedes. He felt his face grow warm. *Chekhov, the bastard.*

"I understand your situation, but my advice is go home. Now. The Bratva treat most foreigners well because they bring in the cash. They don't kill the golden geese. You're an exception. If you don't go now, it's unlikely you'll leave Moscow alive."

Jake didn't respond, so the legal attaché continued, "The Russian mob isn't sophisticated, but sophistication isn't needed when brutality is so effective. Dmitri Chekhov is among the worst of them. Though not part of the old, established Bratva, he's a force of nature. He has such deep government connections I can't inquire about him without him finding out.

"And for ruthlessness, he scores near the top. We received reports a rival gang held up one of his extortion runners. Chekhov not only had the holdup men butchered, but their families were killed as well." Vandagriff got a hard look in his eyes. "Seventeen men, women, and, yes, children. The women and girls were raped before they were murdered."

A sick twist knotted Jake's stomach. *Barbaric. And this man has Alexandr.* He studied the photograph and swallowed. "I'll be careful, but I have to save my son."

Vandagriff nodded. "I figured you wouldn't give up. Oh, and someone else who needs to watch his back is Sidor Borisov."

Jake tried to cover his surprise but failed. The implications were clear: the mobster may know about Jake's policeman friend. Sidor could be at risk from inside his own police department because he ran Chekhov's license plate.

He prayed Vandagriff was wrong. "Any idea where they might keep my stepson?"

"No clue. We suspect Chekhov hides a number of children, but they could be together or dispersed, in Moscow or Lord-knows-where. My people are asking around, but nothing so far."

"We won't have any problem with the visas, will we?"

"You're persistent, aren't you? I'll make sure your mother-in-law's application is processed right away. When will she apply?"

"This week."

"The sooner the better. And if by some miracle you rescue the boy, I'll expedite his visa."

"What if we need admission to the Embassy fast?"

"I've alerted the Marine guards. If you make it to the gate, they'll let you in." Vandagriff paused. "That's the limit of what I can do, but I'll give you my beeper number. You never know."

* * *

"You never know," Jake muttered to himself as he walked up Novinsky Boulevard to where Tatyana and Victor waited in the car. He marveled how the city managed to retain its depressing grayness even in summer. He now understood Muscovites' longing for dachas in the country.

As he approached the Lada, smoke billowed from the vehicle. Tatyana and Victor were in full puff. The driver flicked his cigarette onto the pavement when Jake climbed into the back, but the interpreter kept hers. Jake hated the stench but had bigger worries.

The first was how much he should use Victor and Tatyana, and the second, what to tell them? Jake inspected the shopping sack. Undisturbed. He trusted them not to screw up double pay for a month. He stuffed the folder on top of the newspapers Tatyana had purchased for him. The firearm and knife were hidden at the bottom of the bag.

"You not so long. I thought you would be hours like everyone," Tatyana said.

"I only needed to pick something up. Let's drive down Rus Street. After that, I want to go by the New Russia Casino on Tverskaja Street."

In minutes, they bounced by International Friends. The building across the river from the Kremlin was as Natalia described it.

A half-hour later, Tatyana pointed out the New Russia Casino sitting on a corner lot. For anyone sense-deadened by Las Vegas excess, the exterior of Chekhov's business looked more like an upscale pool hall with concrete walls and without first-floor windows. The streaked, old cement structure marked the building as at least thirty years old. A foot-high neon sign flashed by the door even though the place was closed. He ordered Victor to circle the block three times.

Next to the casino was a crowded bakery. On the side street was an adjacent barbershop. The sidewalks were devoid of the usual kiosks and hawkers. Across the avenue, children played and derelicts congregated in a park under a giant bronze statue of a youth thrusting a wreath-shrouded hammer and sickle toward the sky.

He would watch from there.

* * *

Vladimir Motorin sat in his Saab and listened to a new German song on the radio as he staked out the cop's apartment. Sidor Borisov was at work, but he wouldn't be direct in warning the man. Instead, Vladimir would get to him through his wife. He needed to identify her so he could describe her to her husband if necessary. For now, he wanted the woman to see him in his conspicuous automobile and clothes. Part of the Bratva intimidation.

So far, nothing, but she was there because the apartment's windows were open. No one, including policemen, left windows open on any floor unless they were home.

"There she is," he said beneath his breath. The plain-looking woman stuck her head out the kitchen window and fanned herself. She wore an apron over an old, worn housedress. She scanned up and down the narrow road and locked on him. He grinned at her startled expression before she shut the windows and disappeared.

As he debated whether to leave, Sveta Borisova walked out

of the building wearing a flowered dress and carrying a shopping tote. She turned straight toward him. *What is she doing?* The woman stared at the ground, like most Russians, until she drew near. She looked at him as she passed.

"Fuck-your-mother! The bitch read my plate number." He wasn't angry, only irritated. He knew his license would not benefit her or her husband.

He let the woman walk by before he started the engine, made a slow Y-turn, and slammed the accelerator to the floor. He raced forward. She glanced back with terror on her face. He smiled.

She dove behind one of the portable garages as he neared. He watched her roll in the trash through his rearview mirror. "Ha!" He accelerated away through the korpus and laughed at the people frantic to escape his speeding auto. Scaring the Borisova woman was fun, but of course, he would not hit her. To damage such an automobile would be an inexcusable waste, though he enjoyed the *crunch* when he squashed a dog not quick enough to obey the owner's yank on its leash.

Lieutenant Borisov and his frumpy spouse would now mind their own business. If not, next time he would use his gun and wouldn't miss.

CHAPTER 45

I knew this would happen! Why are we involved in this?!" Sidor pounded his fist on the kitchen table, but Sveta remained stoic.

She held his gaze, and her honest eyes gave him a twinge of shame. "Because no one can be allowed to steal children."

Sidor knew his wife felt the emptiness of their childless marriage, so he changed his approach. "But now we are in danger. Jacob Wilder called and warned me to be vigilant. His own FBI told him that I need to be careful! It is because I looked up Chekhov's plates. And now you tell me about a man outside our apartment! This is too much. You *must* leave and visit your sister in Vladivostok."

"I will not!"

"Sveta!" he yelled but caught himself. Her jaw was set, and he regretted raising his voice. She was his anchor in a troubled world. "See what this is doing to us. We are fighting over someone else's difficulties."

"We can help."

"But your life may be in peril!"

"Perhaps we both are, but less than Jacob and Alexandr." Her eyes softened again, and she took his hand. "I understand your concern, but do not be angry. This happened because I pushed you. This is my fault, but I am not a silly woman. We will continue to help Jacob find the boy, and I won't leave you alone in Moscow to do it."

Sidor gave up trying to sway her.

He only wished he hadn't given the extra Makarov to Wilder. Now he needed to appropriate another one and teach

Sveta how to shoot.

Sidor Borisov swore mightily to himself.

* * *

A cool, Sacramento River Delta breeze took the edge off the blistering capitol-city heat. Today would be in the eighties with an evening forecast of seventy-one. To Detective Bill Jackson, cooler weather meant fewer hot tempers, less mayhem, and an easier day.

He pulled through the Taco Bell drive-thru on Franklin Boulevard and ordered tacos and burritos that filled two bags. Five minutes later, he tapped on the side door of a van parked near the deceased Ivan Rublev's dump of an apartment. Jackson spent as much time as possible on Wilder's case because it interested him, though nothing had transpired since the Russian's headlong introduction to baseball. This international extortion and murder plot was of greater magnitude than the rapes, beatings, thefts, and shootings he usually investigated in this gang-infested swath of town.

Two smiles beckoned Jackson inside. He closed the door behind him. "How's it going?"

The older of two FBI agents, a man perhaps thirty-five with brown hair and white-bread appearance, shrugged. "Nothing new, but at least it's not as hot."

Jackson shared the food with the grateful feds.

After they devoured lunch, Jackson shot-the-shit with them while he thumbed through one of the *Playboy* magazines quasi-hidden in a folder.

The younger agent, a sandy-haired, baby-faced man in his late twenties said, "Uh, who's this?"

A sturdy man of average height who wore expensive clothes banged on Rublev's door. The junior agent zoomed in for a close-up.

Two things told Jackson the man was Russian: his round head and the European habit of buttoning the top button of his shirt. The man knocked several times and swiveled to see if anyone watched. He jimmied the lock and entered.

The older agent said, "Here we go," and made a radio call. His partner maximized the screen image from the camera inside the apartment. The black-and-white, fish-eye view was not sharp but clear enough to observe the man's room-to-room inspection.

After confirming Rublev was not there, the man powered on Rublev's PC.

Jackson stared over the agents' shoulders and hoped he wouldn't get a call requiring him to leave.

The young agent checked another monitor and said, "He's checking email."

The man typed on the keyboard, and *The Sacramento Bee*'s home page flashed onto a monitor.

"He's running a search for any news on Rublev."

After a few minutes, the man picked up the telephone. The surveillance equipment recorded his heavily accented words. "Hallo, police? I am try to locate my brother. He is missing."

Jackson laughed. "That takes balls."

The person at the department told the Russian, "Sorry, but we have no information on him." The records clerk had executed the correct procedure for a "tagged" file. Of course Rublev was in their database.

The caller hung up and verified something on the computer before he dialed a number. A woman answered, and they conversed in Russian.

Jackson recognized her voice. Natalia Wilder.

* * *

"Hallo?"

"Natalia Melnikova Wilder?"

"*Da.*"

"What is the status of your steps to save your boy."

She gasped. "What? Who are you?"

"I will ask the questions! Have you followed instructions?"

"My... my husband is dead. A man said me to wait for directions. Please, when can I have my son?"

The man ignored the question. "Do you have the money?"

"*Da.*"

"I will send you directions on what to do."

The call disconnected.

* * *

Bill Jackson listened to the conversation between Natalia and the unidentified man, and though he couldn't understand the language, he guessed the meaning. He informed the FBI agents, "Rublev failed to collect. This guy's the backup."

The senior agent flipped through a stack of photographs. "He's a new one."

"The woman is Natalia Wilder," Jackson said. "I recognize her voice."

"Yeah, we've got her covered."

Jackson looked at the time and frowned. He needed to go back to his own cases.

The man left the apartment, and Jackson asked, "Now what?"

"Hope a team shows up to tail this guy, but no one's responded yet."

"You mean you might lose him?"

The two feds glanced at each other. The senior one said, "*We* can't follow him without him knowing we're agents, can we? We'd be, ah, too conspicuous."

Right, Jackson thought. *Two clean-cut, white boys would be as obvious as I would be at a white supremacist rally.* "Well, I sure as hell can."

Both agents said, "Go for it!"

Jackson slipped out to the sidewalk and followed the mutt. The man disappeared behind a graffiti-scarred building. Many neighborhood eyes tracked the comparatively well-dressed man and him. The detective increased his pace to not fall too far behind. The man turned another corner toward a parking area.

That's when the yells started.

Then screams.

Jackson sprinted, gun drawn, and peeked around the corner at nine black teenagers trying to strip a new Volvo. The kids spotted him and scattered like cockroaches. One had a bleeding gash on his upper arm. Another clutched a car stereo like a football. Two kicked something on the ground before they ran.

Jackson moved closer. The Russian he'd tailed writhed on a bed of shattered glass and asphalt. The man held a bloody knife, and his midsection was blood-soaked.

The man raised his blade as Jackson pointed his pistol and showed his badge. "Drop it."

The man complied and grabbed his stomach.

Jackson pulled out his cell and phoned the FBI.

CHAPTER 46

Moscow's afternoon drifted into an evening full of aggressive mosquitoes. Jake wished he'd brought his insect repellent. Too late now. He had to contend with the belligerent insects until Tatyana and Victor returned.

Tatyana had been agitated when they dropped him off three hours earlier at the park near the New Russia Casino. With Jake dressed in old clothes and a wig, they knew something was going on. Tatyana objected mightily when he told them to pick him up after dark. She wanted an explanation. Jake knew he couldn't hold her off much longer. He realized he would not succeed without her and Victor's help. If at all.

Jake shifted his sore butt on the concrete bench. Before sunset, children had romped with their dogs under the enormous statue while old men played chess, but they were since replaced by a rougher element. Young and middle-aged Muscovites drank, smoked, and laughed. Jake lifted his vodka bottle filled with water and took a swallow. In his shopping bag were binoculars, night-vision goggles, a knife, and the Makarov.

A voice from behind said, "Nice disguise."

Jake turned as Ted Vandagriff, the legal attaché, walked up. "You scared the crap out of me! Your get-up isn't bad, either."

Vandagriff came around the bench and sat next to Jake. He also wore old workman's clothes and carried an unlabeled bottle. "This isn't a location to look like the cover of *GQ*."

"How did you find me?" Vandagriff's wrinkled forehead smoothed for an instant, and a twinkle lit his eyes. "Right, you're the FBI," Jake said.

Vandagriff took a drink and passed his bottle to Jake, who sipped the tasteless distilled water. He handed it back as Vandagriff said, "Since you're so determined to get yourself killed, I thought we would at least keep tabs on you. You might turn up something to assist our investigation."

"Comforting."

Vandagriff slid a little closer. "Here's some info. First, I checked out your driver and interpreter because you can't be too cautious. They appear clean. He's ex-army, and the military hates the mafia more than anyone. If the generals ever take over, there will be a lot of dead Bratva.

"Your translator is a university graduate and ambitious with nothing criminal in her background. You should still be careful, though."

Jake had a thought. "Do you think they might want to come to the US?"

Vandagriff gave him a sideways glance. After a long pause, he said, "Everyone wants to go to the Promised Land. It could be arranged if they help close this case."

"Thanks. I need them."

"Assuming you can do this at all, which you can't." Vandagriff chuckled and continued, "Well, not to give you any encouragement but we are making progress. We're monitoring email and telephone connections, and we've located nine hitters in the US so far. The tricky part is keeping these guys from killing anyone until we grab Chekhov."

"When will that be?"

Vandagriff said with exasperation, "A preliminary idea is to lure him to a country where we can capture and extradite him. Nothing firm, though."

"Appreciate the info."

Vandagriff turned and stared Jake in the eyes. "Since you're going ahead with this, I'm trying to run some interference. If Chekhov is looking somewhere else, he might not notice you."

"Thank you! What are you doing?"

"Remember I told you about the clash between Chekhov and another gang? Let's say I gave the other leader an incentive to strike back. I suspect they'll use people from another city to do the dirty work so they can claim innocence."

"Holy shit, how'd you do that?"

Vandagriff stood. "Dollars buy everything here, Jake. Besides, if it helps nail this guy, the money's chicken feed. I gotta go. Stay alive." He walked into the darkness.

Jake felt gratitude and relief. The Legal Attaché was not as hide-bound as he first appeared.

He swatted away the bugs and scrutinized the casino. The neon sign had been on solid for more than an hour, and customers wandered in. The people who patronized Chekhov's gaming house were decked in better attire than the typical Muscovite. Many were Europeans and Asians with a few easy-to-identify Americans. Lights glowed in the shade-covered upstairs windows.

A black Mercedes pulled to the curb, and Jake gripped the field glasses. A tall, broad-shouldered man with shaved head stepped out of the German auto followed by Chekhov. No mistake. That was the mobster and his bodyguard. They strode inside.

Jake's face burned in anger as he put the binocs in his sack. "*Oomph!*"

The air in Jake's lungs blasted out of him from a painful jab in the ribcage. He turned to see a policeman standing next to him, nightstick readied for a head blow. The heavyset cop stretched the fabric of his light-blue uniform and white leather belt. Jake cursed himself. He had been so absorbed with Chekhov he didn't see him coming. *Damn!*

The officer barked something unintelligible. Jake shrugged to indicate his lack of understanding. The policeman growled something else and indicated with his nightstick for Jake to stand. He did and held out his open hands in a peaceful gesture. He believed he could be in jail in need of medical attention within the hour.

Jake motioned with his finger to wait, reached into his shirt pocket, and removed his passport. The policeman snatched it, and his eyes registered disbelief that it was American. He was further surprised when he opened the document to the photo. Three crisp, hundred-dollar bills, more than a policeman's wages for six months, lay folded inside.

Jake wanted to swat at the mosquitoes that attacked his head and neck but stayed still. This was not a time for sudden movements. After a pause, the policeman thrust back the passport, minus the cash.

Without a word, he moved on. Only then did Jake register his numerous mosquito bites, and sweat drenched him.

He slumped back down on the bench.

A grim-faced Tatyana stomped toward him. "You are foolish man. How did you deal with policeman?"

Jake rubbed his fingers together in the universal sign for money.

She nodded, but her face remained stern. She lit a cigarette. "Are you hungry?" Then, as if his response was irrelevant, she added, "Let's go eat."

Ten minutes later, Jake and Tatyana were across a table in a small restaurant. Victor waited in the Lada with a chunk of bread and can of beer. Other than one group smoking and drinking their way through dinner on the other side of the room, Jake and Tatyana were the only patrons.

She blew smoke toward the ceiling without taking her eyes off him. She tapped the ash into the tin tray. "I told you it was stupid to be out alone. If you are arrested, I will never find you. What would your wife think of such foolishness?"

"She understands what I'm doing."

She responded with an edge of annoyance in her voice.

"And what is that?"

A sullen waitress in a short red dress deposited their drinks and left.

Jake took a long drink. He marveled at how wonderful the beer tasted, licked his lips, and stared at Tatyana. She focused on him through her thick spectacles. "I'm here to rescue my stepson. The man who owns the New Russia Casino kidnapped him."

Jake drank again and observed her over the rim of his glass. Her stare was more distant.

"This is dangerous," she said.

"As hazardous as it gets."

They locked eyes, and an ash fell from her neglected cigarette. He was not sure what she thought until she spoke.

"Then you require our help, but I tell you double our fee is not enough."

"How about resident visas to the United States, including Victor's family, and money to start a new life? Say twenty-thousand dollars each."

Her chubby face registered shock. "You can do this?"

"Yes. I'll give you both a grand in advance. Help me save Alexandr, and you'll have the chance to build new lives in America."

Her eyes went wide. "My answer is 'yes!' I will speak to Victor."

"Either he agrees or doesn't, but he needs to decide tonight. He can keep the money as long as he stays quiet. I'm risking everything to get my stepson. Chekhov can't discover what I'm doing, understand?"

She took a drag and crinkled her eyes. "*Da.*"

CHAPTER 47

The discussion between Tatyana and Victor on the ride from the restaurant was lively. Jake sensed they both comprehended the danger, but the promise of life in the US with cash had them hooked. Victor glanced back and smiled. "*Spasibo.*"

Jake nodded and gave Victor a thumbs up.

After paying them at his apartment, Jake peeled off the wig and scratched his red stubble before he took a beer out of the refrigerator. He pulled out the subnotebook and logged onto the Internet. His spirits rose when he read the email from Agent Moore about Natalia being contacted. Perhaps the nightmare would be over soon.

He opened the next message.

The thug who called her was in the hospital and under arrest. He hadn't had time to inform Chekhov the first portion of Jake's money was ready and available. Jake pounded his fist on the table.

"Shit!"

***

Jake called Natalia. She was weak and sore, which stoked his anger. They talked over thirty minutes. Then he responded to emails from Sergey, Raj, and Agent Moore.

Jake spent the remaining hours searching Moscow maps on the dream he might find a location for dozens of children. Futile exercise, but what else could he do while he waited?

Tatyana phoned to say she and Victor were on their way, so he powered down and hid the computer. He applied his insect repellent before carrying his shopping bag downstairs to wait for them.

Both the translator and driver were in better spirits that evening. They grinned, and the ever-stoic Victor was ebullient. A shiny watch glistened on his wrist. Jake noticed Tatyana had a new purse.

"Is true a person can become rich in America?" Tatyana asked.

"Of course, but it is not guaranteed. There are poor people in the US as well as wealthy, with most in between. But, if you work hard and are smart, you can build a beautiful life for yourself. I read somewhere, 'the only place success comes before sweat is in the dictionary.' That describes how to succeed."

Tatyana used a shiny gold-accented lighter to fire up a smoke. "I told Victor. For him, the US was always enemy, but he is intelligent as well as proud. He hopes he can have decent life for his family. Like when he commanded in the Army, he wants trucks."

"Tell him that if he helps me rescue my stepson, his reward will cover the down payment on the first truck in his fleet."

After an exchange in Russian, Victor extended his hand. "*Spasibo*."

Jake took the hearty handshake and spoke to Tatyana, "What would you like to do in The States?"

"I think I will work with an international organization. Many companies invest here. That would be beneficial for me."

"I agree."

They made one stop at a kiosk selling Cuban cigars. Jake wanted something to help keep the irritating mosquitos at bay during tonight's surveillance.

They reached the park at dusk. The children and old codgers had gone home, and rougher males clustered in drinking groups. Victor parked the Lada. Tatyana and Jake walked to a bench facing the concrete casino. As the shadows deepened, the ember of Victor's cigarette was visible half a block away.

The bugs assaulted them the instant they climbed out of the car, so Jake lit a cigar. The taste was mellow, but his eyes watered, and he needed to spit after every puff. At least the smoke kept away the mosquitos and made him immune to Tatyana's ever-present cigarettes.

Jake told her the story of what Natalia and Alexandr had gone through and what was supposed to have been his demise.

At the end she said, "You are still foolish man, but now I understand."

Worry crossed her eyes, and he looked to follow her stare. The cop from the night before was about ten yards away and coming towards them. He barked something. Tatyana said, "Our identifications."

They gave him their papers. The officer checked Jake's first and grunted his gratification. Three more bills crumpled in a fat hand as he gave back the passport. He scrutinized Tatyana's papers and flipped them at her. Nothing interesting there.

Without a word, he sauntered away.

Tatyana grumbled in disgust. "They are all criminals."

"That's the only criminal I'm concerned about." Jake motioned with his head to the Mercedes in front of the casino.

He raised the binoculars to the same scene as the night before. Jake imagined crosshairs on the back of Chekhov's head. Could he execute a man? He had killed Rublev in self-defense and suffered no regret, but killing someone in cold blood?

He pushed the thought away. Chekhov had a pattern, which satisfied him to know. But Jake still did not know how to locate Alexandr.

Moments later, the light came on in the structure's second-story corner windows. The shades were open. Chekhov sat at a desk. The angle of his torso and glow on his face indicated he worked at a computer. An idea sparked in Jake's mind.

"How long would it take for you to change into nice clothes and for us to get back here?" he asked

"Two hours. Why?"

He strode to the Lada. "Because we're going gambling!"

CHAPTER 48

Jake puffed a fresh Cuban and surveyed the gaming area like a general sizing up a battlefield before the fight started. He guessed there were more Rolexes in the room than the planet's largest jewelry store.

He wore a suit and blew smoke toward the ceiling to announce his arrival as a successful American businessman. Tatyana's dress fit the look of a businessman's translator. He wondered how many businessmen carried pistols and knives in their waistbands.

Despite the building's drab exterior, the inside was bright and spacious. Two enormous gentlemen in tuxedoes stood guard at the front door. They smiled and nodded welcome, but their purpose was clear to Jake. Control unruly guests and deny undesirables entry. A small rock band belted out music in the back. Dice, roulette, and card tables were crowded with men and a smattering of women. The two bustling bartenders poured drinks, and some of the most beautiful females Jake had ever seen sat along the bar. The stunning ladies, the oldest perhaps nineteen, wore revealing cocktail dresses. *Are their dates gambling?*

Tatyana seemed to read his thoughts and whispered, "They are working girls, prostitutes."

He tried not to let surprise register on his face.

More than one head turned toward him. He displayed a self-confident smile though his insides twisted. Upstairs was the murderous man who had his son.

Jake's head itched under one of the wigs Sergey had purchased for him, and his eyes burned from the stogie. *This is no time to worry about comfort. Alexandr's life is at stake.*

He strode to the roulette table and took a seat. Four other gamblers, including three Japanese, bantered with each other. Tatyana stood just behind his left shoulder.

People stared at him, and the attention increased when he counted out a thousand dollars. The croupier exchanged the cash for chips. Jake took another puff, and a crystal ashtray appeared at his right along with a shapely waitress in a tight, strapless blue dress. Tatyana translated, "Would you like a cocktail?"

"Mineral water, please."

The dazzling woman jotted his order on a napkin. Her sparkling eyes told Jake he had been tagged as an American.

He proceeded to bet. The cocktail waitress delivered his water, and he tipped her a chip worth about fifty bucks. She beamed at him as he went back to roulette.

Between spins, he studied the room. Patrons would approach a working girl, and they would disappear up a staircase at the back. After a half-hour or so, they would return. From time-to-time girls would circulate and troll for business, so he was not surprised when he felt a light touch on his arm. A sweet voice asked, "Having good luck?"

He smiled and gave the woman an appraising glance. Reddish-brunette hair. Buxom. Flawless face. "Yes, I am. What's your name?"

"Galina. Would you like more luck?"

"Perhaps."

The woman ran her fingertips across his shoulder. "I can blow up your mind."

Jake swallowed the urge to roar with laughter. But "blow up your mind" might be a euphemism for rough Russian sex. "I think you mean you can 'blow' my mind."

"*Da.*"

Jake stacked bets on the seven, eleven, and thirteen.

"Well, Galina, I'm here to gamble for now but maybe in a

few hours. Here, thank you for coming by." He pressed two chips into her soft hand. From her puzzled expression, she didn't understand all he said, so Tatyana explained. She blew him a kiss and moved back to her perch at the bar.

Jake winked at Tatyana and continued to gamble, sometimes winning.

Something else Jake noted was men who came in and went straight to the stairs in the back. Some sported expensive suits. They would leave after a short time. *Chekhov's lieutenants?*

At ten o'clock, the band stopped, and a loud tuxedoed man who spoke like a game show host took the microphone on the stage. On a small table beside him sat a vase with a single red rose. Several players drifted to the back while others observed over their shoulders but didn't move from the tables.

"What's this about?"

"This is famous in Moscow. They do this here every night." Tatyana said with excitement.

"Do what?"

"Auction the flower."

"You mean, like, it goes to the highest bidder?"

"Yes. Sometimes it sells for over one thousand dollars."

"For one bud?"

Tatyana nodded.

"Why so much?"

"Because the winner gives the flower to any prostitute he chooses. She is his for the night."

"The whole night?"

"For such money, of course."

At the conclusion of the lively bidding, a Japanese man walked forward to claim the bud amid clapping and rowdy catcalls. "He paid over eight hundred dollars," Tatyana said.

The man took the bloom to the tallest prostitute. She towered over him, and, arm-in-arm, the pair ascended the stairs to a chorus of cheers and whistles. An American shouted something about climbing Mt. Fuji.

I wonder if she'll blow up his mind.

* * *

Three hours before dawn, and girls still entertained guests. Occasional giggles, squeals, and laughs filtered down the hall to his office. Chekhov made a final check of his Internet messages.

He was annoyed that the pace of target deaths had decreased. Less income flowed into his German accounts. One aggravation was the dead Jacob Wilder. The insurance payout should have been collected, but Rublev had disappeared. Chekhov had heard nothing from Mikhail Novoy, whom he dispatched from Los Angeles to find out what the fuck was going on with that flaming asshole, Rublev. Unless he received his money soon, Alexandr Melnikov would not see his mother again.

Based on a call from the orphanage, the boy didn't deserve to join his mother. He was caught again stealing food for himself and other children. Chekhov understood the head woman disciplined harshly but hoped the brat was not too damaged. He wanted cash from the mother, but he would sell the whelp if necessary. A severe beating from the overzealous head woman would depress the price he could get for him.

Chekhov shouted, "Enter!" at the knock on his door.

Vladimir Motorin came in and shut the door behind him. "Any more problems with the Georgian?" Motorin asked.

Chekhov gave a rare smile and tapped the ash off his Marlboro. "No. The message you sent in blood was received. I don't expect him to hit us again. For now. What about the policeman, Sidor Borisov?"

"The man inquired about your license, nothing more."

Chekhov's eyes hardened. "I still don't like it."

"I frightened his wife. If he becomes an issue, they will be dead. I will monitor this myself."

"Excellent. Now, what is the status of your accounts?"

223

CHAPTER 49

Victor's nudge brought Jake out of uncomfortable slumber. He slept folded across the Lada's back seat. A moment passed before he remembered where he was. Victor pointed and said, "Chekhov *mashina*."

Jake sat up, and his cramped joints protested. His head throbbed and his mouth tasted like ash. They had left the casino well past midnight and watched the front door from a block away. Jake wanted to know where Chekhov lived.

He focused on the building. The neon light by the door was off, but second-floor lights still glowed. He picked up the night vision goggles and saw the bodyguard open the Mercedes' door. Chekhov climbed in, and the luxury sedan drove away.

"Follow him!" Jake said.

Victor cranked the ignition, and they lurched into the street. Like most Moscow drivers, he didn't turn on his headlights.

They kept up for five blocks, but the Benz took a right and vanished. The Lada was no match for the German automobile.

"What do you want to do now?" Tatyana asked.

"Sleep in a real bed." He thought for a minute. "Here's some things I want you to buy today." He dictated a list and gave her a wad of bills.

"Why do you need these things?"

"Because tonight, I'm buying the rose."

* * *

Jake did not sleep well and awoke exhausted at dawn. After

coffee and a hot shower, he waited until an appropriate time to make some calls, the first to Sidor Borisov.

"Morning, Sidor. I wanted to catch you before work." Jake told him about the hospitalized second mobster in Sacramento.

Sidor's voice carried an irritated edge. "So, there is nothing new. You will still go ahead with this madness?"

"Yes. Is something wrong?"

"*Da*. They know where I live. A man watched my apartment and tried to hit Sveta with his *mashina*."

A chill slid through Jake. "I am *so* sorry."

"You need to stop this."

Jake's shoulders sagged. "I cannot, my friend."

"I don't want Sveta in danger."

"I don't, either. Any idea who it was?"

"She told me the man wore a suit, like the man Regina described who asked about your wife in winter."

Jake recalled the parade of well-dressed thugs who visited Chekhov last night. Was the man at Sidor's one of them?

"She got a plate, but I haven't run the number. I don't like what happened when I searched before."

"Give it to me. I'll check," said Jake.

"You can do that?"

"I think so. I don't want the two of you in any more danger because of me."

Sidor softened as he recited the number. "I am sorry. I cannot risk my wife's life."

"I'm concerned about her, too, and you. Thank you, my friend. Goodbye for now."

Jake pressed the call button to dial Ted Vandagriff's pager and paced in the gathering summer heat.

Jakes satphone rang, and the legal attaché greeted him with, "Morning. I understand you had a busy night."

Jake remembered the American who encouraged the auction winner and speculated he was one of the legal attaché's FBI team. "So, you heard about what I was up to, huh?"

"Of course, though I can't say going to the casino was smart."

"And what would you do in my place?"

After a breath of silence, "The same. What's your next move?"

"I'm going back tonight to buy the rose."

"What? Why?"

"To try to access Chekhov's PC."

"Impossible," but there was anticipation in the attaché's voice.

"My friend gave me a super sniffer. If I can download it into the bastard's machine, we'll get every keystroke and message when he logs on the Internet."

"You're crazy, but I hope like hell you succeed. If you step in shit, I can't do much, but anything else you need?"

"Couple of things. The first is a name and address for a license plate. Here's the number. The driver is most likely in Chekhov's gang. He might lead me to the man himself."

"Okay, but Chekhov bounces around from one house to another. He has several, so he doesn't stay in the same bed every night."

Damn. Following the Mercedes wouldn't have provided any information. "One final thing. Where can I rent a vehicle, something powerful?"

"What kind?"

"Suburban, perhaps? Black with the large motor."

"I can arrange that. The General Motors dealer keeps an inventory for Embassy and US company rentals, but it won't be cheap."

"Not a concern."

"It's your money. I still think you're nuts, but I hope you

help us nail this scumbag."

"Me, too, but my first priority is locating my stepson."

* * *

Jake checked the time. Still early enough to phone Natalia, though late yesterday on the other side of the world. He felt compelled to call as he thought about the coming night.

He was alarmed at how despondent she seemed. "You alright, sweetheart?"

"Yes, all is fine," but her voice betrayed her words.

"I trust you believe in whatever I do here, I'm doing for Alexandr and you."

Firmly, she said, "I thank you to try. You are good man, Jacob. Understand I love you."

After their good-byes, he gazed out the window at the brightening day. Deep tiredness overtook him. His body screamed for rest.

In a flash, he realized why Natalia was depressed. He had lost track of the days. Yesterday was Alexandr's birthday.

* * *

Natalia wept after Jacob's call. She was tired, weak, and her soreness and pain were the most she had experienced other than childbirth. The nurse took excellent care of her compared to anything in Russia, and Veronika came by frequently to cheer her up, but her feelings were low. Alexandr's absence was bad enough, but not celebrating his fifth birthday cleaved her heart.

And there was no escape from the fear Jacob could die trying to find her son. The thought was unbearable.

Natalia could do nothing other than pray all would be well. That, and heal as fast as she could.

CHAPTER 50

The sat phone's incessant ring startled Jake awake in late afternoon. He answered with a groggy, "Yeah."

"Jake, Ted Vandagriff. I've got those items you asked for."

Jake tried to shake his grogginess and retrieved a pen and paper. "Shoot."

"First, the tag. The car belongs to a Vladimir Motorin at 33-9 Melodija Street. Ritzy neighborhood, at least by Moscow standards. He's one of Chekhov's rising stars."

So, Chekhov knows about Sidor. Damn! "Do you have a picture?"

"No, but he has the reputation of being a sharp dresser. Vicious bastard, too, from what we hear. He may have directed the recent slaughter I told you about. I understand he sometimes hangs out at a pastry shop not far from the Embassy. I'll see if we can catch him on film."

"Thanks. What about the Suburban rental?"

"That's the other reason I called. The vehicle is at the dealership on Mechnikova Street. Your credit card better have a high limit."

Jake yawned. "Anything else?"

"No, but good luck."

* * *

The Suburban's rental was indeed expensive, but Jake laughed at Victor's fountain of excited words. He acted like a biplane pilot given the controls of a jumbo jet. He pointed out each of the electronic displays. Jake speculated the man also visualized his first semi-tractor/trailer in The States.

The Suburban projected an almost sinister presence with

its dark, tinted glass. The kind of transportation a successful businessman would use.

Tatyana seemed enlivened, too. She sat in the passenger seat and added her own comments to Victor's animated appraisal. Jake smiled from the second row. "Let's go."

"Where?" she asked.

"It's early. Let's take the scenic route. Thirty-three-dash-nine Melodija."

Victor guided the brawny SUV to the boulevard. His cigarette-stained smile grew when the truck surged ahead, the engine undaunted by the vehicle's size.

Jake smiled, too. The smooth ride was decadent compared to the cramped, cranky Lada.

When they arrived, the evening sun cast shadows down Melodija Street, a narrow, cobblestone passage. The quiet enclave was different from other Moscow areas. The old buildings were clean and recently painted. Modern apartments with barred windows.

They cruised past Motorin's home. The lights inside glowed.

A man appeared at the window. Jake couldn't make out the face because the man was backlit.

Victor drove at the same pace and took the next corner. Jake took a breath.

"Let's go to the casino."

He didn't know what he had achieved but felt better. For once, he had something on the mobsters. He knew where one of them lived.

* * *

Motorin heard a throaty-sounding vehicle approach as he tried to figure out his stolen computer. He should be careful staring out his window, but the American SUV was rare here.

Rival mob bosses might own such vehicles for their personal use, but they would never risk luxury machines when hitting another gang. Still, Motorin wondered if word had spread that he had led the execution of the Georgian's thieves and their families. That might set him up for revenge. Possible, but doubtful. The gangs would not be so obvious or stupid to attack him at his home. Because of his rising status under Chekhov, his boss would retaliate with force. Still, he must be vigilant.

The SUV moved up the street, rounded the corner, and its rumble faded. Motorin had strained to see the license, but the running lights were off. He closed the curtains, retrieved his Walther Model 4, and stuffed it into his waistband.

* * *

"Let's test the phones," Jake said. Tatyana gave him the cellphone she had purchased earlier that day. He programmed it with his number and set his phone to emit a single chirp when she called. He handed the cell back. "Here. Now press recall and zero-one."

She did, and Jake's phone chirped. "Hello."

He guessed she thought it weird to use technology to talk to a person two feet away. She grinned but didn't answer.

He hung up. "Perfect. What about the rest?"

She handed him three small, triangular envelopes, which he put into his suit pocket next to Sergey's diskette as they arrived at the New Russia Casino.

Jake expected to be nervous but wasn't. Determination ruled. He climbed out of the Suburban, lit a fresh cigar, and strode into the casino.

The same scene as before, only busier and smokier. Stunning teenage prostitutes sat along the long bar. Gamblers played at the tables, and bartenders poured drinks as musicians at the back thumped out American-sounding tunes.

He again went to the roulette table, converted a thousand dollars, and proceeded to play the red. He had dropped about four hundred yesterday, which he figured categorized him as an important guest. That earned a smile from the pit boss and prompt delivery of his mineral water. A parade of gorgeous working girls, including Galina, soon materialized. She again ran the tips of her fingers across his shoulder. "You having luck?"

"No, I am not."

"I can change luck."

The woman had the face of a Hollywood starlet. Light blue eyes set off by her reddish-brunette hair. Full lips. Perfect facial symmetry. He told her, "Perhaps you can. Would you like a rose?"

Tatyana translated, and the woman beamed. "I like rose." Galina rubbed his shoulder with her hand.

Jake forced his mind back to the game, and she returned to her perch near the bar. Jake took a draw from the cigar. His eyes burned, and the acrid taste was enough for him to push aside thoughts of Galina.

Tatyana stood at his side as time crawled toward ten o'clock. He was down about three hundred dollars but paid little attention as he noted the string of visitors to Chekhov's upstairs office. *Is one Vladimir Motorin?*

Victor would alert Tatyana if the car with the number Sidor gave him pulled up.

At long last, the music stopped, and the same tuxedoed man took the microphone. On the riser sat the vase with a red rose. Several people drifted to the back, Jake and Tatyana among them.

The auction began, and Jake cheered the participants on.

When the bidders were down to three, Jake whispered in Tatyana's ear, and she entered the contest for him. She announced the first amount. A New Russian dropped out, but a Japanese gentleman and a blond German kept bidding. After two more rounds, the Japanese man sucked air, shook his head, and literally bowed out.

The German puffed out his chest and bid again. This brought gasps from the audience. Tatyana's retort caused some to whistle in disbelief. The German reddened and went higher.

Tatyana countered, and the man didn't respond.

The auctioneer pointed to Jake with excited fanfare, and the crowd clapped.

"Pay him a thousand, four hundred dollars...and good luck," she said.

Jake stepped forward to accept the bud while Tatyana ordered Dom Perignon for him. He counted out the money and traded for the flower. A path opened for him as he went to the lineup. All the girls sat with legs crossed, heads back, and breasts up. An incredible choice.

He went to the smiling Galina and presented her the bud, which she accepted as cheers and whistles erupted. Jake helped her off her stool and picked up the bottle and two fluted glasses.

The band started to grind out their songs, and people went back to their games. Jake and Galina walked hand-in-hand up the stairs.

CHAPTER 51

W hat your name?" Galina asked in broken English.
"Michael."

At the landing, he glanced down the hall toward Chekhov's office to orient himself. A light shone under the door. *Where are the security cameras? I expected a mob boss would have them.* As he thought about it, even the casino was devoid of cameras. *Strange.*

Galina tugged him the other way and guided him to one of the rooms with subdued lighting, a bed, chair, dresser, and small bathroom.

She wrapped her arms around him the moment they were inside.

He put his hands on her shoulders. "Wait. We have all night."

She backed up and smiled.

Jake raised the bottle. "Drink?"

She nodded. "Wait." She went into the bathroom and shut the door.

He struggled with the bottle's foil and wire. His fingers couldn't move fast enough. *Pop!* He fumbled with two of the packets from Tatyana and tapped the yellowish powder into one of the glasses. *Now the hard part.* He poured the champagne in her glass, but he couldn't let it overflow.

Galina came out, and he almost dropped the bottle. She wore nothing but a sheer, see-through robe. She was no more than seventeen, perhaps sixteen, and a descendent of an exceptional gene pool.

This entire situation is fucked up. She was probably forced into prostitution at a very early age. Poor girl.

"You like, Michael?"

Jake's mouth was dry. "*Da!*" He placed the flute in her soft hand.

She moved close to him while he concentrated on filling his own glass. His hands shook.

That difficult task accomplished, they touched flutes, and he toasted, "To luck!"

"*Da*, to luck."

They each took a sip, and he emptied his glass, wanting her to do the same. She did and frowned. The drug must have an aftertaste. He refilled her glass, and she again followed his lead and drank most of the pale-yellow bubbly. That time her face registered delight.

Her full lips parted in an impish smile, and she tugged at his tie. She slipped it off in an instant.

To stop her, he put his arms around her and drew her to him. He didn't want her to undress him, but before he could stop her, she gave him a kiss that seemed as if it would suck the enamel off his teeth. Her quick hands were busy down below.

She soon had her hand in his fly, and she went to her knees with an anticipatory smile.

Crap, now what do I do?

He reached down and eased her to her feet. "Please, I want to take our time."

He wasn't sure how much she understood, but she went to the bed, took off the robe, and reclined.

Jake peeled off his jacket and kept the weapons in his waistband hidden from her. He eased the Makarov and knives into the inside pockets of the coat. He shed his shirt and undershirt.

How far do I go before she falls asleep?

He shed both socks as her face changed from anticipation to dreamy softness. He thought for a second and finished undressing. He wanted her to see him in full arousal as her blue eyes blinked and closed. She needed to believe they'd had intercourse.

Though aroused, he remained in control. *I love you, Natalia.* He dressed and covered her gorgeous, sleeping body with a sheet.

He sat in the chair and anticipated a protracted night.

* * *

Jake dozed in the uncomfortable seat rather than stretch out on the bed by Galina. After what seemed hours, the cellphone chirped.

Tatyana said, "He's gone."

He shook off his tiredness. "Thanks."

Tired or not, Alexandr's life depended on the next minutes. Jake slipped into the hallway. Giggles and grunts came from other rooms, but the hallway was empty.

He crept as softly as a mouse to the office door. He tried the knob. It turned. *Unbelievable.* He'd been prepared to shimmy the lock with a credit card or knife.

Jake entered and pulled the door shut. In the faint circle of illumination from his small flashlight, he went to the computer, an obsolete model with limited capabilities. *Perhaps the best available in post-Soviet Russia.*

Okay, Sergey, let's see what you can do.

He put the diskette into the drive with a *click* and powered on the monitor and PC. The machine *beeped* and booted from Sergey's disk with more noise than Jake's heightened senses anticipated. Several lines of code scrolled up the screen, and an odometer displayed: "Time to complete: ten minutes."

Ten minutes! What have you done to me, Sergey?

Hollow curse. His best software engineer had given him a

sophisticated tool to help find Alexandr. But ten minutes was a monumental risk.

"Time to complete: nine minutes."

He scanned the office. *So, this is the bastard's operations center.* The room stank of cigarettes. What appeared to be sex stains marred the couch.

"Time to complete: eight minutes."

He tried the desk drawers. Most were unlocked, but their contents were labeled in Russian. He didn't want Chekhov to know he had been there, so he didn't disturb anything.

"Time to complete: seven minutes."

He searched the small closet. Nothing but clothes.

"Time to complete: six minutes."

He opened the file cabinet drawers. Nothing of interest in the first two, but he found bundles of letters crammed into the third.

"Time to complete: five minutes."

Jake thumbed through the mail and froze. One bundle contained letters from Natalia to her mother. He recognized his wife's handwriting. The bastard had somehow intercepted their mail. *Why did he keep these instead of tossing them?*

"Time to complete: three minutes."

He stuffed Natalia's packet into his jacket pocket.

"Time to complete: two minutes."

A door creaked open. Footfalls.

Oh, shit!

Jake yanked out the Makarov and cocked the hammer.

"Time to complete: one minute."

Come on, come on!

The footsteps faded. A customer must have finished with a prostitute. Jake put away the pistol.

The display showed, "Task complete."

About damned time.

Jake ejected the disk, powered off the computer and monitor, and hurried to the door. He peeked down the empty hallway. *Almost outta here!*

CHAPTER 52

Halfway to the stairs, Jake froze. Someone with heavy footfalls climbed the stairs.

Jake retrieved the combat knife and concealed the blade behind his leg.

He rushed toward Galina's room, but one of the oversized doormen reached the landing and rounded from the staircase. Caught. The only thing behind Jake was Chekhov's office. "I'm looking for the toilet."

The twenty-something hulk's dark eyes narrowed. He advanced, flexed his broad shoulders, and towered over Jake by at least four inches. The man smirked.

Jake held up his one empty hand. "Sorry, where is the restroom?"

The man growled something and shoved him backward. Hard.

"Please..."

The man pushed again with his left hand and balled his right into a massive fist.

Jake's anger exploded.

The guard grabbed Jake's hair and started to swing but was astounded when the wig came off in his hand. At that moment, a loud crash came up from the casino. Then came the sound of yells and shattered glass. The guard hesitated.

Jake thrust the knife deep under the doorman's breast-bone.

The man gasped and tried to punch again, but Jake rammed him against the wall with all his strength and stabbed him again and again. The man was muscled and outweighed Jake by fifty pounds or more, but the punishing blade dominated.

He clutched at Jake as he slid to the floor. Blood flowed from his heart. His smirk had been replaced by frozen fear.

Jake fought to breathe. He hadn't noticed until that moment he was panting.

Blood spread on the landing and seeped down the stairs.

Jake wanted to wipe his bloody hands but knew he had to get away quickly. Now. Rather than putting the blood-soaked knife back in his waistband, he rubbed fingerprints off the handle and placed it on the lifeless thug. It was a Soviet blade. Perhaps the Russian origin would provide some misdirection.

Streaks of blood had splashed Jake's clothes, but he couldn't do anything about it other than peel off the jacket. He replaced the wig and descended to the gaming area. Tatyana joined him. They hustled around the tumble of a damaged blackjack table, overturned stools, and astonished players. Chips were scattered across the floor and attacked by the prostitutes to claim them.

Inside, Jake shook with fright.

* * *

"What the hell was that fight all about?" Jake asked as Victor accelerated from the curb.

"A man went wild," Tatyana said. "Yelled he'd been cheated and broke stool over table. Huge struggle. Doorman took his money and threw him out. Exciting."

"I'm sure." *And the timing was impeccable.*

"Did you get stabbed?" Tatyana asked. "Need a hospital? You have blood everywhere."

"Not my blood."

Jake felt both weary and stoked. He had installed the spyware and murdered a man. No, not a man, a criminal who was part of the gang who held Alexandr. He told Tatyana, "I had difficulty, but everything went as planned. Now we need to wait for him to log onto the Internet."

Victor said, "No *mashina* with number."

The news on Motorin was of little importance now that Sergey's code was in Chekhov's PC. Jake had executed the most crucial job and killed a man without regret. *Damn right I don't have remorse.*

* * *

Back at his apartment, Jake cut up, bagged, and disposed of his blood-soaked clothes on a nearby building's trash heap. He made three calls before bed. The first because he wanted to hear her voice, which was again encouraging and strong. "I love you so, Natalia."

The second went to Sergey. "Ten minutes! You trying to get me killed?!"

"I surprised, too. Must be slow machine. Program calculates time to compress files and segment them to send in background mode. Chekhov won't know."

Jake's modest pique evaporated. If the machine stored that much information, the payoff might be significant. And he couldn't have done it without Sergey. "It was close, but I made it in and out. If Chekhov follows his routine, we should receive the first data dump tomorrow." *If he keeps to his pattern after finding a dead man near his office.*

"I happy it worked."

"Me, too, my friend. I owe you one."

Jake dialed Vandagriff's beeper. After several minutes, his satphone rang. The legal attaché sounded anxious. "How'd it go?"

"I had trouble getting out. Do you know if the police were called?"

"They were not. It was only a fracas. You can thank one of my team. He started the diversion when the doorman headed up the stairs. Cost him two cracked ribs and a swallowed tooth."

"Ouch! Please pass on my appreciation and condolences. He saved my ass. I have a concern about a hefty package, uh, dispatched upstairs."

"Oh? I don't know about that, but police were not summoned."

Jake didn't comment, so Vandagriff added, "So what now?"

"We wait to find out what Chekhov's computer tells us. With luck, plenty."

* * *

Vladimir Motorin sipped his favorite café's rich coffee and ate his morning pastry. He examined the foreign embassy workers for new fashions and was pleased he hadn't been required to visit Chekhov in the middle of the night. Vladimir's boss now focused on nighttime activities. The Bratva leader ceded daylight operations to his lieutenants, though he monitored everything. Motorin guessed the child kidnap scheme was more profitable than protection.

A flash caught his eye. Another flash.

He prided himself in being conscious of everything around him, but daydreaming about the bride racket had caused him to not pay attention to the foreigners who posed for photos.

He turned away before the camera flashed again and cursed his inattentiveness. That might have been a gun instead of a camera.

The group left in their loose-fitting clothes and jabbered in English. He preferred the more tailored, European styles.

His phone buzzed. "*Da?*"

"Come to the casino. Now!" Chekhov shrieked.

CHAPTER 53

Six of Chekhov's men stood outside the casino when Motorin pulled to the curb. Inside, he found wrecked furniture and broken glass. Two old babushkas scrubbed away blood on the upstairs hall floor and staircase. From Chekhov's office came curses, a slap, and sobs.

He walked in as Chekhov towered over Galina. She slumped on the couch, her face red with the pattern of his hand. Two bodyguards leaned against the wall. Chekhov screamed at the prostitute, "Tell me again! The truth!"

She fought for control but didn't succeed. "He is American. He came here two nights. Last night he bought the rose. His name is Michael."

"Did he fuck you?!"

She sobbed. "I think so. Uh, I fell asleep."

She dissolved into sobs, and Chekhov turned away, disgusted. "Stupid *shlyukha*," he muttered.

"What's the problem?" Motorin asked.

Chekhov scowled, walked to his desk, and sat. He slammed down his fist and pointed to the old Soviet army knife sitting in front of him. "Someone stabbed one of my men in the hallway. I suspect it was the American. He came up here to screw Galina, but she doesn't remember a fucking thing because she slept!"

Motorin's eyes locked with his boss. "An American SUV passed my apartment yesterday. And I think Americans took my photo this morning at a café."

Chekhov hammered his desk again and yelled at the universe.

Motorin had never seen the man in such uncontrolled fury.

* * *

The Mariupol Hotel sat one block off Red Square. Victor showed the armed guard his identification before he was allowed to drive through the gate. He parked the Suburban at the front entrance. Jake and Tatyana got out and walked up the stone steps into the high-ceilinged lobby. The interior had a dark wood wainscot, and the floors were marble.

Two men approached them. They wore light-blue jackets, navy slacks, and carried radios. Metal emblems clipped to their jacket pockets read "Security" in Russian, English, German, and Japanese.

The men spoke, and Tatyana translated. "Identifications." She explained they were here to pick up a guest, Stuart Baxter, as Jake presented his passport.

One man radioed. He told them in passable English, "Mr. Baxter is called. He will come. Please wait here." He motioned them to velour high-backed chairs. The guards moved off but kept them in sight.

Stuart Baxter's deep voice resonated through the room, "Jake! Great to see you." The broker was dressed in slacks with a gray polo shirt that emphasized his graying temples.

Jake shook Baxter's hand and introduced Tatyana. "Ready to eat?"

"I am! My body clock's all fouled up. I feel like I missed a meal somewhere along the way."

"Well, I think you'll find the food delicious and the portions enormous."

The two security men bid them goodbye when the trio exited. Jake, Stu, and Tatyana walked to the waiting SUV.

"Nice ride!" Baxter said.

"I need something powerful because Chekhov drives a Mercedes."

Baxter nodded. "I called Natalia before I left. She told me about the guy in Sacramento sliced up by shit-head kids stealing his radio. Too bad. You might have paid the ransom and been done with this nightmare."

"Not after what they did to Natalia, and they still have Alexandr."

Baxter cocked his head but said nothing as they climbed into the Suburban.

Jake opened an envelope and pulled out several photos. "This is one of the criminals. I picked these up from the embassy on our way over."

"Sharp dresser. Is he the man at the top?"

"No, but we think he participated in Alexandr's kidnapping. That should be confirmed this morning. He watched my friends' apartment earlier this week."

Baxter frowned. "Sounds messy."

Jake reflected a moment. "Definitely." He changed the subject. "Your flight okay?"

"Long. And when I got to my room, the concierge called to recommend female companionship. He offered the hotel's selection of girls and asked what type I prefer. The expense would be added to my bill. Unbelievable!"

"Welcome to Moscow."

"Well, *that's* a new definition of the term 'room service.'"

Over dinner at a seafood restaurant, Baxter asked about the search for Alexandr. Jake told him about the escapade with Galina and Chekhov's PC but left out that he killed a guard.

"Hmm," Baxter responded. "So, if he logs on the Internet, you might learn where they're holding your stepson?"

"I sure hope so. Losing Alexandr would devastate Natalia."

Baxter raised his glass of so-so Ukrainian wine. "Here's to

success."

* * *

Natalia picked up on the second ring. The caller was the rough, familiar voice from Moscow. "Mrs. Wilder, I call about your boy. He continues to steal, and he gets the belt. Tell him to behave."

"I will. I will. I'll do whatever you say."

"He is alive for now. Where is my money?"

She sounded startled. "I am ready to pay, but no one contacted me."

"What? Do not lie to me."

"*Nyet.* I have heard nothing."

"Fuck-your-mother! So, you have the money?"

"*Da.*"

"Listen. Wire five-hundred-thousand dollars today to Bundesbank in Munich. Write down the account information." He dictated the number.

"But it is Saturday here. Our banks are closed."

After a pause, "If the half-million is not deposited by Tuesday, your son is dead. This is the first payment. I will give you another amount when the estate is settled. Here, speak to the little turd."

"Mama?"

"Alexandr! Oh, *moi syn.* You will be with me soon, I promise."

"I am scared. When will they let me go?"

"Not much longer. And do not cause trouble. I love you."

The man came back on the line and shouted, "Enough! Send the money!"

"Please don't hurt him. You will get paid."

Natalia wept after the man hung up. She ached from her surgery and was overwhelmed with guilt. Her husband and son were in danger because she had lied. "Foolish woman!" she cried out.

* * *

Victor drove back to the Mariupol after dinner, and Baxter and Jake were quieter than they'd been on the way to the restaurant.

"So, what's your next move?" Stu asked.

"Keep searching. I couldn't live with myself or look Natalia in the eye if I didn't do everything possible to save Alexandr."

"If you want help, call me." A sad expression slipped across Baxter's face. "I came here to talk to Yelena and tell her I understand what happened. I'm not sure why this is so important to me. I plan to see her tomorrow."

"Does she know you're coming?"

"No, I don't want to take the chance she'll refuse to meet. Better to show up, I think."

"I wish you luck. Do you want a ride or use the Suburban?"

Baxter shook his head. "Nah, I'll rent something. The road signs are easy to follow. Do you think they rent BMWs here?"

Jake chuckled despite his dismal mood. "Stu, *everything* is available here. All it takes is a pile of cash or a high-limit credit card."

CHAPTER 54

Back at the apartment, Jake called Natalia.

"Hallo, Jacob?"

"Hi, sweetheart!"

Natalia's voice overflowed with fear and despair. "The man telephoned from Russia! He said me to send half-million to German bank. If the deposit is not there Tuesday, Alexandr... they kill him."

Jake's face burned, unsure if he felt elation or dread beneath his seething rage. If the man received the money, he should free Alexandr. At least he hoped so. But there wasn't much time. "Don't worry. Sergey will help with the transfer. Everything will be okay. He gave you an account?"

"Da. Munich's Bundesbank, 74-331-938."

He scribbled on a napkin. "I think this is good news. Do your FBI agents know about the bank?

"Da. I am so sorry about the cost."

"Don't worry about that, sweetheart. I love you too."

He pressed the "end" button. "Fuck!"

His heart felt as hard as granite.

* * *

The Internet was slow tonight, but this was not unusual. Dimitri Chekhov tapped his fingers on his desk as he waited to retrieve his emails. The slowness irritated him.

The disappearances of two of his men, Ivan Rublev and Mikhail Novoy, worried him. *Where the fuck are they?* Of greater alarm was their failure to collect Wilder's insurance payout.

He had taken a risk when he called the bitch himself, but it was unavoidable.

And the Americans, were they getting wise? Did this relate to the policeman asking about his license? He dialed Motorin and told him to find out and do so quickly.

One of his lieutenants rushed into the office, out of breath. "What?"

"Twenty of our businesses! They're on fire!"

He glared at the man. "What?! The *fucking* Georgians."

* * *

Jake awoke groggy after a restless night of anticipation. The morning sky lightened to a hazy, brownish-blue. He took a long walk to exercise and daydreamed of strolling with Natalia, Alexandr and Silky. Back at his apartment, he read his email. If Chekhov used his computer last night, Sergey should have useful information.

And what a report!

The supersniffer had indeed siphoned off Chekhov's files. Victim names. Staggering dollar amounts. Identities of his hit men. Bank account numbers. Everything but the one thing he wanted most. Alexandr's location.

His satphone rang.

"Moore here. Good morning." The connection was as clear as if the call was from the next room, not the other side of the world. The FBI man sounded elated.

"Yes, it is. The data dump is fantastic, but I still don't know where to find my stepson."

"We're working on that. Don't give up."

Jake answered more sharply than he intended, "Who said anything about giving up?"

Moore continued in a quieter tone, "Sergey's retrieval was magnificent. We have everything to roll up the operation and arrest Chekhov. Now we'll try to lure him out of Russia."

"How?"

"Let's say we think he'll head for Germany if his accounts have problems. Oh, and on your wife's bank transfer, we'll restrict it. The funds will be sent, but he won't be able to withdraw or move it. You'll get the money back once we nail him."

"Wow, thanks. I'm sorry I sounded angry."

"No worries. This is the least we can do. You risked your butt to hand us what we need to prosecute these bastards." The agent seemed to sense Jake's thoughts. "We're doing everything we can to locate your stepson."

"But what if you capture Chekhov before we get Alexandr?"

"All a matter of timing. You must realize there are other husbands, wives, and children in jeopardy here. We have to capture him as soon as we can, but if we don't locate the kids first, we will once he's in custody."

"How can you be certain?"

Moore was silent longer than Jake liked. "You're right. We're confident but there is no guarantee."

"I can't take the chance. I have to keep searching. Wouldn't you do the same?"

"Yeah, I sure as hell would."

* * *

Stuart Baxter felt awed by Moscow's miles of similar-looking apartment towers. Jake was correct in that he had no trouble renting the car, but he had difficulty locating where Yelena Sands lived. The street signs and maps were more difficult to read than he expected, and he navigated through yet another maze of drab concrete structures before deciding he arrived at the right address. He parked in the small lot of a neighborhood grocery and walked down the footpath between a set of apartments bathed in late-morning sun. Children romped in a playground at the center of the complex, and their squeals and laughter echoed off the buildings in the warm summer air.

This is the place. Yelena sat at a bench, and, though she had her back to him, he recognized her. Brownish-blonde hair pulled up on her head and held with combs. Slender white neck he had seen so many times at Stephen's restaurant and on outings together.

Baxter stopped and turned to stone from indecision. *Should I go through with this? Will my presence hurt her more?*

She called something toward the playground, and a girl of about ten replied. He studied the child. She inherited her mother's hair and smile. He grieved for Stephen and the terrible choice this woman had to make. His anger for Chekhov seethed.

Yelena busied herself with something on her lap.

Stu moved his feet. He came up behind her. She knitted a sweater. At first, he couldn't think what to say. She glanced up to watch the child play.

He took a breath and prayed he did the right thing. He softly said, "Beautiful daughter, like her mother."

She spun toward him in shock. Her hand went to her mouth. Panic filled her eyes.

They stared at each other a long moment before he said, "You have nothing to fear, but I want to tell you something." Her soft brown eyes remained wide and her speechless lips moved behind her hand.

"With you, Stephen was the happiest he'd been in his life. I know for certain because he was my best friend."

Her eyes welled with tears, and her hand dropped to her lap as the child ran to her side. The little girl also shared Yelena's eyes.

Baxter's courage faltered, but he pressed on. "I wanted you to know I think he would understand this was not your fault. He was a fine man, and you made him better."

Her trembling voice was as sweet as he remembered. "You came all this way to tell me this?"

"Yes, yes I did."

"How did you find out?"

"It's a long story, but I think you should hear it."

Yelena looked at her daughter and smiled. "First, this is Alena."

"Hello, Alena." The shy girl dropped her eyes and hid behind her mom.

"May I sit down?" Stuart asked.

CHAPTER 55

The slap of the baseball in Jake's mitt stung. Sidor threw with heat, the same as Jake had done the past half-hour. He sensed they both worked off their frustrations while Sveta and Regina prepared dinner.

Jake had cruised Moscow streets the entire day in a vain attempt to find where Alexandr might be hidden. Irrational, yes, but what else was he supposed to do?

As evening shadows darkened the narrow road by the Borisovs' apartment, Jake aimed and fired a perfect shot. He imagined the first-base umpire yelling, "Yerrrr OUT!"

Sveta called from the window. "Jacob! Telephone!" She held up his cellphone, which he'd left upstairs.

He jogged past Sidor, who followed him. She handed him the phone at the apartment door. "Hello?"

"Jake, this is Stu. I've spent the day with Yelena Sands and her daughter."

"How'd that go?"

"Well, I think. We both needed this, especially Yelena. She carries a lot of guilt. Anyway, I have something that may help. One of our FBI people tried to interview her a couple of weeks ago, but she didn't tell him anything. I take it people here are afraid of any kind of police.

"Anyway, Yelena's eleven-year-old, Alena, says all the children are in one place, a building with a dormitory and play yard. It's surrounded by a high cement wall with an iron gate in front. She also says there's a power plant nearby. She's not clear where but thinks it is in the north of the city because they take them in and out only at night, and they cover their eyes."

"Stuart, this is fantastic!"

"I'm heading back to the hotel. Call me if you need me."

"I won't hesitate, my friend."

Jake dialed Ted Vandagriff's pager and relayed to Sidor what Baxter told him. Sidor rushed to snatch a map from the bookshelf as he informed Sveta and Regina of the news.

Jake's cell chirped. Vandagriff. "What's up?"

Jake relayed Baxter's info.

After a moment of scribbling notes, the legal attaché said, "Terrific. I'll have my people check. You stay put."

"I can't. If you discover anything, call me."

Jake went to the kitchen table cleared of dishes for the now unimportant meal. While Sidor, Sveta and Regina chattered and drew red circles on the map, Jake called Tatyana and directed her to pick him up immediately.

Sidor's face broke into a hopeful smile under his thick mustache. "Eighteen power plants in the north section of city. More there than anywhere else. We can check most tonight."

"What do you think is the best approach?"

Sidor spoke with professional authority. "If we locate the place, we will require help. I will contact my squad, and they will come here where we have a telephone. You search. If you find the place, we will come."

"I have a better idea. When Tatyana and Victor arrive, I'll give you my cellphone. I'll have the satphone. You hunt, too. We can cover the area twice as fast."

"That will work," Sidor said.

Sveta announced, "I will go with Jacob."

Sidor almost exploded but stopped when he saw his wife's determined stare.

Regina stated she would come, too.

* * *

Sunday should be a relaxed night for Dmitri Chekhov. The casino was not busy, and most of the girls had the day off to rest. He typically checked emails, screwed one of his women, and went out with friends.

This wasn't a normal Sunday night. Frustration overwhelmed him. Twenty of his protected businesses had burned last night, and he had discovered little about those responsible other than vague rumors about a St. Petersburg gang. He assumed the Georgian was behind it, but Istomin called him saying he was not responsible. From what Chekhov could determine, that appeared true. If not the Georgians, who? Was a St. Petersburg faction trying to move in? Was this the start of a war? Time to retire to Finland?

And what about the apparent loss of two of his men in California? He anticipated attrition, but not two in such a short time. What if the Americans had uncovered his bride business? "Shit."

He turned on his PC and logged onto the Internet, which was again slow. Unusual for Sunday, but so many people were on the network now that delays were frequent. The slowness irritated him, but that was the least of the night's concerns.

He emailed all his overseas men and ordered them to confirm they were alright. Next, he reviewed his incoming messages. Twenty-four, but no communication from Rublev or Novoy. He called them but no answers. *Fuck!*

The sixteenth message was from one of his insiders at Bundesbank's wire transfer desk, which never closed. Still, a weekend message was strange.

He opened the email and read it. "Fuck-your-mother! Fuck, fuck, fuck!"

His cash from the Wilder woman had arrived, but the deposit had a "pending" status and was on hold.

The whelp is doomed.

Chekhov called the orphanage. "Get the Melnikov kid

ready. This is his last night."

The head woman asked, "Can I give him the belt? He has caused much trouble."

"Do whatever you want, but I want him alive." He would personally strangle the whelp while the mother listened on the phone.

The grandmother would be killed as well. He called one of his lieutenants and ordered Regina's execution.

And Natalia Melnikova Wilder would suffer the price for her betrayal. Chekhov pounded out an email directive.

CHAPTER 56

Jake, Sveta, and Regina bounded into the Suburban as Victor screeched to a stop. Jake tossed his second cell to Sidor. Sveta carried the map and barked directions the instant the doors closed.

Eighteen areas to check. They had to move.

Sidor glared at them as they pulled away, displeased about Sveta going along. He had been unable to dissuade her.

They raced out of the complex to a street. Tatyana and Victor listened to the description of the area where the kids were probably kept. The directions communicated, the women fell silent. Regina gave Jake a hopeful smile. He took her hand and smiled back.

They searched ten square blocks around the closest power generation facility. Nothing. They rushed to the next one.

Jake's satphone rang. "Agent Moore here. We have a problem. Chekhov found out there's a hold on your wife's fund transfer."

"What?!"

"Sergey's sniffer forwarded us the contents of an email from someone at the bank. This guy has hooks everywhere, but the point is, he knows."

Jake squeezed the phone so tightly his hand ached. "We need to find Alexandr."

"Agree. I'll call Vandagriff at the embassy. And, Jake, he also sent emails to Rublev and Novoy telling them to murder your wife after he calls her again. Don't worry, she's safe, and those two hitmen won't receive messages. Thought you should know." Moore hung up.

Jake cursed to himself. "Faster, faster!"

He noticed a reflection off a car's windshield far behind them, though most Russian drivers navigated at night without headlights. *Is someone following us?* He looked back but couldn't see anything definite on the dark streets.

The cell chirped. Jake expected more bad news. "Yes?"

"Ted Vandagriff. We caught a break. One of my men knows the north area well. He remembers a place like the one you described near the generation facility on Lenskaya Road."

Jake shouted, "Lenskaya Road!" to Victor.

Sveta checked the map under the ceiling light. "Number twelve!"

They took the next corner fast, fishtailed, and almost went up on two tires. "Got it!" Jake said. "We're on our way there."

"Jake, we might be able to run a little interference, but we can't do anything overt to help. The place is so far from the embassy my people can't catch up with you anyway. We can't call the police because so many of them are corrupt."

"Understand. Be ready to get us into the embassy compound."

"We expect you. I hope this is the right place."

They did eighty on the straightaways.

"We'll know in a few minutes."

Jake pressed the recall number for his cellphone. "Sidor, Chekhov issued an order to murder Natalia. I assume he's done the same for Regina. Be extra careful, just in case."

"Not good, Jacob."

"Nope, but we think we know where the kids are. Near the plant on Lenskaya Road."

"On the way with my squad."

One more call to make. Jake dialed the Hotel Mariupol and left a message for Stuart Baxter about the possible location.

* * *

Dmitri Chekhov gave his prostitute a final, climactic thrust as his phone continued its incessant ring. He slid off her, wiped himself with a towel, and picked up the receiver. "What?!"

Vladimir Motorin's voice betrayed anxiety. "I will execute the policeman, Sidor Borisov. I observed his home. The Melnikova woman's mother, the policeman's wife, and the American left in the SUV that went by my apartment. I'm following, but they are moving fast."

"American? What American?"

"The red-haired man who met Natalia Melnikova months ago."

"Fuck-your-mother! Jacob Wilder!" he yelled. *The sonofawhore and his bitch deceived me. Wilder is alive and here.* "Don't you dare lose them. You will pay a high price if he gets away."

Motorin swore to himself. He knew Dmitri would murder him if he lost Wilder. "I won't. I think they are going to the orphanage."

"Stay with them and call me if something changes. I will let the headmistress know trouble is coming, though there is probably little the old hag can do about it. I am bringing more men. Kill Wilder and the others if you can."

* * *

Victor stopped the Suburban near the barred gate. The place was as Yelena Sands' daughter described. A nearby power station belched smoke and ash into the air, and an enormous hot-water pipe snaked along the wall and over the entrance.

Jake pulled out his night vision goggles and surveyed the complex. Nothing but connected buildings. Off to the side was an empty playground.

"I'm going in," Jake said, but his companions erupted in an animated argument.

When the discussion ended, Tatyana said, "I open. We all

go in."

She was out before Jake could stop her and ran faster than he thought she could. Tatyana swung the barrier open and climbed back into the vehicle. Victor drove into the compound. A few rooms at the front of the building had lights on, but the rest were dark. At the back, they turned around and parked facing the street for a quick getaway.

"You stay here. I'll go in alone," Jake said, but when he climbed out, so did the three women. The air was hot and thick with a sulfurous stench.

He found a locked door at the back and shimmied it with a knife. He pulled the Makarov out of his waistband and eased inside. Regina, Sveta, and Tatyana followed.

All four of them froze.

CHAPTER 57

Enough light filtered through the windows to see rows of cots filled with children. The room stank of sweat, urine, and fear. Most youngsters' eyes sparkled in the night.

My God, so many of them.

Sveta choked back emotion. Regina gasped.

Jake motioned for them to split up, and they worked their way through the aisles whispering, "Alexandr Melnikov! Alexandr Melnikov!"

No answer.

Jake's chest constricted. *Where is he?!*

They gathered at the back of the room. *Is there another dorm?*

Most children were awake now, and many wept. The kids watched them in fearful silence.

Jake tried one more time. "Alexandr Melnikov!"

Jakes stepson wasn't there, and he feared they'd arrived too late. He also wondered if Alexandr had been there at all.

A small girl of perhaps five slipped out of bed and came toward them. She whispered something in Russian, and Tatyana said, "She will show us."

She took Tatyana's hand and tugged her through a door into a long corridor. Regina, Sveta, and Jake stayed close.

A door opened at Jake's right, and he spun, Makarov raised. An old babushka almost fainted from fright. Sveta growled something, and the old woman lowered her eyes and shut the door.

As they hurried along the hall, faint sounds grew louder. A child's screams. Jake sprinted ahead. He kicked in the door to the room where the sound emanated.

A woman with a thick belt stood over a crying boy. The

child's bottom was a mass of angry, bleeding welts. The wild woman looked up in surprise. Jake clobbered her face with the heavy Makarov. Hard.

He tried to swing the pistol around to aim at her, but not in time. She attacked him and spouted Russian expletives.

He wrestled the belt from her and walloped her with it. He flogged her until she fell to the floor next to a desk. He couldn't help himself. He reached far back and whacked her again.

"Alexandr!" Regina screamed as she entered and lifted the boy into her arms. Alexandr bawled as Regina pulled up her grandson's pants. Tatyana, Sveta, and the girl were wide-eyed in the doorway.

"Let's go!" Jake said.

He ran out of the room and took the girl's hand. A gun-shot exploded. He looked back at the woman. She slumped on the floor with a revolver in her hand. A red blotch expanded on her blouse.

Smoke curled from the barrel of the pistol in Sveta's hand. "*Suka!*" She spit on the dead woman.

Jake held the girl's hand and the Makarov with his other as they rushed down the hallway. Regina clutched whimper-ing Alexandr. Tatyana was winded and struggled to keep up. Sveta jogged past Tatyana with grim determination.

They charged through the dormitory on their way to the exit.

"*Stoy!*" Halt! came a soft-spoken, firm command from the shadows three yards away. The man used a boy around seven as a human shield.

Enough light shone to catch the glint of a gun. The shape of the man's head, the cut of his chin, and his shadowed face caused Jake to say, "Motorin, I assume."

A sinister voice whispered, "*Da.*"

There was nothing gentle about the Russian's meaning or

the forceful motions with his pistol. Sveta's weapon *clunked* to the floor. Jake dropped his on the cot next to him.

Motorin spoke and aimed at Jake's chest.

Trucks rumbled as Sidor's men arrived. The flash of headlights through the windows bathed the room in light.

Motorin squinted and turned his head to shield his eyes.

In that time-slowed instant, Jake thought about grabbing the Makarov, aiming, and shooting before Motorin killed him. *But I've never fired a gun.*

He thought of his years fielding grounders at shortstop and third base and smoking fastballs the one-hundred-twenty-seven feet to first. Ten feet was nothing. He went with muscle memory.

Jake scooped up his pistol like a hot line drive, visualized the first baseman's glove, and threw with everything he had.

End-over-end, the pistol flew the short distance to Motorin's face.

Thwack!

The pistol struck hammer-first.

Motorin stumbled back and collapsed on his back on the cement floor. His head bounced twice.

The child fell with him and landed on Motorin's torso. He yelped, slid off the body, and ran toward the others.

Regina, Sveta, and Tatyana led the kids to the door as Jake stood over Motorin. Lifeless eyes stared at nothing. Blood seeped from the deep dimple in his forehead.

I can still throw a bullet to first, asshole.

He retrieved his, Sveta's, and Motorin's guns.

Sidor charged in with four of his armed men and called, "Sveta!"

Someone turned on a light, which lit the room with a dim glow. Dozens of youngsters cowered in bunches. Some hid behind their beds.

Jake lifted the little girl in his arms and sprinted to the

door. She clung tight to his neck.

"Thanks! We're going to the embassy!" he told Sidor.

Sveta was at her husband's side, and Sidor said, "We will meet you there."

Orders were bellowed. Children began crowding out the door. Officers carried the smallest.

Outside, three trucks with canvas-covered beds idled. As the first group of kids was hoisted into the back of the lorries, Jake sprinted around the corner with the child to the Suburban. Tatyana, Regina, and Alexandr were already inside.

He jumped in and bellowed, "Go!"

The SUV sprayed gravel as it sped to the street, but a dingy-brown car blocked their exit. Victor turned on the headlights. Four men holding automatic carbines tried to climb out of their car and shielded their eyes from the Suburban's intense light.

Victor stomped the accelerator and rammed into the vehicle behind its back wheels. The Suburban cut through its trunk like a train through papier-mâché.

The brown car rocketed into the insulated pipe and disappeared in an explosion of steam and boiling water.

As Jake glanced back at the scalding fountain, a black Mercedes rocketed through the spray and gained on them.

"We've got company," Jake said. "How long to the embassy?"

Tatyana conversed with a focused Victor. "At this speed, fifteen minutes...if we don't crash."

Regina embraced Alexandr and cooed soft words. He watched Jake with familiar, smoky-blue eyes. Jake winked, and Alexandr did his best to copy by blinking both eyes.

The little girl peeked at Jake. She appeared frightened but happy to be away from that place.

"What's your name?" he asked.

"Katya," Alexandr said for her. He added something else. Tatyana explained, "They are friends."

He smiled. "Hello, Katya."

They hurled through intersections and over trolley tracks.

The back window shattered. The women and girl screamed. Jake leaned over and pushed Regina and the kids down.

The Benz closed the gap between them. More gunfire came from the car.

Jake elbowed out the Suburban's rear window and fired back.

The car swerved and dropped back but soon came at them again.

"Tatyana, tell Victor to slam on the brakes."

Victor did as he was told.

The Mercedes plowed into their back bumper. A slug pinged off the Suburban's taillight. Jake fired twice.

The Mercedes moved back but again surged forward.

"Stop!"

Jake braced himself as the Suburban decelerated. The Mercedes crashed into them and nose-dived under the Suburban.

Jake saw the driver's face three feet away. He fired three times at the man. Red spotted the inside of the windshield.

"Go! Go, Victor!"

They scraped off Chekhov's car, lurched ahead, and accelerated away.

Victor pushed ninety miles an hour down the boulevard along the Jauza River.

Inside the Mercedes, the guard shoved the dead driver onto the street and took his place at the wheel. The crumpled Benz came after the Suburban again. A moment later Chekhov leaned out and blasted away.

A round ripped through the tailgate and punched through the upholstery not two inches from Jake. "Everyone alright?"

Two frightened female "Da's" responded.

"How much longer, Tatyana?"

"Five minutes," the terrified interpreter replied.

Victor veered to dodge the gunshots but kept hurtling along the riverside thoroughfare. At the junction of the Jauza and Moscow Rivers, he fishtailed west past Red Square and the Kremlin. He turned and took the loop to Novinsky Boulevard.

The US Embassy loomed in sight.

But the Mercedes was directly behind them again.

Victor bellowed something and locked the wheels into a controlled skid. The Suburban stopped in a cloud of acrid tire smoke at the corner of the US compound wall.

The Mercedes skidded to a halt. The bodyguard burst out of the car and shot from behind his door.

Bullets tore into the Suburban.

Something stung Jake's cheek, and he recoiled.

He popped up to shoot, but the man and door vanished in an ear-splitting explosion of twisted metal.

CHAPTER 58

After Stu Baxter received Jake's message, he located Lenskaya Road on his street map, oriented himself, and sped as fast as he dared. The 7-series BMW was responsive as he red-lined through the gears.

He turned at the Jauza River and headed north. Moments later, he spotted the black Suburban race the opposite direction across the water with a Mercedes sedan on its tail. Gunfire echoed.

"Damn!"

Baxter blasted through the curves before he roared onto a bridge and charged over the river. On the far side, he cut in front of another vehicle to continue his pursuit.

He guessed their destination and knew how to handle a BMW.

On Novinsky Boulevard, three blocks away, he watched the vehicles slide to smoky stops. More gunshots. Two men in the Benz fired on Jake's Suburban.

Baxter switched off his lights and floored the gas pedal.

The Mercedes' driver door opened. The oversized man fired from behind it and riddled the SUV with holes. The tailgate resembled a sieve.

"Eat shit, asshole!" Stu roared.

Baxter rammed the bodyguard going sixty. A sudden splash of gore covered the BMW's windshield, and the front tire complained under its wrinkled fender.

He flipped on the wipers, fought the complaining BMW into a U-turn and hurled back up the street.

Three Marines protected by riot shields crab-walked to the Suburban. A man leapt out and hid behind the Benz, fired, reloaded, and shot again.

"Chekhov, the bastard."

Stu forced the BMW into another squealing U-turn.

Chekhov was half a block away.

Baxter glanced at the steering column. "What the hell."

He floored the accelerator. "You had my best friend killed, asshole!"

Chekhov turned a moment before impact, eyes wide in disbelief.

Baxter nailed Chekhov dead center against the Benz. Around the airbag, he watched the top half of Chekhov's body catapult into the air.

* * *

Jake watched the bodyguard's crumpled corpse splash to the pavement after the BMW zoomed by. He didn't have time to think about it because Chekhov was out of the car and blasted away from behind the Mercedes. Jake emptied the Makarov, tossed it aside, and pulled out Sveta's pistol. Jake saw Marines with their riot shields grab Alexandr and Katya. Regina, Tatyana, and Victor cowered behind them as they hustled to the embassy. Jake turned and saw the oncoming BMW disappear behind the Mercedes, which rose and vaulted forward. "No, Stuart!"

A chunk of Chekhov's body spurted through the air.

Jake hustled out of the Suburban, and a Marine clutched his arm to yank him into the embassy. Jake wrenched away. "I've got to get Stuart!" He heard sirens and saw flashing blue lights far up the street as he ran to the back of the Mercedes. The BMW's front end was crushed, but the passenger cage was intact. Jake wrestled open the deformed door as the police cars drew closer.

Stuart sat slumped over with the deflated airbag on his

lap. He moved and turned his head. "Christ, Jake, my legs! The steering wheel. My legs!"

Jake saw the steering column was canted upward at an abnormal angle. The wheel was a lopsided oval.

"Come on, Stuart. Let's get out of here!"

Jake reached in and unbuckled Stuart's seatbelt. He dragged his friend out of the car. Stuart couldn't stand, so Jake pulled him toward the embassy.

Six or more police cars bore down on them.

A pair of strong hands wrestled Stuart away from Jake and hoisted him over a broad shoulder. The Marine yelled, "Come on, sir, we have to get inside. We can't trust the police out here."

Jake didn't need convincing.

Two police units slid to a stop next to the wreck as the embassy's steel entrance slammed shut.

Pairs of hands grabbed Jake and hustled him into the building.

Jake smelled the reek of spent gunpowder on his clothes.

The Marine escorted him into a small infirmary where a doctor and nurse dressed Alexandr's wounds. Stuart was stretched on an examination table.

Jake asked, "Is everyone okay? Is anyone hurt?"

The doctor said, "Nothing serious."

Alexandr lay bravely on an examination table while the nurse worked on his backside. Jake knelt down and said, "Hello, Alexandr, I'm Jake."

Alexandr smiled and then grimaced when the nurse touched a sensitive spot. Jake tousled his hair.

Ted Vandagriff entered the infirmary. Jake shook Vandagriff's extended hand as the legal attaché said, "Glad you made it, Jake. This has been a busy night and it's a long way from over. The Ambassador is on the phone with the Russian interior minister. US citizens and their dependents were attacked by Russian criminals. It'll take some sorting out, but there shouldn't be a problem.

"I called headquarters to inform them Chekhov is dead. A flash message has been transmitted to all our field offices. We'll have his whole network shut down in a day, two at the most. They are all under surveillance."

"Excellent! And there's no issues with the visas for Tatyana and Victor and his family?"

"No. They'll stay here until the paperwork is done, just a day or so. We'll ship over their belongings along with Regina's once everyone is settled. Victor went to get his family. They should be back in about an hour."

Jake grinned, but his smile faded. "I worry about the Borisovs, though."

Vandagriff said, "I think they'll be okay. Chekhov wasn't part of the established Mafia. He was an outsider. Most of the other mob boys will probably think Sidor helped do them a favor."

Vandagriff rubbed his forehead and asked, "Where're the other kids, do you know?"

"Last I saw, Sidor was loading them into trucks."

"Damn! Do you know where he's taking them? We need to get everyone to the embassy, quick."

"Why don't you ask him?" Jake pulled the satphone out of his pocket, pressed the speed dial, and handed the phone to Vandagriff.

Jake walked over to Stuart. He was hurt, but he lay still while the doctor examined him. "How you doing, Stu?"

"I won't be jogging tomorrow. You make it through this mess? There's blood on your face."

Jake realized his left cheek stung. He wiped his hand across it, and his fingers were red. "Just a scratch, I guess."

"Looks more like a bullet graze to me." Stuart painfully

laughed. "Us Americans are a lot tougher than they think."

"All we need is a reason to be," Jake answered.

* * *

Early afternoon in Milpitas, which meant it was after midnight in Moscow, and Natalia didn't expect a call from Jacob. But it was him, and she heard excitement in his voice.

"Hi, sweetheart! Our son would like to talk with you."

CHAPTER 59

The adrenaline drained from Jake's body and weariness seeped in, so he walked to the noisy canteen for coffee. Sixty-two excited children packed the room. Sidor had brought them in through the delivery entrance, and the cafeteria was opened to assemble them in one place. They devoured chocolate milk, sandwiches, cookies, and fruit. They were all thin and hungry.

Jake filled a cup from the urn and observed the kids. A few seemed bewildered but most were happy. They smiled and chattered. They'd been told they would soon reunite with their mothers. Katya drank her milk alone at one of the tables. She had a trace of a smile on her face.

Everything seemed under control. Vandagriff dispatched men to his and Regina's apartments to pick up their essential belongings.

Jake sipped the hot, black brew and wandered over to the infirmary. He asked the tired doctor, "How's Baxter?"

"His legs are badly bruised but not broken. I put him on painkillers. Also, Alexandr is not seriously hurt, but he'll be scarred on his backside."

Jake's vision darkened as he remembered the encounter with the wild-haired woman. His jaw clenched.

"I've given him a tetanus shot and antibiotics. He'll be bouncing around in a couple days."

"Thanks, doc."

"You need to see a plastic surgeon about that graze on your cheek. The scar will be worse if you don't."

Jake reached up to touch the bandage on his face. "I'll do that."

He intercepted Tatyana after her visa interview. "Thank you for all your help. We couldn't have done it without you and Victor."

She wore the euphoria of one who had escaped death. "I so scared, but now all okay. I think."

"You'll like The States."

The translator grinned. "Yes, America!"

He caught up with the Borisovs before they headed home. He shook Sidor's hand and hugged Sveta. "This is a miracle you made possible," he said.

Sidor smiled, happy the excitement was over. "We were lucky, all of us." He sighed. "We must leave now. I have endless reports and explanations to complete for my superiors."

"Well, thank you both again. Sidor, keep your mitt limber."

"I will, Jacob Wilder!"

Ted Vandagriff touched Jake's arm and said, "I think we're all set but we had difficulty at your mother-in-law's. A carload of Chekhov's men waited there. We brought in the Militia, who took them by surprise. Messy."

From Vandagriff's face, Jake guessed the mob boys were the mess.

"We chartered a flight for you. You'll be in Frankfurt by daylight."

"What about the other children?"

"We want to make sure Chekhov's organization is dismantled before they leave. You know, keep them safe. That shouldn't take long."

Jake nodded. "The girl with us, Katya?"

"The mom and stepdad are in Atlanta. She'll go out with the others as soon as everything is secure."

"Do me a favor? When you can, send me her parents' email address."

"Will do."

Jake's smile was lopsided because of the bandage. "She helped us a lot and is Alexandr's friend."

* * *

Marines loaded the van to take Jake, Alexandr, and Regina to the airport. Stu wasn't there. Jake found him in the infirmary. Baxter lay on the examination table with ice packs stacked on his legs.

"You ready to go? We're about to leave," Jake said.

Stuart said in his deep voice, "Nah, I changed my mind. I think I'll stick around Moscow a few more days. I promised Yelena and Alena a nice dinner."

Jake smiled and patted him on the shoulder. "Well, tell Yelena I hope to meet her someday."

"Who knows? Maybe you will."

* * *

The van pulled out and turned onto Novinsky Boulevard. Jake noted the spectators behind barricades. News crews milled under floodlights, and investigators poked through the wrecked vehicles. The scene was now guarded by the Militia instead of the regular police. A Militia escort formed up in front and behind the van.

He watched Alexandr and smiled. His stepson lay across his and Regina's laps, close to slumber.

As the convoy headed to Sheremetyevo Airport, Jake stroked Alexandr's head.

* * *

Natalia had pushed herself since Jacob left. She refused to just lie in bed to recuperate. But it was so painful to walk. The first day, she managed only a few steps. By the third day, she moved from room to room upstairs. On the weekend, she negotiated the stairs and brewed tea.

Then came yesterday's call. Alexandr was safe. She had wept with joy. Her son was hurt, but she would be with him and Mama soon.

Jacob saved them. If he could go to the other side of the world to rescue her family, she would be at the airport to greet them. Natalia felt sore and tired, but she had to meet Jacob, Alexandr, and Mama.

The female FBI agent counseled her, "You are still too weak to travel."

Natalia respected the advice, but, on this, she would not negotiate. "I go. Even if I take myself."

The other Agent called Moore, who drove her to the airport.

* * *

The flight from Frankfurt to San Francisco seemed interminable to Jake. He wanted to be home with Natalia.

Regina coddled and whispered to the boy and later read the letters from Chekhov's office. Tears welled in her eyes. Though Jake couldn't communicate verbally with his mother-in-law, he was happy she was with them.

As much as Jake had thought about being a father to Alexandr, the dream had come to life.

The plane took its long looping curve down to San Francisco. Alexandr and Regina gawked wide-eyed out the windows.

They were home.

Jake carried Alexandr up the ramp with the boy's arms wrapped around his neck.

Agent Moore waited for them at the gate, flanked by immigration and customs officials. "Jake! Welcome back. Please come with me. The Customs Inspector will retrieve your luggage."

"Sure." Jake fished the tags from his pocket, careful not to aggravate Alexandr's wounds.

They followed Agent Moore to a small office where their passports were stamped. Moore escorted them to a room attached to security.

Blessed pandemonium! Natalia and Regina squealed. Natalia scooped Alexandr out of Jake's arms. She winced from her surgery, and her face showed pain. Jake knew she had to hold her son, no matter what. She embraced Regina, too.

Jake relieved Natalia of Alexandr and hugged her. Though better than when he last saw her, she remained pale and fragile. Tears streamed down her cheeks.

She gazed into his eyes and touched his bandage. "Thank you, Jacob, oh, thank you."

"I told you everything would be alright, didn't I?"

"*Da*. I love you."

"Those are nice words to hear."

"They true."

CHAPTER 60

A lexandr's belated birthday party was in full bedlam. The Wilder backyard was packed with adults and children. Happy, screaming kids romped on rented inflatable playhouses and slides, monitored by Regina to ensure no one got squashed. Silky navigated the crush of people, mostly staying close to Alexandr, though she did not pass up a pat from guests. Parents talked and laughed in groups around the food tables, punch bowls, and beer kegs.

Alexandr and Regina had been home a month, but Jake and Natalia delayed the celebration until everyone could attend. Tatyana Filiminova was here, talking to one of Jake's engineers. She had found a job as a translator at a software company hoping to do business in Russia. Jake expected her to be successful.

Victor, his wife, and daughter had driven over from Sacramento, where they had settled because of its established Russian community and central transportation location. Jake wasn't surprised Victor purchased a Suburban, though an older model. Jake had happily cosigned a loan for Victor to buy a used tractor/trailer. He had no doubt Victor would expand his new trucking business. He had already landed his first contract with Land O'Lakes out of Minnesota.

Mark and Nina Osborne flew in from Atlanta with Katya, who stuck to Alexandr almost as closely as Silky. The Osbornes stayed at the now-crowded house, which was wonderful. Jake wanted the two young friends to share as many good times as possible after what they experienced in Moscow.

Raj Gupta, his family, Jake's coworkers, and softball team members and their families mingled and ate. Jake chuckled about his nickname around the office. Wild Man Wilder. The scar on his cheek added to the persona.

Jill Anderson from Standard Mutual and the reporter from the *Mercury-News* were in an animated discussion at the back fence. The newswoman had done all right. She sold the exclusive about "The Russian gang and the computer guy who took it down" to the New York Times. He had laughed at the hyperbole but felt some pride. The story went national, and he and Natalia were featured on two morning shows. The reporter also wanted to work with them on a book deal.

The FBI took two and a half days to roll up Chekhov's US operation after Jake left Moscow. No one escaped.

Fifty-two children were now reunited with their mothers and American stepfathers across the country.

Detective Bill Jackson came over from Sacramento and talked with Detective Phelps and FBI Agent Moore.

Jake walked up to them. "Bill, thanks for coming down and for your help."

"Glad to be here. Besides, Moore here is trying to talk me into applying for a job with The Bureau. Cornrows in the FBI! Imagine that!"

Jake guessed the man had decided to join. "Sounds like a smart move."

Agent Moore smiled and said, "I was telling Bill and Lonnie I received confirmation last night from the attorney general's office that Chekhov's eleven wise guys are facing maximum penalties under RICO. The files from their computers and the victims' statements are irrefutable. The mutts are doomed."

"Can't say I'm sorry."

"Me neither. On a somber note, we're working with Treasury to get the extortion money returned to the women whose husbands were killed. Not sure how much we can get."

Jake stared at his shoes and shook his head. "Well, it could have been a lot worse."

"Indeed."

"And I'm holding you to your promise, Jake, to help with Youth Baseball," Phelps said.

Jake glanced over at Natalia, who was busy at the food tables with Nina Osborne. "I keep my promises."

Jake moved on to chat with Stuart Baxter and Yelena Sands. Her daughter was somewhere in the flock of happy children. Stu had told him that Yelena took some convincing to return to Red Bluff, but Jake believed they both made the right decision. He passed his fingers down the scar on his cheek knowing he, too, had made a winning choice.

He caught up with Sergey on his way to the beer kegs. "Jacob! Sveta Borisova called. I cannot believe it, but they will adopt boy. Russians never take other children, but she insisted to Sidor that if Americans can adopt them, they would, too. She always wanted a family, and Sidor will now have someone to throw baseball with."

"Fantastic news!"

Natalia tugged his sleeve. "Come, Jacob. Time for presents!" She took his hand, and he followed her through the crowd.

Once the children were herded into a group, Natalia encouraged Alexandr to take his place at the table piled with gifts. In just a month, he had grown, which amazed Jake. Now he understood his friends' frequent complaint, "They grow so fast!" Silky lay on the grass to the left of the birthday boy, and Katya stood at his right with an excited smile.

The kids went wild as Alexandr tore into each package in amazement. Many took pictures while Veronika wrote a list of the gifts and the givers. Natalia handed Alexandr a small, square box. "This is one of presents from Papa."

He opened the gift. "*Myach!*"

"This, son, is a baseball."

ABOUT ATMOSPHERE PRESS

Founded in 2015, Atmosphere Press was built on the principles of Honesty, Transparency, Professionalism, Kindness, and Making Your Book Awesome. As an ethical and author-friendly hybrid press, we stay true to that founding mission today.

If you're a reader, enter our giveaway for a free book here:

SCAN TO ENTER
BOOK GIVEAWAY

If you're a writer, submit your manuscript for consideration here:

SCAN TO SUBMIT
MANUSCRIPT

And always feel free to visit Atmosphere Press and our authors online at atmospherepress.com. See you there soon!

ABOUT THE AUTHOR

DR. RICHTER has received national writing awards and earned a bachelor's degree from UC Berkeley, a master's degree, an MBA, and a Ph.D.

He is president of the San Antonio Writers Guild and past-president of the California Writers Club. He is an active member of the Writer's League of Texas.

Dr. Richter moderates a weekly, multi-state, online critique session and is an international writing contest judge.

Doc has written seven novels and is working on his eighth.